HIRA SINGH

HIRA SINGH

By

TALBOT MUNDY

AUTHOR OF

"Rung Ho!," "King – of the Khyber Rifles,"
"The Winds of the World," "The Eye of Zeitoon,"
"The Ivory Traoil," "Guns of the Gods," etc.

GYAN

Published by

GYAN

Gyan Publishing House
5, Ansari Road
Daryaganj, New Delhi-110002
Phone: 011-47034999, 9811692060
E-mail: books@gyanbooks.com

Distribution Network
gyanbooks.com
India, USA, Canada, UK, Australia, France

ISBN : 978-81-212-9812-4 (PB)
First Published, 1917

2nd Impression 2023

Printed at: Gyan Press, Delhi.

HIRA SINGH
Author: TALBOT MUNDY

The Germans cheered and laughed, but we made never a sound

HIRA SINGH

By TALBOT MUNDY

Author of

"Rung Ho!," "King—of the Khyber Rifles," "The Winds of the World," "The Eye of Zeitoon," "The Ivory Trail," "Guns of the Gods," etc.

Frontispiece by
JOSEPH CLEMENT COLL

One hundred Indian troops of the British Army have arrived at Kabul, Afghanistan, after a four months' march from Constantinople. The men were captured in Flanders by the Germans and were sent to Turkey in the hope that, being Mohammedans, they might join the Turks. But they remained loyal to Great Britain and finally escaped, heading for Afghanistan. They now intend to join their regimental depot in India, so it is reported.

New York Times, July, 1915.

PREFACE

I take leave to dedicate this book to Mr. Elmer Davis, through whose friendly offices I was led to track down the hero of these adventures and to find the true account of them even better than the daily paper promised.

Had Ranjoor Singh and his men been Muhammadans their accomplishment would have been sufficiently wonderful. For Sikhs to attempt what they carried through, even under such splendid leadership as Ranjoor Singh's, was to defy the very *nth* degree of odds. To have tried to tell the tale otherwise than in Hira Singh's own words would have been to varnish gold. Amid the echoes of the roar of the guns in Flanders, the world is inclined to overlook India's share in it all and the stout proud loyalty of Indian hearts. May this tribute to the gallant Indian gentlemen who came to fight our battles serve to remind its readers that they who give their best, and they who take, are one.

T. M.

HIRA SINGH

Hira Singh

CHAPTER I

Let a man, an arrow, and an answer each go straight. Each is his own witness. God is judge.
—EASTERN PROVERB.

A Sikh who must have stood about six feet without his turban—and only imagination knows how stately he was with it—loomed out of the violet mist of an Indian morning and scrutinized me with calm brown eyes. His khaki uniform, like two of the medal ribbons on his breast, was new, but nothing else about him suggested rawness. Attitude, grayness, dignity, the unstudied strength of his politeness, all sang aloud of battles won. Battles with himself they may have been—but they were won.

I began remembering ice-polished rocks that the glaciers once dropped along Maine valleys, when his quiet voice summoned me back to India and the convalescent camp beyond whose outer gate I stood. Two flags on lances formed the gate and the boundary line was mostly imaginary; but one did not trespass, because at about the point where vision no longer pierced the mist there stood a sentry, and the grounding of a butt on gravel and now and then a cough announced others beyond him again.

"I have permission," I said, "to find a certain

Risaldar-major Ranjoor Singh, and to ask him questions."

He smiled. His eyes, betraying nothing but politeness, read the very depths of mine.

"Has the sahib credentials?" he asked. So I showed him the permit covered with signatures that was the one scrap of writing left in my possession after several searchings.

"Thank you," he said gravely. "There were others who had no permits. Will you walk with me through the camp?"

That was new annoyance, for with such a search as I had in mind what interest could there be in a camp for convalescent Sikhs? Tents pitched at intervals—a hospital marquee—a row of trees under which some of the wounded might sit and dream the day through—these were all things one could imagine without journeying to India. But there was nothing to do but accept, and I walked beside him, wishing I could stride with half his grace.

"There are no well men here," he told me. "Even the heavy work about the camp is done by convalescents."

"Then why are you here?" I asked, not trying to conceal admiration for his strength and stature.

"I, too, am not yet quite recovered."

"From what?" I asked, impudent because I felt desperate. But I drew no fire.

"I do not know the English name for my complaint," he said. (But he spoke English better than I, he having mastered it, whereas I was only born to its careless use.)

"How long do you expect to remain on the sick list?" I asked, because a woman once told me that the way to make a man talk is to seem to be interested in himself.

"Who knows?" said he.

He showed me about the camp, and we came to a stand at last under the branches of an enormous mango tree. Early though it was, a Sikh non-commissioned officer was already sitting propped against the trunk with his bandaged feet stretched out in front of him—a peculiar attitude for a Sikh.

"That one knows English," my guide said, nodding. And making me a most profound salaam, he added: "Why not talk with him? I have duties. I must go."

The officer turned away, and I paid him the courtesy due from one man to another. It shall always be a satisfying memory that I raised my hat to him and that he saluted me.

"What is that officer's name?" I asked, and the man on the ground seemed astonished that I did not know.

"Risaldar-major Ranjoor Singh bahadur!" he said.

For a second I was possessed by the notion of running after him, until I recalled that he had known my purpose from the first and that therefore his purpose must have been deliberate. Obviously, I would better pursue the opportunity that in his own way he had given me.

"What is your name?" I asked the man on the ground.

"Hira Singh," he answered, and at that I sat down beside him. For I had also heard of Hira Singh.

He made quite a fuss at first because, he said, the dusty earth beneath a tree was no place for a sahib. But suddenly he jumped to the conclusion I must be American, and ceased at once to be troubled about my dignity. On the other hand, he grew perceptibly less distant. Not more friendly, perhaps, but less guarded.

"You have talked with Sikhs in California?" he asked, and I nodded.

"Then you have heard lies, sahib. I know the burden of their song. A bad Sikh and a bad Englishman alike resemble rock torn loose. The greater the height from which they fall, the deeper they dive into the mud. Which is the true Sikh, he who marched with us or he who abuses us? Yet I am told that in America men believe what hired Sikhs write for the German papers.

"No man hired me, sahib, although one or two have tried. When I came of age I sought acceptance in the army, and was chosen among many. When my feet are healed I shall return to duty. I am a true Sikh. If the sahib cares to listen, I will tell him truth that has not been written in the papers."

So, having diagnosed my nationality and need, he proceeded to tell me patiently things that many English are in the dark about, both because of the censorship and because of the prevailing superstition that the English resent being told—he stabbing and sweeping at the dust with a broken twig and making little heaps and dents by way of illustration,—I sitting silent, brushing away the flies.

Day after day I sought him soon after dawn when they were rolling up the tent-flaps. I shared the curry and chapatties that a trooper brought to him at noon, and I fetched water for him to drink from time to time. It was dusk each day before I left him; so that, what with his patience and my diligence, I have been able to set down the story as he told it, nearly in his own words.

But of Risaldar-major Ranjoor Singh bahadur in the flesh, I have not had another glimpse. I went in search of him the very first evening, only to learn that he had "passed his medical" that afternoon and had returned at once to active service.

* * *

We Sikhs have a proverb, sahib, that the ruler and the ruled are one. That has many sides to it, of which one is this: India having many moods and minds, the British are versatile. Not altogether wise, for who is? When, for instance, did India make an end of wooing foolishness? Since the British rule India, they may wear her flowers, but they drink her dregs. They may bear her honors, but her blame as well. As the head is to the body, the ruler and the ruled are one.

Yet, as I understand it, when this great war came there was disappointment in some quarters and surprise in others because we, who were known not to be contented, did not rise at once in rebellion. To that the answer is faith finds faith. It is the great gift of the British that they set faith in the hearts of other men.

There were dark hours, sahib, before it was made

known that there was war. The censorship shut down on us, and there were a thousand rumors for every one known fact. There had come a sudden swarm of Sikhs from abroad, and of other men—all hirelings—who talked much about Germany and a change of masters. There were dark sayings, and arrests by night. Men with whom we talked at dusk had disappeared at dawn. Ranjoor Singh, not yet bahadur but risaldar-major, commanding Squadron D of my regiment, Outram's Own, became very busy in the bazaars; and many a night I followed him, not always with his knowledge. I intended to protect him, but I also wished to know what the doings were.

There was a woman. Did the sahib ever hear of a plot that had not a woman in it? He went to the woman's house. In hiding, I heard her sneer at him. I heard her mock him. I would have doubted him forever if I had heard her praise him, but she did not, and I knew him to be a true man.

Ours is more like the French than the British system; there is more intercourse between officer and non-commissioned officer and man. But Ranjoor Singh is a silent man, and we of his squadron, though we respected him, knew little of what was in his mind. When there began to be talk about his knowing German, and about his secrecy, and about his nights spent at HER place, who could answer? We all knew he knew German.

There were printed pamphlets from God-knows-where, and letters from America, that made pretense at explanations; and there were spies who whispered. My voice, saying I had listened and seen and that I trusted, was as a quail's note when the monsoon bursts. None heard. So that in the end I held my tongue. I even began to doubt.

Then a trooper of ours was murdered in the bazaar, and Ranjoor Singh's servant disappeared. Within an hour Ranjoor Singh was gone, too.

Then came news of war. Then our officers came among us to ask whether we are willing or not to take a hand in this great quarrel. Perhaps in that hour if they had not asked us we might have judged that we and they were not one after all.

But they did ask, and let a man, an arrow, and an answer each go straight, say we. Our Guru tells us Sikhs should fight ever on the side of the oppressed; the weaker the oppressed, the more the reason for our taking part with them. Our officers made no secret about the strength of the enemy, and we made none with them of our feeling in the matter. They were proud men that day. Colonel Kirby was a very proud man. We were prouder than he, except when we thought of Ranjoor Singh.

Then, as it were out of the night itself, there came a message by word of mouth from Ranjoor Singh saying he will be with us before the blood shall run. We were overjoyed at that, and talked about it far into the night; yet when dawn had come doubt again had hold of us, and I think I was the only Sikh in the regiment ready to swear to his integrity. Once, at least a squadron of us had loved him to the death because we thought him an example of Sikh honor. Now only I and our British officers believed in him.

We are light cavalry. We were first of all the

Indian regiments to ride out of Delhi and entrain at a station down the line. That was an honor, and the other squadrons rode gaily, but D Squadron hung its head. I heard men muttering in the ranks and some I rebuked to silence, but my rebukes lightened no man's heart. In place of Ranjoor Singh rode Captain Fellowes, promoted from another squadron, and noticing our lack of spirit, he did his best to inspire us with fine words and manly bearing; but we felt ashamed that our own Sikh major was not leading us, and did not respond to encouragement.

Yet when we rode out of Delhi Gate it was as if a miracle took place. A stiffening passed along the squadron. A trooper caught sight of Ranjoor Singh standing beside some bullock carts, and passed the word. I, too, saw him. He was with a Muhammadan bunnia, and was dressed to resemble one himself.

The trooper who was first to see him—a sharp-eyed man—he died at Ypres—Singh means lion, sahib—now recognized the man who stood with him. "That bunnia," said he, "is surely none other than the European who gave us the newspaper clippings about Sikhs not allowed to land in Canada. See—he is disguised like a fool. Are the police asleep," said he, "that such thieves dare sun themselves?"

It was true enough, sahib. The man in disguise was German, and we remembered again that Ranjoor Singh knew German. From that moment we rode like new men—I, too, although I because I trusted Ranjoor Singh now more than ever; they, because they trusted no longer at all, and he can shoulder what seem certainties whom doubt unmans. No word, but a thought that a man could feel passed all down the line, that whatever our officer might descend to being, the rank and file would prove themselves faithful to the salt. Thenceforward there was nothing in our bearing to cause our officers anxiety.

You might wonder, sahib, why none broke ranks to expose both men on the spot. I did not because I trusted Ranjoor Singh. I reasoned he would never have dared be seen by us if he truly were a traitor. It seemed to me I knew how his heart must burn to be riding with us. They did not because they would not willingly have borne the shame. I tell no secret when I say there has been treason in the Punjab; the whole world knows that. Yet few understand that the cloak under which it all made headway was the pride of us true ones, who would not own to treason in our midst. Pride and the shadow of shame are one, sahib, but who believes it until the shame bears fruit?

Before the last squadron had ridden by, Captain Warrington, our adjutant, also caught sight of Ranjoor Singh. He spurred after Colonel Kirby, and Colonel Kirby came galloping back; but before he could reach Delhi Gate Ranjoor Singh had disappeared and D Squadron was glad to the last man.

"Let us hope he may die like a rat in a hole and bring no more shame on us!" said Gooja Singh, and many assented.

"He said he will be with us before the blood shall run!" said I.

"Then we know whose blood shall run first!" said the trooper nearest me, and those who heard him laughed. So I held my tongue. There is no need of argument while a man yet lives to prove himself. I had charge of the party that burned that trooper's body. He was one of the first to fall after we reached France.

Colonel Kirby, looking none too pleased, came trotting back to us, and we rode on. And we entrained. Later on we boarded a great ship in Bombay harbor and put to sea, most of us thinking by that time of families and children, and some no doubt of money-lenders who might foreclose on property in our absence, none yet suspecting that the government will take steps to prevent that. It is not only the British officer, sahib, who borrows money at high interest lest his shabbiness shame the regiment.

We were at sea almost before the horses were stalled properly, and presently there were officers and men and horses all sick together in the belly of the ship, with chests and bales and barrels broken loose among us. The this-and-that-way motion of the ship caused horses to fall down, and men were too sick to help them up again. I myself lay amid dung like a dead man—yet vomiting as no dead man ever did—and saw British officers as sick as I laboring like troopers. There are more reasons than one why we Sikhs respect our British officers.

The coverings of the ship were shut tight, lest the waves descend among us. The stench became worse than any I had ever known, although I learned to know a worse one later; but I will speak of that at the proper time. It seemed to us like a poor beginning and that thought put little heart in us.

But the sickness began to lessen after certain days, and as the movements grew easier the horses were able to stand. Then we became hungry, who had thought we would never wish to eat again, and double rations were served out to compensate for days when we had eaten nothing. Then a few men sought the air, and others—I among them—went out of curiosity to see why the first did not return. So, first by dozens and then by hundreds, we went and stood full of wonder, holding to the bulwark for the sake of steadiness.

It may be, sahib, that if I had the tongue of a woman and of a priest and of an advocate—three tongues in one—I might then tell the half of what there was to wonder at on that long journey. Surely not otherwise. Being a soldier, well trained in all subjects becoming to a horseman but slow of speech, I can not tell the hundredth part.

We—who had thought ourselves alone in all the sea—were but one ship among a number. The ships proceeded after this manner—see, I draw a pattern—with foam boiling about each. Ahead of us were many ships bearing British troops—cavalry, infantry and guns. To our right and left and behind us were Sikh, Gurkha, Dogra, Pathan, Punjabi, Rajput—many, many men, on many ships. Two and thirty ships I counted at one time, and there was the smoke of others over the sky-line!

Above the bulwark of each ship, all the way along it, thus, was a line of khaki. Ahead of us that was helmets. To our right and left and behind us it was turbans. The men of each ship wondered at all the others. And most of all, I think, we wondered at the great gray war-ships plunging in the distance; for none knew whence they had come; we saw none in Bombay when we started. It was not a sight for the tongue to explain, sahib, but for a man to carry in his heart. A sight never to be forgotten. I heard no more talk about a poor beginning.

We came to Aden, and stopped to take on coal and water. There was no sign of excitement there, yet no good news. It was put in Orders of the Day that the Allies are doing as well as can be expected pending arrival of reenforcements; and that is not the way winners speak. Later, when we had left Aden behind, our officers came down among us and confessed that all did not go well. We said brave things to encourage them, for it is not good that one's officers should doubt. If a rider doubts his horse, what faith shall the horse have in his rider? And so it is with a regiment and its officers.

After some days we reached a narrow sea—the Red Sea, men call it, although God knows why—a place full of heat and sand-storms, shut in on either hand by barren hills. There was no green thing anywhere. There we passed islands where men ran down to the beach to shout and wave helmets—unshaven Englishmen, who trim the lights. It must have been their first intimation of any war. How else can they have known of it? We roared back to them, all of the men on all of the ships together, until the Red Sea was the home of thunder, and our ships' whistles screamed them official greeting through the din. I spent many hours wondering what those men's thoughts might be.

Never was such a sight, sahib! Behind our ships was darkness, for the wind was from the north and the funnels belched forth smoke that trailed and spread. I watched it with fascination until one day Gooja Singh came and watched beside me near the stern. His rank was the same as mine, although I was more than a year his senior. There was never too much love between us. Step by step I earned promotion first, and he was jealous. But on the face of things we were friends. Said he to me after a long time of gazing at the smoke, "I think there is a curtain drawn. We shall never return by that road!"

I laughed at him. "Look ahead!" said I. "Let us leave our rear to the sweepers and the crows!"

Nevertheless, what he had said remained in my mind, as the way of dark sayings is. Yet why should the word of a fool have the weight of truth? There are things none can explain. He proved right in the end, but gained nothing. Behold me; and where is Gooja Singh? I made no prophecy, and he did. Can the sahib explain?

Day after day we kept overtaking other ships, most of them hurrying the same way as ourselves. Not all were British, but the crews all cheered us, and we answered, the air above our heads alive with waving arms and our trumpets going as if we rode to the king of England's wedding. If their hearts burned as ours did, the crews of those ships were given something worth remembering.

We passed one British ship quite close, whose captain was an elderly man with a gray beard. He so waved his helmet that it slipped from his grasp and went spinning into the sea. When we lost him in our smoke his crew of Chinese were lowering a boat to recover the helmet. We heard the ships behind us roaring to him. Strange that I should wonder to this day whether those Chinese recovered the helmet! It looked like a good new one. I have wondered about it on the eve of action, and in the trenches, and in the snow on outpost duty. I wonder about it now. Can the sahib tell me why an old man's helmet should be a memory, when so much that was matter of life and death has gone from mind? I see that old man and his helmet now, yet I forget the feel of Flanders mud.

We reached Suez, and anchored there. At Suez lay many ships in front of us, and a great gray battle-ship saluted us with guns, we all standing to attention while our ensigns dipped. I thought it strange that the battle-ship should salute us first, until I recalled how when I was a little fellow I once saw a viceroy salute my grandfather. My grandfather was one of those Sikhs who marched to help the British on the Ridge at Delhi when the British cause seemed lost. The British have long memories for such things.

Later there came an officer from the battle-ship and there was hot argument on our upper bridge. The captain of our ship grew very angry, but the officer from the battle-ship remained polite, and presently he took away with him certain of our stokers. The captain of our ship shouted after him that there were only weaklings and devil's leavings left, but later we discovered that was not true.

We fretted at delay at Suez. Ships may only enter the canal one by one, and while we waited some Arabs found their way on board from a small boat, pretending to sell fruit and trinkets. They assured us that the French and British were already badly beaten, and that Belgium had ceased to be. To test them, we asked where Belgium was, and they did not know; but they swore it had ceased to be. They advised us to mutiny and refuse to go on to our destruction.

They ought to have been arrested, but we were enraged and drove them from the ship with blows. We upset their little boat by hauling at the rope with which they had made it fast, and they were forced to swim for shore. One of them was taken by a shark, which we considered an excellent omen, and the others were captured as they swam and taken ashore in custody.

I think others must have visited the other ships with similar tales to tell, because after that, sahib, there was something such as I think the world never saw before that day. In that great fleet of ships we were men of many creeds and tongues—Sikh, Muhammadan, Dorga, Gurkha (the Dogra and Gurkha be both Hindu, though of different kinds), Jat, Punjabi, Rajput, Guzerati, Pathan, Mahratta—who can recall how many! No one language could have sufficed to explain one thought to all of us—no, nor yet ten languages! No word passed that my ear caught. Yet, ship after ship became aware of closer unity.

All on our knees on all the ships together we prayed thereafter thrice a day, our British officers standing bareheaded beneath the upper awnings, the chin-strap marks showing very plainly on their cheeks as the way of the British is when they feel emotion. We prayed, sahib, lest the war be over before we could come and do our share. I think there was no fear in all that fleet except the fear lest we come too late. A man might say with truth that we prayed to more gods than one, but our prayer was one. And we received one answer.

One morning our ship got up anchor unexpectedly and began to enter the canal ahead of all the ships bearing Indian troops. The men on the other ships bayed to us like packs of wolves, in part to give encouragement but principally jealous. We began to expect to see France now at any minute—I, who can draw a map of the world and set the chief cities in the proper place, being as foolish as the rest. There lay work as well as distance between us and France.

We began to pass men laboring to make the canal banks ready against attack, but mostly they had no news to give us. Yet at one place, where we tied to the bank because of delay ahead, a man shouted from a sand-dune that the kaiser of Germany has turned Muhammadan and now summons all Islam to destroy the French and British. Doubtless he mistook us for Muhammadans, being neither the first nor the last to make that mistake.

So we answered him we were on our way to Berlin to teach the kaiser his new creed. One man threw a lump of coal at him and he disappeared, but presently we heard him shouting to the men on the ship behind. They truly were Muhammadans, but they jeered at him as loud as we.

After that our officers set us to leading horses up and down the deck in relays, partly, no doubt, to keep us from talking with other men on shore, but also for the horses' sake. I remember how flies came on board and troubled the horses very much. At sea we had forgotten there were such things as flies, and they left us again when we left the canal.

At Port Said, which looks like a mean place, we stopped again for coal. Naked Egyptians—big black men, as tall as I and as straight—carried it up an inclined plank from a float and cast it by basketfuls through openings in the ship's side. We made up a purse of money for them, both officers and men contributing, and I was told there was a coaling record broken.

After that we steamed at great speed along another sea, one ship at a time, just as we left the canal, our ship leading all those that bore Indian troops. And now there were other war-ships—little ones, each of many funnels—low in the water, yet high at the nose—most swift, that guarded us on every hand, coming and going as the sharks do when they search the seas for food.

A wonder of a sight, sahib! Blue water—blue water—bluest ever I saw, who have seen lake water in the Hills! And all the ships belching black smoke, and throwing up pure white foam—and the last ship so far behind that only masts and smoke were visible above the sky-line—but more, we knew, behind that again, and yet more coming! I watched for hours at a stretch without weariness, and thought again of Ranjoor Singh. Surely, thought I, his three campaigns entitled him to this. Surely he was a better man than I. Yet here was I, and no man knew where he was. But when I spoke of Ranjoor Singh men spat, so I said nothing.

After a time I begged leave to descend an iron ladder to the bowels of the ship, and I sat on the lowest rung watching the British firemen at the furnaces. They cursed me in the name of God, their teeth and the whites of their eyes gleaming, but their skin black as night with coal dust. The sweat ran down in rivers between ridges of grime on the skin of their naked bellies. When a bell rang and the fire doors opened they glowed like pictures I have seen of devils. They were shadows when the doors clanged shut again. Considering them, I judged that they and we were one.

I climbed on deck again and spoke to a risaldar. He spoke to Colonel Kirby. Watching from below, I saw Colonel Kirby nod—thus, like a bird that takes an insect; and he went and spoke to the captain of the ship. Presently there was consultation, and a call for volunteers. The whole regiment responded. None, however, gave me credit for the thought. I think that risaldar accepted praise for it, but I have had no opportunity to ask him. He died in Flanders.

We went down and carried coal as ants that build a hill, piling it on the iron floor faster than the stokers could use it, toiling nearly naked like them lest we spoil our uniforms. We grew grimy, but the ship shook, and the water boiled behind us. None of the other ships was able to overtake us, although we doubted not they all tried.

There grew great good will between us and the stokers. We were clumsy from inexperience, and they full of laughter at us, but each judged the spirit with which the other labored. Once, where I stood directing near the bunker door, two men fell on me and covered me with coal. The stokers laughed and I was angry. I had hot words ready on my tongue, but a risaldar prevented me.

"This is their trade, not ours," said he. "Look to it lest any laugh at us when the time for our own trade comes!" I judged that well spoken, and remembered it.

There came at last a morning when the sun shone through jeweled mist—a morning with scent in it that set the horses in the hold to snorting—a dawn that smiled, as if the whole universe in truth were God's. A dawn, sahib, such as a man remembers to judge other dawns by. That day we came in sight of France.

Doubtless you suppose we cheered when we saw Marseilles at last. Yet I swear to you we were silent. We were disappointed because we could see no enemy and hear no firing of great guns! We made no more commotion than the dead while our ship steamed down the long harbor entrance, and was pushed and pulled by little tugs round a corner to a wharf. A French war-ship and some guns in a fort saluted us, and our ship answered; but on shore there seemed no excitement and our hearts sank. We thought that for all our praying we had come too late.

But the instant they raised the gangway a French officer and several British officers came running up it, and they all talked earnestly with Colonel Kirby on the upper bridge—we watching as if we had but an eye and an ear between us. Presently all our officers were summoned and told the news, and without one word being said to any of us we knew there was neither peace as yet, nor any surpassing victory fallen to our side. So then instantly we all began to speak at once, even as apes do when sudden fear has passed.

There were whole trains of trucks drawn up in the street beside the dock and we imagined we were to be hurried at once toward the fighting. But not so, for the horses needed rest and exercise and proper food before they could be fit to carry us. Moreover, there were stores to be offloaded from the ships, we having brought with us many things that it would not be so easy to replace in a land at war. Whatever our desire, we were forced to wait, and when we had left the ship we were marched through the streets to a camp some little distance out along the Estague Road. Later in the day, and the next day, and the next, infantry from the other ships followed us, for they, too, had to wait for their stores to be offloaded.

The French seemed surprised to see us. They were women and children for the most part, for the grown men had been called up. In our country we greet friends with flowers, but we had been led to believe that Europe thinks little of such manners. Yet the French threw flowers to us, the little children bringing arms full and baskets full.

Thenceforward, day after day, we rode at exercise,

keeping ears and eyes open, and marveling at France. No man complained, although our very bones ached to be on active service. And no man spoke of Ranjoor Singh, who should have led D Squadron. Yet I believe there was not one man in all D Squadron but thought of Ranjoor Singh all the time. He who has honor most at heart speaks least about it. In one way shame on Ranjoor Singh's account was a good thing, for it made the whole regiment watchful against treachery.

Treachery, sahib—we had yet to learn what treachery could be! Marseilles is a half-breed of a place, part Italian, part French. The work was being chiefly done by the Italians, now that all able-bodied Frenchmen were under arms. And Italy not yet in the war!

Sahib, I swear to you that all the spies in all the world seemed at that moment to be Italian, and all in Marseilles at once! There were spies among the men who brought our stores. Spies who brought the hay. Spies among the women who walked now and then through our lines to admire, accompanied by officers who were none too wide-awake if they were honest. You would not believe how many pamphlets reached us, printed in our tongue and some of them worded very cunningly.

There were men who could talk Hindustanee who whispered to us to surrender to the Germans at the first opportunity, promising in that case that we shall be well treated. The German kaiser, these men assured us, had truly turned Muhammadan; as if that were anything to Sikhs, unless perhaps an additional notch against him! I was told they mistook the

Muhammadans in another camp for Sikhs, and were spat on for their pains!

Nor were all the spies Italians, after all. Our hearts went out to the French. We were glad to be on their side—glad to help them defend their country. I shall be glad to my dying day that I have struck a blow for France. Yet the only really dangerous man of all who tried to corrupt us in Marseilles was a French officer of the rank of major, who could speak our tongue as well as I. He said with sorrow that the French were already as good as vanquished, and that he pitied us as lambs sent to the slaughter. The part, said he, of every wise man was to go over to the enemy before the day should come for paying penalties.

I told what he had said to me to a risaldar, and the risaldar spoke with Colonel Kirby. We heard—although I do not know whether it is true or not—that the major was shot that evening with his face to a wall. I do know that I, in company with several troopers, was cross-examined by interpreters that day in presence of Colonel Kirby and a French general and some of the general's staff.

There began to be talk at last about Ranjoor Singh. I heard men say it was no great wonder, after all, that he should have turned traitor, for it was plain he must have been tempted cunningly. Yet there was no forgiveness for him. They grew proud that where he had failed they could stand firm; and there is no mercy in proud men's minds—nor much wisdom either.

At last a day came—too soon for the horses, but

none too soon for us—when we marched through the streets to entrain for the front. As we had marched first out of Delhi, so we marched first from Marseilles now. Only the British regiments from India were on ahead of us; we led the Indian-born contingent.

French wives and children, and some cripples, lined the streets to cheer and wave their handkerchiefs. We were on our way to help their husbands defend France, and they honored us. It was our due. But can the sahib accept his due with a dry eye and a word in his throat? Nay! It is only ingratitude that a man can swallow unconcerned. No man spoke. We rode like graven images, and I think the French women wondered at our silence. I know that I, for one, felt extremely willing to die for France; and I thought of Ranjoor Singh and of how his heart, too, would have burned if he had been with us. With such thoughts as swelled in my own breast, it was not in me to believe him false, whatever the rest might think.

D Squadron proved in good fortune that day, for they gave us a train of passenger coaches with seats, and our officers had a first-class coach in front. The other squadrons, and most of the other regiments, had to travel in open trucks, although I do not think any grumbled on that score. There was a French staff officer to each train, and he who rode in our train had an orderly who knew English; the orderly climbed in beside me and we rode miles together, talking all the time, he surprising me vastly more than I him. We exchanged information as two boys that play a game—I a move, then he a move, then I again, then he.

The game was at an end when neither could think of another question to ask; but he learned more than I. At the end I did not yet know what his religion was, but he knew a great deal about mine. On the other hand, he told me all about their army and its close association between officers and men, and all the news he had about the fighting (which was not so very much), and what he thought of the British. He seemed to think very highly of the British, rather to his own surprise.

He told me he was a pastry cook by trade, and said he could cook chapatties such as we eat; and he understood my explanation why Sikhs were riding in the front trains and Muhammadans behind—because Muhammadans must pray at fixed intervals and the trains must stop to let them do it. He understood wherein our Sikh prayer differs from that of Islam. Yet he refused to believe I am no polygamist. But that is nothing. Since then I have fought in a trench beside Englishmen who spoke of me as a savage; and I have seen wounded Germans writhe and scream because their officers had told them we Sikhs would eat them alive. Yes, sahib; not once, but many times.

The journey was slow, for the line ahead of us was choked with supply trains, some of which were needed at the front as badly as ourselves. Now and then trains waited on sidings to let us by, and by that means we became separated from the other troop trains, our regiment leading all the others in the end by almost half a day. The din of engine whistles became so constant that we no longer noticed it.

But there was another din that did not grow

familiar. Along the line next ours there came hurrying in the opposite direction train after train of wounded, traveling at great speed, each leaving a smell in its wake that set us all to spitting. And once in so often there came a train filled full of the sound of screaming. The first time, and the second time we believed it was ungreased axles, but after the third time we understood.

Then our officers came walking along the footboards, speaking to us through the windows and pretending to point out characteristics of the scenery; and we took great interest in the scenery, asking them the names of places and the purposes of things, for it is not good that one's officers should be other than arrogantly confident.

We were a night and a day, and a night and a part of a day on the journey, and men told us later we had done well to cross the length of France in that time, considering conditions. On the morning of the last day we began almost before it was light to hear the firing of great guns and the bursting of shells—like the thunder of the surf on Bombay Island in the great monsoon—one roar without intermission, yet full of pulsation.

I think it was midday when we drew up at last on a siding, where a French general waited with some French and British officers. Colonel Kirby left the train and spoke with the general, and then gave the order for us to detrain at once; and we did so very swiftly, men, and horses, and baggage. Many of us were men of more than one campaign, able to judge by this and by that how sorely we were needed. We knew what it means when the reenforcements look fit for the work in hand. The French general came and shook hands again with Colonel Kirby, and saluted us all most impressively.

We were spared all the business of caring for our own baggage and sent away at once. With a French staff officer to guide us, we rode away at once toward the sound of firing—at a walk, because within reasonable limits the farther our horses might be allowed to walk now the better they would be able to gallop with us later.

We rode along a road between straight trees, most of them scarred by shell-fire. There were shell-holes in the road, some of which had been filled with the first material handy, but some had to be avoided. We saw no dead bodies, nor even dead horses, although smashed gun-carriages and limbers and broken wagons were everywhere.

To our right and left was flat country, divided by low hedges and the same tall straight trees; but far away in front was a forest, whose top just rose above the sky-line. As we rode toward that we could see the shells bursting near it.

Between us and the forest there were British guns, dug in; and away to our right were French guns—batteries and batteries of them. And between us and the guns were great receiving stations for the wounded, with endless lines of stretcher-bearers like ants passing to and fro. By the din we knew that the battle stretched far away beyond sight to right and left of us.

Many things we saw that were unexpected. The

speed of the artillery fire was unbelievable. But what surprised all of us most was the absence of reserves. Behind the guns and before the guns we passed many a place where reserves might have sheltered, but there were none.

There came two officers, one British and one French, galloping toward us. They spoke excitedly with Colonel Kirby and our French staff officer, but we continued at a walk and Colonel Kirby lit a fresh cheroot. After some time there came an aeroplane with a great square cross painted on its under side, and we were ordered to halt and keep quite still until it went away. When it was too far away for its man to distinguish us we began to trot at last, but it was growing dusk when we halted finally behind the forest —dusky and cloudy, the air full of smoke from the explosions, ill-smelling and difficult to breathe. During the last three-quarters of a mile the shells had been bursting all about us, but we had only lost one man and a horse—and the man not killed.

As it grew darker the enemy sent up star-shells, and by their light we could sometimes see as plainly as by daylight. British infantry were holding the forest in front of us and a road that ran to right of it. Their rifle-fire was steady as the roll of drums. These were not the regiments that preceded us from India; they had been sent to another section of the battle. These were men who had been in the fighting from the first, and their wounded and the stretcher-bearers were surprised to see us. No word of our arrival seemed to reach the firing line as yet. Men were too busy to pass news.

Over our heads from a mile away, the British and French artillery were sending a storm of shells, and the enemy guns were answering two for one. And besides that, into the forest, and into the trench to the right of it that was being held by the British infantry there was falling such a cataract of fire that it was not possible to believe a man could live. Yet the answering rifle-fire never paused for a second.

I learned afterward the name of the regiment in the end of the trench nearest us. With these two eyes in the Hills I once saw that same regiment run like a thousand hares into the night, because it had no supper and a dozen Afridi marksmen had the range. Can the sahib explain? I think I can. A man's spirit is no more in his belly than in the cart that carries his belongings; yet, while he thinks it is, his enemies all flourish.

We dismounted to rest the horses, and waited behind the forest until it grew so dark that between the bursting of the star-shells a man could not see his hand held out in front of him. Now and then a stray shell chanced among us, but our casualties were very few. I wondered greatly at the waste of ammunition. My ears ached with the din, but there seemed more noise wrought than destruction. We had begun to grow restless when an officer came galloping at last to Colonel Kirby's side and gave him directions with much pointing and waving of the arm.

Then Colonel Kirby summoned all our officers, and they rode back to tell us what the plan was. The din was so great by this time that they were obliged to explain anew to each four men in turn. This was the plan:

The Germans, ignorant of our arrival, undoubtedly believed the British infantry to be without support and were beginning to press forward in the hope of winning through to the railway line. The infantry on our right front, already overwhelmed by weight of artillery fire, would be obliged to evacuate their trench and fall back, thus imperiling the whole line, unless we could save the day.

Observe this, sahib: so—I make a drawing in the dust. Between the trench here, and the forest there, was a space of level ground some fifty or sixty yards wide. There was scarcely more than a furrow across it to protect the riflemen—nothing at all that could stop a horse. At a given signal the infantry were to draw aside from that piece of level land, like a curtain drawn back along a rod, and we were to charge through the gap thus made between them and the forest. The shock of our charge and its unexpectedness were to serve instead of numbers.

Fine old-fashioned tactics, sahib, that suited our mind well! There had been plenty on the voyage, including Gooja Singh, who argued we should all be turned into infantry as soon as we arrived, and we had dreaded that. Each to his own. A horseman prefers to fight on horseback with the weapons that he knows.

Perhaps the sahib has watched Sikh cavalry at night and wondered how so many men and horses could keep so still. We had made but little noise hitherto, but now our silence was that of night itself.

We had but one eye, one ear, one intellect among us. We were one! One with the night and with the work ahead!

One red light swinging near the corner of the forest was to mean BE READY! We were ready as the fuse is for the match! Two red lights would mean that the sidewise movement by the infantry was under way. Three lights swinging together were to be our signal to begin. Sahib, I saw three red lights three thousand times between each minute and the next!

The shell-fire increased from both sides. Where the British infantry lay was such a lake of flame and din that the very earth seemed to burst apart; yet the answering rifle-fire was steady—steady as the roll of drums. Then we truly saw one red light, and "EK!" said we all at once. *Ek* means *one,* sahib, but it sounded like the opening of a breech-block. "Mount!" ordered Colonel Kirby, and we mounted.

While I held my breath and watched for the second light I heard a new noise behind me, different from the rest, and therefore audible—a galloping horse and a challenge close at hand. I saw in the light of a bursting shell a Sikh officer, close followed by a trooper on a blown horse. I saw the officer ride to Colonel Kirby's side, rein in his charger, and salute. At that instant there swung two red lights, and "DO!" said the regiment. *Do* means *two,* sahib, but it sounded like the thump of ordnance. "Draw sabers!" commanded Colonel Kirby, and the rear ranks drew. The front-rank men had lances.

By the light of a star-shell I could plainly see the Sikh officer and trooper. I recognized the charger—

a beast with the devil in him and the speed of wind. I recognized both men. I thought a shell must have struck me. I must be dead and in a new world. I let my horse edge nearer, not believing—until ears confirmed eyes. I heard Colonel Kirby speak, very loud, indeed, as a man to whom good news comes.

"Ranjoor Singh!" said he; and he took him by the hand and wrung it. "Thank God!" he said, speaking from the heart as the British do at times when they forget that others listen. "Thank God, old man! You've come in the nick of time!"

So I was right, and my heart leapt in me. He was with us before the blood ran! Every man in the squadron recognized him now, and I knew every eye had watched to see Colonel Kirby draw saber and cut him down, for habit of thought is harder to bend than a steel bar. But I could feel the squadron coming round to my way of thinking as Colonel Kirby continued talking to him, obviously making him an explanation of our plan.

"Join your squadron, man—hurry!" I heard Colonel Kirby say at last, for taking advantage of the darkness I had let my horse draw very near to them. Now I had to rein back and make pretense that my horse had been unruly, for Ranjoor Singh came riding toward us, showing his teeth in a great grin, and Captain Fellowes with a word of reproof thrown back to me spurred on to meet him.

"Hurrah, Major Ranjoor Singh!" said Captain Fellowes. "I'm damned glad to see you!" That was a generous speech, sahib, from a man who must now yield command of the squadron, but Captain Fellowes had a heart like a bridegroom's always. He must always glory in the squadron's luck, and he loved us better than himself. That was why we loved him. They shook hands, and looked in each other's eyes. Ranjoor Singh wheeled his charger. And in that same second we all together saw three red lights swinging by the corner.

"TIN!" said we, with one voice. *Tin* means *three,* sahib, but it sounded rather like the scream of a shell that leaves on its journey.

My horse laid his ears back and dug his toes into the ground. A trumpet sounded, and Colonel Kirby rose in his stirrups:

"Outram's Own!" he yelled, "by squadrons on number One—"

But the sahib would not be interested in the sequence of commands that have small meaning to those not familiar with them. And who shall describe what followed? Who shall tell the story of a charge into the night, at an angle, into massed regiments of infantry advancing one behind another at the double and taken by surprise?

The guns of both sides suddenly ceased firing. Even as I used my spurs they ceased. How? Who am I that I should know? The British guns, I suppose, from fear of slaying us, and the German guns from fear of slaying Germans; but as to how, I know not. But the German star-shells continued bursting overhead, and by that weird light their oncoming infantry saw charging into them men they had never seen before out of a picture-book!

God knows what tales they had been told about

us Sikhs. I read their faces as I rode. Fear is an ugly weapon, sahib, whose hilt is more dangerous than its blade. If our officers had told us such tales about Germans as their officers had told them about us, I think perhaps we might have feared to charge.

Numbers were as nothing that night. Speed, and shock, and unexpectedness were ours, and lies had prepared us our reception. D Squadron rode behind Ranjoor Singh like a storm in the night—swung into line beside the other squadrons—and spurred forward as in a dream. There was no shouting; no war-cry. We rode into the Germans as I have seen wind cut into a forest in the hills—downward into them, for once we had leapt the trench the ground sloped their way. And they went down before us as we never had the chance of mowing them again.

So, sahib, we proved our hearts—whether they were stout, and true, as the British had believed, or false, as the Germans planned and hoped. That was a night of nights—one of very few such, for the mounted actions in this war have not been many. Hah! I have been envied! I have been called opprobrious names by a sergeant of British lancers, out of great jealousy! But that is the way of the British. It happened later, when the trench fighting had settled down in earnest and my regiment and his were waiting our turn behind the lines. He and I sat together on a bench in a great tent, where some French artists gave us good entertainment.

He offered me tobacco, which I do not use, and rum, which I do not drink. He accepted sweetmeats from me. And he called me a name that would make the sahib gulp, a word that I suppose he had picked up from a barrack-sweeper on the Bengal side of India. Then he slapped me on the back, and after that sat with his arm around me while the entertainment lasted. When we left the tent he swore roundly at a newcomer to the front for not saluting me, who am not entitled to salute. That is the way of the British. But I was speaking of Ranjoor Singh. Forgive me, sahib.

The horse his trooper-servant rode was blown and nearly useless, so that the trooper died that night for lack of a pair of heels, leaving us none to question as to Ranjoor Singh's late doings. But Bagh, Ranjoor Singh's charger, being a marvel of a beast whom few could ride but he, was fresh enough and Ranjoor Singh led us like a whirlwind beckoning a storm. I judged his heart was on fire. He led us slantwise into a tight-packed regiment. We rolled it over, and he took us beyond that into another one. In the dark he re-formed us (and few but he could have done that then)—lined us up again with the other squadrons—and brought us back by the way we had come. Then he took us the same road a second time against remnants of the men who had withstood us and into yet another regiment that checked and balked beyond. The Germans probably believed us ten times as many as we truly were, for that one setback checked their advance along the whole line.

Colonel Kirby led us, but I speak of Ranjoor Singh. I never once saw Colonel Kirby until the fight was over and we were back again resting our horses behind the trees while the roll was called. Throughout the fight—and I have no idea whatever how long it lasted—I kept an eye on Ranjoor Singh and spurred in his wake, obeying the least motion of his saber. No, sahib, I myself did not slay many men. It is the business of a non-commissioned man like me to help his officers keep control, and I did what I might. I was nearly killed by a wounded German officer who seized my bridle-rein; but a trooper's lance took him in the throat and I rode on untouched. For all I know that was the only danger I was in that night.

A battle is a strange thing, sahib—like a dream. A man only knows such part of it as crosses his own vision, and remembers but little of that. What he does remember seldom tallies with what the others saw. Talk with twenty of our regiment, and you may get twenty different versions of what took place—yet not one man would have lied to you, except perhaps here and there a little in the matter of his own accomplishment. Doubtless the Germans have a thousand different accounts of it.

I know this, and the world knows it: that night the Germans melted. They were. Then they broke into parties and were not. We pursued them as they ran. Suddenly the star-shells ceased from bursting overhead, and out of black darkness I heard Colonel Kirby's voice thundering an order. Then a trumpet blared. Then I heard Ranjoor Singh's voice, high-pitched. Almost the next I knew we were halted in the shadow of the trees again, calling low to one another, friend's voice seeking friend's. We could scarcely hear the voices for the thunder of artillery that had begun again; and whereas formerly the German gun-fire had been greatest, now we thought the British and French fire had the better of it. They had been reenforced, but I have no notion whence.

The infantry, that had drawn aside like a curtain to let us through, had closed in again to the edge of the forest, and through the noise of rifle-firing and artillery we caught presently the thunder of new regiments advancing at the double. Thousands of our Indian infantry—those who had been in the trains behind us—were coming forward at a run! God knows that was a night—to make a man glad he has lived!

It was not only the Germans who had not expected us. Now, sahib, for the first time the British infantry began to understand who it was who had come to their aid, and they began to sing—one song, all together. The wounded sang it, too, and the stretcher-bearers. There came a day when we had our own version of that song, but that night it was new to us. We only caught a few words—the first words. The sahib knows the words—the first few words? It was true we had come a long, long way; but it choked us into silence to hear that battered infantry acknowledge it.

Color and creed, sahib. What are color and creed? The world has mistaken us Sikhs too long for a breed it can not understand. We Sikhs be men, with the hearts of men; and that night we knew that our hearts and theirs were one. Nor have I met since then the fire that could destroy the knowledge, although efforts have been made, and reasons shown me.

But my story is of Ranjoor Singh and of what he

did. I but tell my own part to throw more light on his. What I did is as nothing. Of what he did, you shall be the judge—remembering this, that he who does, and he who glories in the deed are one. Be attentive, sahib; this is a tale of tales!

CHAPTER II

Can the die fall which side up it will? Nay, not if it be honest.—EASTERN PROVERB.

Many a league our infantry advanced that night, the guns following, getting the new range by a miracle each time they took new ground. We went forward, too, at the cost of many casualties—too many in proportion to the work we did. We were fired on in the darkness more than once by our own infantry. We, who had lost but seventy-two men killed and wounded in the charge, were short another hundred when the day broke and nothing to the good by it.

Getting lost in the dark—falling into shell-holes—swooping down on rear-guards that generally proved to have machine guns with them—weary men on hungrier, wearier horses—the wonder is that a man rode back to tell of it at dawn.

One-hundred-and-two-and-seventy were our casualties, and some two hundred horses—some of the men so lightly wounded that they were back in the ranks within the week. At dawn they sent us to the rear to rest, we being too good a target for the enemy by daylight. Some of us rode two to a horse. On our way to the camp the French had pitched for us we passed through reenforcements coming from another section of the front, who gave us the right of way, and we took the salute of two divisions of French infantry who, I suppose, had been told of the service we had rendered. Said I to Gooja Singh, who sat on my horse's rump, his own beast being disemboweled, "Who speaks now of a poor beginning?" said I.

"I would rather see the end!" said he. But he never saw the end. Gooja Singh was ever too impatient of beginnings, and too sure what the end ought to be, to make certain of the middle part. I have known men on outpost duty so far-seeing that an enemy had them at his mercy if only he could creep close enough. And such men are always grumblers.

Gooja Singh led the grumbling now—he who had been first to prophesy how we should be turned into infantry. They kept us at the rear, and took away our horses—took even our spurs, making us drill with unaccustomed weapons. And I think that the beginning of the new distrust of Ranjoor Singh was in resentment at his patience with the bayonet drill. We soldiers are like women, sahib, ever resentful of the new—aye, like women in more ways than one; for whom we have loved best we hate most when the change comes.

Once, at least a squadron of us had loved Ranjoor Singh to the death. He was a Sikh of Sikhs. It had been our boast that fire could not burn his courage nor love corrupt him, and I was still of that mind; but not so the others. They began to remember how he had stayed behind when we left India. We had all seen him in disguise, in conversation with that German by the Delhi Gate. We knew how busy he had been in the bazaars while the rumors flew. And the trooper who had stayed behind with him, who had joined us with him at the very instant of the charge that night, died in the charge; so that there was none to give explanation of his conduct. Ranjoor Singh himself was a very rock for silence. Our British officers said nothing, doubtless not suspecting the distrust; for it was a byword that Ranjoor Singh held the honor of the squadron in his hand. Yet of all the squadron only the officers and I now trusted him—the Sikh officers because they imitated the British; the British because faith is a habit with them, once pledged, and I—God knows. There were hours when I did distrust him—black hours, best forgotten.

The war settled down into a siege of trenches, and soon we were given a section of a trench to hold. Little by little we grew wise at the business of tossing explosives over blind banks—we, who would rather have been at it with the lance and saber. Yet, can a die fall which side up it will? Nay, not if it be honest! We were there to help. We who had carried coal could shovel mud, and as time went on we grumbled less.

But time hung heavy, and curiosity regarding Ranjoor Singh led from one conjecture to another. At last Gooja Singh asked Captain Fellowes, and he said that Ranjoor Singh had stayed behind to expose a German plot—that having done so, he had hurried after us. That explanation ought to have satisfied every one, and I think it did for a time. But who could hide from such a man as Ranjoor Singh that the squadron's faith in him was gone? That knowledge made him savage. How should we know that he had been forbidden to tell us what had kept him? When he set aside his pride and made us overtures, there was no response; so his heart hardened in him,

Secrecy is good. Secrecy is better than all the lame explanations in the world. But in this war there has been too much secrecy in the wrong place. They should have let him line us up and tell us his whole story. But later, when perhaps he might have done it, either his pride was too great or his sense of obedience too tightly spun. To this day he has never told us. Not that it matters.

The subtlest fool is the worst, and Gooja Singh's tongue did not lack subtlety on occasion. He made it his business to remind the squadron daily of its doubts, and I, who should have known better, laughed at some of the things he said and agreed with others. One is the fool who speaks with him who listens. I have never been rebuked for it by Ranjoor Singh, and more than once since that day he has seen fit to praise me; but in that hour when most he needed friends I became his half-friend, which is worse than enemy. I never raised my voice once in defense of him in those days.

Meanwhile Ranjoor Singh grew very wise at this trench warfare, Colonel Kirby and the other British officers taking great comfort in his cunning. It was he who led us to tie strings to the German wire entanglements, which we then jerked from our trench, causing them to lie awake and waste much ammunition. It was he who thought of dressing turbans on the end of poles and thrusting them forward at the hour before dawn when fear and chill and darkness have done their worst work. That started a panic that cost the Germans eighty men.

I think his leadership would have won the squadron back to love him. I know it saved his life. We had all heard tales of how the British soldiers in South Africa made short work of the officers they did not love, and it would have been easy to make an end of Ranjoor Singh on any dark night. But he led too well; men were afraid to take the responsibility lest the others turn on them. One night I overheard two troopers considering the thought, and they suspected I had overheard. I said nothing, but they were afraid, as I knew they would be. Has the sahib ever heard of "left-hand casualties"? I will explain.

We Sikhs have a saying that in fear there is no wisdom. None can be wise and afraid. None can be afraid and wise. The men at the front, both Indian and British—French, too, for aught I know—who feared to fight longer in the trenches were seized in those early days with the foolish thought of inflicting some injury on themselves—not very severe, but enough to cause a spell of absence at the base and a rest in hospital. Folly being the substance of that idea, and most men being right-handed, such self-inflicted wounds were practically always in the hand or foot and always on the left side. The ambulance men knew them on the instant.

Those two fools of my squadron wounded themselves with bullets in the left hand, forgetting that their palms would be burned by the discharge. I was sent to the rear to give evidence against them (for I saw them commit the foolishness). The cross-examination we all three underwent was clever—at the hands of a young British captain, who, I dare swear, was suckled by a Sikh nurse in the Punjab. In less than thirty minutes he had the whole story out of us; and the two troopers were shot that evening for an example.

That young captain was greatly impressed with the story we had told about Ranjoor Singh, and he called me back afterward and asked me a hundred questions more—until he must have known the very color of my entrails and I knew not which way I faced. To all of this a senior officer of the Intelligence Department listened with both ears, and presently he and the captain talked together.

The long and short of that was that Ranjoor Singh was sent for; and when he returned to the trench after two days' absence it was to work independently of us—from our trench, but irrespective of our doings. Even Colonel Kirby now had no orders to give him, although they two talked long and at frequent intervals in the place Colonel Kirby called his funk-hole. It was now that the squadron's reawakening love for Ranjoor Singh received the worst check of any. We had almost forgotten he knew German. Henceforward he conversed in German each day with the enemy.

It is a strange thing, sahib,—not easy to explain—but I, who have achieved some fluency in English and might therefore have admired his gift of tongues, now began to doubt him in earnest—hating myself the while, but doubting him. And Gooja Singh, who had talked the most and dropped the blackest hints against him, now began to take his side.

And Ranjoor Singh said nothing. Night after night he went to lie at the point where our trench and the enemy's lay closest. There he would talk with some one whom we never saw, while we sat shivering in the mud. Cold we can endure, sahib, as readily as any; it is colder in winter where I come from than anything I felt in Flanders; but the rain and the mud depressed our spirits, until with these two eyes I have seen grown men weeping.

They kept us at work to encourage us. Our spells in the trench were shortened and our rests at the rear increased to the utmost possible. Only Ranjoor Singh took no vacation, remaining ever on the watch, passing from one trench to another, conversing ever with the enemy.

We dug and they dug, each side laboring everlastingly to find the other's listening places and to blow them up by means of mining, so that the earth became a very rat-run. Above-ground, where were only ruin and barbed wire, there was no sign of activity, but only a great stench that came from bodies none dared bury. We were thankful that the wind blew oftenest from us to them; but whichever way the wind blew Ranjoor Singh knew no rest. He was ever to be found where the lines lay closest at the moment, either listening or talking. We understood very well that he was carrying out orders given him at the rear, but that did not make the squadron or the regiment like him any better, and as far as that went I was one with them; I hated to see a squadron leader stoop to such intrigues.

It was plain enough that some sort of intrigue was making headway, for the Germans soon began to toss over into our trench bundles of printed pamphlets, explaining in our tongue why they were our best friends and why therefore we should refuse to wage war on them. They threw printed bulletins that said, in good Punjabi, there was revolution from end to end of India, rioting in England, utter disaster to the British fleet, and that our way home again to India had been cut by the German war-ships. They must have been ignorant of the fact that we received our mail from India regularly. I have noticed this about the Germans: they are unable to convince themselves that any other people can appreciate the same things they appreciate, think as swiftly as they, or despise the terrors they despise. That is one reason why they must lose this war. But there are others also.

One afternoon, when I was pretending to doze in a niche near the entrance to Colonel Kirby's funk-hole, I became possessed of the key to it all; for Colonel Kirby's voice was raised more than once in anger. I understood at last how Ranjoor Singh had orders to deceive the Germans as to our state of mind. He was to make them believe we were growing mutinous and that the leaven only needed time in which to work; this of course for the purpose of throwing them off their guard.

My heart stopped beating while I listened, for what man hears his honor smirched without wincing? Even so I think I would have held my tongue, only that Gooja Singh, who dozed in a niche on the other side of the funk-hole entrance, heard the same as I.

Said Gooja Singh that evening to the troopers round about: "They chose well," said he. "They picked a brave man—a clever man, for a desperate venture!" And when the troopers asked what that might mean, he asked how many of them in the Punjab had seen a goat tied to a stake to lure a panther. The suggestion made them think. Then, pretending to praise him, letting fall no word that could be thrown back in his teeth, he condemned Ranjoor Singh for a worse traitor than any had yet believed him. Gooja Singh was a man with a certain subtlety. A man with two tongues, very dangerous.

"Ranjoor Singh is brave," said he, "for he is not afraid to sacrifice us all. Many officers are afraid to lose too many men in the gaining of an end, but not so he. He is clever, for who else would have thought of making us seem despicable to the Germans in order to tempt them to attack in force at this point? Have ye not noticed how to our rear all is being made ready for the defense and for a counter-attack to follow? We are the bait. The battle is to be waged over our dead bodies."

I corrected him. I said I had heard as well as he, and that Colonel Kirby was utterly angry at the defamation of those whom he was ever pleased to call "his Sikhs." But that convinced nobody, although it did the colonel sahib no harm in the regiment's opinion—not that he needed advocates. We were all ready to die around Colonel Kirby at any minute. Even Gooja Singh was ready to do that.

"Does the colonel sahib accept the situation?" one of the troopers asked.

"Aye, for he must," said Gooja Singh; and I could not deny it. "Ranjoor Singh went over his head and orders have come from the rear." I could not deny that either, although I did not believe it. How should I, or any one, know what passed after Ranjoor Singh had been sent for by the Intelligence officers? I was his half-friend in those days, sahib. Worse than his enemy—unwilling to take part against him, yet unready to speak up in his defense. Doubtless my silence went for consent among the troopers.

The end of the discussion found men unafraid. "If the colonel sahib is willing to be bait," said they, "then so be we, but let us see to it that none hang back." And so the whole regiment made up its mind to die desperately, yet with many a sidewise glance at Ranjoor Singh, who was watched more carefully than I think he guessed in those days. If he had tried to slip back to the rear it would have been the end of him. But he continued with us.

And all this while a great force gathered at our rear—gathered and grew—Indian and British infantry. Guns by the fifty were brought forward under cover of the night and placed in line behind us. Ranjoor Singh continued talking with the enemy, lying belly downward in the mud, and they kept throwing printed stuff to us that we turned in to our officers. But the Germans did not attack. And the force behind us grew.

Then one evening, just after dusk, we were all amazed by the news that the assault was to come from our side. And almost before that news had reached us the guns at our rear began their overture, making preparation beyond the compass of a man's mind to grasp or convey. They hurled such a torrent of shells that the Germans could neither move away the troops in front of us nor bring up others to their aid. It did not seem possible that one German could be left alive, and I even felt jealous because, thought I, no work would be left for us to do! Yet men did live—as we discovered. For a night and a day our ordnance kept up that preparation, and then word went around.

Who shall tell of a night attack, from a trench against trenches? Suddenly the guns ceased pounding the earth in front of us and lifted to make a screen of fire almost a mile beyond. There was instant pitch darkness on every hand, and out of that a hundred trumpets sounded. Instantly, each squadron leader leaped the earthwork, shouting to his men. Ranjoor Singh leaped up in front of us, and we followed him, all forgetting their distrust of him in the fierce excitement —remembering only how he had led us in the charge on that first night. The air was thick with din, and fumes, and flying metal—for the Germans were not forgetting to use artillery. I ceased to think of anything but going forward. Who shall describe it?

Once in Bombay I heard a Christian preacher tell of the Judgment Day to come, when graves shall give up their dead. That is not our Sikh idea of judgment, but his words brought before my mind a picture not so much unlike a night attack in Flanders. He spoke of the whole earth trembling and consumed by fire—of thunder and lightning and a great long trumpet call—of the dead leaping alive again from the graves where they lay buried. Not a poor picture, sahib, of a night attack in Flanders!

The first line of German trenches, and the second had been pounded out of being by our guns. The barbed wire had been cut into fragments by our shrapnel. Here and there an arm or a leg protruded from the ground—here and there a head. For two hundred yards and perhaps more there was nothing to oppose us, except the enemy shells bursting so constantly that we seemed to breathe splintered metal. Yet very few were hit. The din was so great that it seemed to be silence. We were phantom men, going forward without sound of footfall. I could neither feel nor think for the first two hundred yards, but ran with my bayonet out in front of me. And then I did feel. A German bayonet barked my knuckles. After that there was fighting such as I hope never to know again.

The Germans did not seem to have been taken by surprise at all. They had made ample preparation. And as for holding us in contempt, they gave no evidence of that. Their wounded were unwilling to surrender because their officers had given out we would torture prisoners. We had to pounce on them, and cut their buttons off and slit their boots, so that they must use both hands to hold their trousers up and could not run. And that took time so that we lagged behind a little, for we took more prisoners than the regiments to right and left of us. The Dogra regiment to our left and the Gurkha regiment to our right gained on us fast, and we became, as it were, the center of a new moon.

But then in the light of bursting shells we saw Colonel Kirby and Ranjoor Singh and Captain Fellowes and some other officers far out in front of us beckoning—calling on us for our greatest effort. We answered. We swept forward after them into the teeth of all the inventions in the world. Mine after mine exploded under our very feet. Shrapnel burst among us. There began to be uncut wire, and men rushed out at us from trenches that we thought obliterated, but that proved only to have been hidden under debris by our gun-fire. Shadows resolved into trenches defended by machine guns.

But we went forward—cavalry, without a spur among us—cavalry with rifles—cavalry on foot—infantry with the fire and the drill and the thoughts of cavalry—still cavalry at heart, for all the weapons they had given us and the trench life we had lived. We remembered, sahib, that the Germans had been educated lately to despise us, and we were out that night to convert them to a different opinion! It seemed good to D Squadron that Ranjoor Singh, who had done the defamation, should lead us to the clearing of our name. Nothing could stop us that night.

Whereas we had been last in the advance, we charged into the lead and held it. We swept on I know not how far, but very far beyond the wings. No means had been devised that I know of for checking the distance covered, and I suppose Headquarters timed the attack and tried to judge how far the advance had carried, with the aid of messengers sent running back. No easy task!

At all events we lost touch with the regiments to right and left, but kept touch with the enemy, pressing forward until suddenly our own shell-fire ceased to fall in front of us but resumed pounding toward our rear. They call such a fire a barrage, sahib. Its purpose is to prevent the enemy from making a counter-attack until the infantry can dig themselves in and secure the new ground won. That meant we were isolated. It needed no staff officer to tell us that, or to bring us to our senses. We were like men who wake from a nightmare, to find the truth more dreadful than the dream.

Colonel Kirby was wounded a little, and sat while a risaldar bound his arm. Ranjoor Singh found a short trench half full of water, and ordered us into it. Although we had not realized it until then, it was raining torrents, and the Germans we drove out of that trench (there were but a few of them) were wetter than water rats; but we had to scramble down into it, and the cold bath finished what the sense of isolation had begun. We were sober men when Kirby sahib scrambled in last and ordered us to begin on the trench at once with picks and shovels that the Germans had left behind. We altered the trench so that it faced both ways, and waited shivering for the dawn.

Let it not be supposed, however, sahib, that we waited unmolested. The Germans are not that kind of warrior. I hold no brief for them, but I tell no lies about them, either. They fight with persistence, bravery, and what they consider to be cunning. We were under rifle-fire at once from before and behind and the flanks, and our own artillery began pounding the ground so close to us that fragments of shell and shrapnel flew over our heads incessantly, and great clods of earth came thumping and splashing into our trench, compelling us to keep busy with the shovels.

Nor did the German artillery omit to make a target of us, though with poor success. More than the half of us lived; and to prove that there had been thought as well as bravery that night we had plenty of ammunition with us. We were troubled to stow the ammunition out of the wet, yet where it would be safe from the German fire.

We made no reply to the shell-fire, for that would have been foolishness; so, doubtless thinking they had the range not quite right, or perhaps supposing that we had been annihilated, the enemy discontinued shelling us and devoted their attention to our friends beyond. But at the same time a battalion of infantry began to feel its way toward us and we grew very busy with our rifles, the wounded crawling through the wet to pass the cartridges. Once there was a bayonet charge, which we repelled.

Those who had not thrown away their knapsacks to lighten themselves had their emergency rations, but about half of us had nothing to eat whatever. It was perfectly evident to all of us from the very first that unless we should receive prompt aid at dawn our case was as hopeless as death itself. So much the more reason for stout hearts, said we, and our bearing put new heart into our officers.

When dawn came the sight was not inspiriting. Dawn amid a waste of Flanders mud, seen through a rain-storm, is not a joyous spectacle in any case. Consider, sahib, what a sunny land we came from, and pass no hasty judgment on us if our spirits sank. It was the weather, not the danger that depressed us. I, who was near the center of the trench, could see to right and left over the ends, and I made a hasty count of heads, discovering that we, who had been a regiment, were now about three hundred men, forty of whom were wounded.

I saw that we were many a hundred yards away from the nearest British trench. The Germans had crept under cover of the darkness and dug themselves in anew between us and our friends. Before us was a trench full of infantry, and there were others to right and left. We were completely surrounded; and it was not an hour after dawn when the enemy began to shout to us to show our hands and surrender. Colonel Kirby forbade us to answer them, and we lay still as dead men until they threw bombs—which we answered with bullets.

After that we were left alone for an hour or two, and Colonel Kirby, whose wound was not serious, began passing along the trench, knee-deep in the muddy water, to inspect us and count us and give each man encouragement. It was just as he passed close to me that a hand-grenade struck him in the thigh and exploded. He fell forward on me, and I took him across my knee lest he fall into the water and be smothered. That is how it happened that only I overheard what he said to Ranjoor Singh before he died. Several others tried to hear, for we loved Colonel Kirby as sons love their father; but, since he lay with his head on my shoulder, my ear was as close to his lips as Ranjoor Singh's, to whom he spoke, so that Ranjoor Singh and I heard and the rest did not. Later I told the others, but they chose to disbelieve me.

Ranjoor Singh came wading along the trench,

stumbling over men's feet in his hurry and nearly falling just as he reached us, so that for the moment I thought he too had been shot. Besides Colonel Kirby, who was dying in my arms, he, and Captain Fellowes, and one other risaldar were our only remaining officers. Colonel Kirby was in great pain, so that his words were not in his usual voice but forced through clenched teeth, and Ranjoor Singh had to stoop to listen.

"Shepherd 'em!" said Colonel Kirby. "Shepherd 'em, Ranjoor Singh!" My ear was close and I heard each word. "A bad business. They did not know enough to listen to you at Headquarters. Don't waste time blaming anybody. Pray for wisdom, and fear nothing! You're in command now. Take over. Shepherd 'em! Good-by, old friend!"

"Good-by, Colonel sahib," said Ranjoor Singh, and Kirby sahib died in that moment, having shed the half of his blood over me. Ranjoor Singh and I laid him along a ledge above the water and it was not very long before a chance shell dropped near and buried him under a ton of earth. Yes, sahib, a British shell.

Presently Ranjoor Singh waded along the trench to have word with Captain Fellowes, who was wounded rather badly. I made busy with the men about me, making them stand where they could see best with least risk of exposure and ordering spade work here and there. It is a strange thing, sahib, but I have never seen it otherwise, that spade work—which is surely the most important thing—is the last thing troopers will attend to unless compelled. They will comb their beards, and decorate the trench with colored stones and draw names in the mud, but the all-important digging waits. Sikh and Gurkha and British and French are all alike in that respect.

When Ranjoor Singh came back from his talk with Captain Fellowes he sent me to the right wing under our other risaldar, and after he was killed by a grenade I was in command of the right wing of our trench.

The three days that followed have mostly gone from memory, that being the way of evil. If men could remember pain and misery they would refuse to live because of the risk of more of it; but hope springs ever anew out of wretchedness like sprouts on the burned land, and the ashes are forgotten. I do not remember much of those three days.

There was nothing to eat. There began to be a smell. There was worse than nothing to drink, for thirst took hold of us, yet the water in the trench was all pollution. The smell made us wish to vomit, yet what could the empty do but desire? Corpses lay all around us. No, sahib, not the dead of the night before's fighting. Have I not said that the weather was cold? The bombardment by our own guns preceding our attack had torn up graves that were I know not how old. When we essayed to re-bury some bodies the Germans drove us back under cover.

That night, and the next, several attempts were made to rush us, but under Ranjoor Singh's command we beat them off. He was wakeful as the stars and as unexcited. Obedience to him was so comforting that men forgot for the time their suspicion and distrust. When dawn came there were more dead bodies round about, and some wounded who called piteously for help. The Germans crawled out to help their wounded, but Ranjoor Singh bade us drive them back and we obeyed.

Then the Germans began shouting to us, and Ranjoor Singh answered them. If he had answered in English, so that most of us could have understood, all would surely have been well; I am certain that in that case the affection, returning because of his fine leadership, would have destroyed the memory of suspicion. But I suppose it had become habit with him to talk to the enemy in German by that time, and as the words we could not understand passed back and forth even I began to hate him. Yet he drove a good bargain for us.

Instead of hand-grenades the Germans began to throw bread to us—great, flat, army loaves, Ranjoor Singh not showing himself, but counting aloud as each loaf came over, we catching with great anxiety lest they fall into the water and be polluted. It took a long time, but when there was a good dry loaf for each man, Ranjoor Singh gave the Germans leave to come and carry in their wounded, and bade us hold our fire. Gooja Singh was for playing a trick but the troopers near him murmured and Ranjoor Singh threatened him with death if he dared. He never forgot that.

The Germans who came to fetch the wounded laughed at us, but Ranjoor Singh forbade us to answer, and Captain Fellowes backed him up.

"There will be another attack from our side presently," said Captain Fellowes, "and our friends will answer for us."

I shuddered at that. I remembered the bombardment that preceded our first advance. Better die at the hands of the enemy, thought I. But I said nothing. Presently, however, a new thought came to me, and I called to Ranjoor Singh along the trench.

"You should have made a better bargain," said I. "You should have compelled them to care for our wounded before they were allowed to take their own!"

"I demanded, but they refused," he answered, and then I wished I had bitten out my tongue rather than speak, for although I believed his answer, the rest of the men did not. There began to be new murmuring against him, led by Gooja Singh; but Gooja Singh was too subtle to be convicted of the responsibility.

Captain Fellowes grew aware of the murmuring and made much show thenceforward of his faith in Ranjoor Singh. He was weak from his wound and was attended constantly by two men, so that although he kept command of the left wing and did ably he could not shout loud enough to be heard very far, and he had to send messages to Ranjoor Singh from mouth to mouth. His evident approval had somewhat the effect of subduing the men's resentment, although not much, and when he died that night there was none left, save I, to lend our leader countenance. And I was only his half-friend, without enough merit in my heart truly to be the right-hand man I was by right of seniority. I was willing enough to die at his back, but not to share contempt with him.

The day passed and there came another day, when the bread was done, and there were no more German wounded straddled in the mud over whom to strike new bargains. It had ceased raining, so we could catch no rain to drink. We were growing weak from weariness and want of sleep, and we demanded of Ranjoor Singh that he lead us back toward the British lines.

"We should perish on the way," said he.

"What of it?" we answered, I with the rest. "Better that than this vulture's death in a graveyard!"

But he shook his head and ordered us to try to think like men. "The life of a Sikh," said he, "and the oath of a Sikh are one. We swore to serve our friends. To try to cut our way back would be but to die for our own comfort."

"You should have led us back that first night, when the attack was spent," said Gooja Singh.

"I was not in command that first night," Ranjoor Singh answered him, and who could gainsay that?

At irregular intervals British shells began bursting near us, and we all knew what they were. The batteries were feeling for the range. They would begin a new bombardment. Now, therefore, is the end, said we. But Ranjoor Singh stood up with his head above the trench and began shouting to the Germans. They answered him. Then, to our utter astonishment, he tore the shirt from a dead man, tied it to a rifle, and held it up.

The Germans cheered and laughed, but we made never a sound. We were bewildered—sick from the stink and weariness and thirst and lack of food. Yet I swear to you, sahib, on my honor that it had not entered into the heart of one of us to surrender. That we who had been first of the Indian contingent to board a ship, first to land in France, first to engage the enemy, should now be first to surrender in a body seemed to us very much worse than death. Yet Ranjoor Singh bade us leave our rifles and climb out of the trench, and we obeyed him. God knows why we obeyed him. I, who had been half-hearted hitherto, hated him in that minute as a trapped wolf hates the hunter; yet I, too, obeyed.

We left our dead for the Germans to bury, but we dragged the wounded out and some of them died as we lifted them. When we reached the German trench and they counted us, including Ranjoor Singh and three-and-forty wounded there were two-hundred-and-three-and-fifty of us left alive.

They led Ranjoor Singh apart. He had neither rifle nor saber in his hand, and he walked to their trench alone because we avoided him. He was more muddy than we, and as ragged and tired. He had stood in the same foul water, and smelt the same stench. He was hungry as we. He had been willing to surrender, and we had not. Yet he walked like an officer, and looked like one, and we looked like animals. And we knew it, and he knew it. And the Germans recognized the facts.

He acted like a crowned king when he reached the trench. A German officer spoke with him earnestly, but he shook his head and then they led him away. When he was gone the same officer came and spoke to us in English, and I understanding him at once, he bade me tell the others that the British must have witnessed our surrender. "See," said he, "what a bombardment they have begun again. That is in the hope of slaying you. That is out of revenge because you dared surrender instead of dying like rats in a ditch to feed their pride!" It was true that a bombardment had begun again. It had begun that minute. Those truly had been ranging shells. If we had stayed five minutes longer before surrendering we should have been blown to pieces; but we were in no mood to care on that account.

The Germans are a simple folk, sahib, although they themselves think otherwise. When they think they are the subtlest they are easiest to understand. Understanding was reborn in my heart on account of that German's words. Thought I, if Ranjoor Singh were in truth a traitor then he would have leaped at a chance to justify himself to us. He would have repeated what that German had urged him to tell us. Yet I saw him refuse.

As they hurried him away alone, pity for him came over me like warm rain on the parched earth, and when a man can pity he can reason. I spoke in Punjabi to the others and the German officer thought I was translating what he told me to say, yet in truth I reminded them that man can find no place where God is not, and where God is is courage. I was senior now, and my business was to encourage them. They took new heart from my words, all except Gooja Singh, who wept noisily, and the German officer was pleased with what he mistook for the effect of his speech.

"Tell them they shall be excellently treated," said he, seizing my elbow. "When we shall have won this war the British will no longer be able to force natives of India to fight their battles for them."

I judged it well to repeat that word for word. There are over ten applicants for every vacancy in such a regiment as ours, and until Ranjoor Singh ordered our surrender, we were all free men—free givers of our best; whereas the Germans about us were all conscripts. The comparison did no harm.

We saw no more of our wounded until some of them were returned to us healed, weeks later; but from them we learned that their treatment had been good. With us, however, it was not so, in spite of the promise the German officer had made. We were hustled along a wide trench, and taken over by another guard, not very numerous but brutal, who kicked us without excuse. As we went the trenches were under fire all the time from the British artillery. The guards swore it was our surrender that had drawn the fire, and belabored us the more on that account.

At the rear of the German lines we were herded in a quarry lest we observe too much, and it was not until after dark that we were given half a loaf of bread apiece. Then, without time to eat that which had been given to us, we were driven off into the darkness. First, however, they took our goatskin overcoats away, saying they were too good to be worn by savages. A non-commissioned officer, who could speak good English, was sent for to explain that point to us.

After an hour's march through the dark we were herded into some cattle trucks that stood on a siding behind some trees. The trucks did not smell of cattle, but of foul garments and unwashed men. Two armed German infantrymen were locked into each truck with us, and the pair in the truck in which I was drove us in a crowd to the farther end, claiming an entire half for themselves. It was true that we stank, for we had been many days and nights without opportunity to get clean; yet they offered us no means of washing—only abuse. I have seen German prisoners allowed to wash before they had been ten minutes behind the British lines.

We were five days in that train, sahib—five days and nights! Our guards were fed at regular intervals, but not we. Once or twice a day they brought us a bucket of water from which we were bidden drink in a great hurry while the train waited; yet often the train waited hours on sidings and no water at all was brought us. For food we were chiefly dependent on the charity of people at the wayside stations who came with gifts intended for German wounded; some of those took pity on us.

At last, sahib, when we were cold and stiff and miserable to the very verge of death, we came to a little place called Oeschersleben, and there the cruelty came to an unexpected end. We were ordered out of the trucks and met on the platform by a German, not in uniform, who showed distress at our predicament and who hastened to assure us in our own tongue that henceforward there would be amends made.

If that man had taken charge of us in the beginning we might not have been suspicious of him, for he seemed gentle and his words were fair; but now his kindness came too late to have effect. Animals can sometimes be rendered tame by starvation and brutality followed by plenty and kindness, but not men, and particularly not Sikhs—it being no part of our Guru's teaching that either full belly or tutored intellect can compensate for lack of goodness. Neither is it his teaching, on the other hand, that a man must wear thoughts on his face; so we did not reject this man's advances.

"There have been mistakes made," said he, "by ignorant common soldiers who knew no better. You shall recuperate on good food, and then we shall see what we shall see."

I asked him where Ranjoor Singh was, but he did not answer me.

We were not compelled to walk. Few of us could have walked. We were stiff from confinement and sick from neglect. Carts drawn by oxen stood near the station, and into those we were crowded and driven to a camp on the outskirts of the town. There comfortable wooden huts were ready, well warmed and clean—and a hot meal—and much hot water in which we were allowed to bathe.

Then, when we had eaten, doctors came and examined us. New clothes were given us—German uniforms of khaki, and khaki cotton cloth from which to bind new turbans. Nothing was left undone to make us feel well received, except that a barbed-wire fence was all about the camp and armed guards marched up and down outside.

Being senior surviving non-commissioned officer, I was put in charge of the camp in a certain manner, with many restrictions to my authority, and for about a week we did nothing but rest and eat and keep the camp tidy. All day long Germans, mostly women and children but some men, came to stare at us through the barbed-wire fence as if we were caged animals, but no insults were offered us. Rather, the women showed us kindness and passed us sweetmeats and strange food through the fence until an officer came and stopped them with overbearing words. Then, presently, there was a new change.

A week had gone and we were feeling better, standing about and looking at the freshly fallen snow, marking the straight tracks made by the sentries outside the fence, and thinking of home maybe, when new developments commenced.

Telegrams translated into Punjabi were nailed to the door of a hut, telling of India in rebellion and of men, women and children butchered by the British in cold blood. Other telegrams stated that the Sikhs of India in particular had risen, and that Pertab Singh, our prince, had been hanged in public. Many other lies they posted up. It would be waste of time to tell them all. They were foolishness—such foolishness as might deceive the German public, but not us who had lived in India all our lives and who had received our mail from home within a day or two of our surrender.

There came plausible men who knew our tongue and the argument was bluntly put to us that we ought to let expediency be our guide in all things. Yet we were expected to trust the men who gave us such advice!

Our sense of justice was not courted once. They

made appeal to our bellies—to our purses—to our lust—to our fear—but to our righteousness not at all. They made for us great pictures of what German rule of the world would be, and at last I asked whether it was true that the kaiser had turned Muhammadan. I was given no answer until I had asked repeatedly, and then it was explained how that had been a rumor sent abroad to stir Islam; to us, on the other hand, nothing but truth was told. So I asked, was it true that our Prince Pertab Singh had been hanged, and they told me yes. I asked them where, and they said in Delhi. Yet I knew that Pertab Singh was all the while in London.

I asked them where was Ranjoor Singh all this while, and for a time they made no answer, so I asked again and again. Then one day they began to talk of Ranjoor Singh.

They told us he was being very useful to them, in Berlin, in daily conference with the German General Staff, explaining matters that pertained to the intended invasion of India. Doubtless they thought that news would please us greatly. But, having heard so many lies already, I set that down for another one, and the others became all the more determined in their loyalty from sheer disgust at Ranjoor Singh's unfaithfulness. They believed and I disbelieved, yet the result was one.

At night Gooja Singh held forth in the hut where he slept with twenty-five others. He explained—although he did not say how he knew—that the Germans have kept for many years in Berlin an office for the purpose of intrigue in India—an office manned by Sikh traitors. "That is where Ranjoor Singh will be," said he. "He will be managing that bureau." In those days

Gooja Singh was Ranjoor Singh's bitterest enemy, although later he changed sides again.

The night-time was the worst. By day there was the camp to keep clean and the German officers to talk to; but at night we lay awake thinking of India, and of our dead officer sahibs, and of all that had been told us that we knew was lies. Ever the conversation turned to Ranjoor Singh at last, and night after night the anger grew against him. I myself admitted very often that his duty had been to lead us to our death. I was ashamed as the rest of our surrender.

After a time, as our wounded began to be drafted back to us from hospital, we were made to listen to accounts of alleged great German victories. They told us the German army was outside Paris and that the whole of the British North Sea Fleet was either sunk or captured. They also said that the Turks in Gallipoli had won great victories against the Allies. We began to wonder why such conquerors should seek so earnestly the friendship of a handful of us Sikhs. Our wounded began to be drafted back to us well primed, and their stories made us think, but not as the Germans would have had us think.

Week after week until the spring came we listened to their tales by day and talked them over among ourselves at night; and the more they assured us Ranjoor Singh was working with them in Berlin, the more we prayed for opportunity to prove our hearts. Spring dragged along into summer and there began to be prayers for vengeance on him. I said less than any. Understanding had not come to me fully yet, but it seemed to me that if Ranjoor Singh was really playing traitor, then he was going a tedious way about it. Yet it was equally clear that if I should dare to say one word in his behalf that would be to pass sentence on myself. I kept silence when I could, and was evasive when they pressed me, cowardice struggling with new conviction in my heart.

There came one night at last, when men's hearts burned in them too terribly for sleep, that some one proposed a resolution and sent the word whispering from hut to hut, that we should ask for Ranjoor Singh to be brought to us. Let the excuse be that he was our rightful leader, and that therefore he ought to advise us what we should do. Let us promise to do faithfully whatever Ranjoor Singh should order. Then, when he should have been brought to us, should he talk treason we would tear him in pieces with our hands. That resolution was agreed to. I also agreed. It was I who asked the next day that Ranjoor Singh be brought. The German officer laughed; yet I asked again, and he went away smiling.

We talked of our plan at night. We repeated it at dawn. We whispered it above the bread at breakfast. After breakfast we stood in groups, confirming our decision with great oaths and binding one another to fulfillment—I no less than all the others. Like the others I was blinded now by the sense of our high purpose and I forgot to consider what might happen should Ranjoor Singh take any other line than that expected of him.

I think it was eleven in the morning of the fourth day after our decision, when we had all grown weary of threats of vengeance and of argument as to what each individual man should do to our major's body, that there was some small commotion at the entrance gate and a man walked through alone. The gate slammed shut again behind him.

He strode forward to the middle of our compound, stood still, and confronted us. We stared at him. We gathered round him. We said nothing.

"Fall in, two deep!" commanded he. And we fell in, two deep, just as he ordered.

"'Ten-shun!" commanded he. And we stood to attention.

Sahib, he was Ranjoor Singh!

He stood within easy reach of the nearest man, clothed in a new khaki German uniform. He wore a German saber at his side. Yet I swear to you the saber was not the reason why no man struck at him. Nor were there Germans near enough to have rescued him. We, whose oath to murder him still trembled on our lips, stood and faced him with trembling knees now that he had come at last.

We stood before him like two rows of dumb men, gazing at his face. I have heard the English say that our eastern faces are impossible to read, but that can only be because western eyes are blind. We can read them readily enough. Yet we could not read Ranjoor Singh's that day. It dawned on us as we stared that we did not understand, but that he did; and there is no murder in that mood.

Before we could gather our wits he began to speak to us, and we listened as in the old days when at least a squadron of us had loved him to the very death. A very unexpected word was the first he used.

"Simpletons!" said he.

Sahib, our jaws dropped. Simpletons was the last thing we had thought ourselves. On the contrary, we thought ourselves astute to have judged his character and to have kept our minds uncorrupted by the German efforts. Yet we were no longer so sure of ourselves that any man was ready with an answer.

He glanced over his shoulder to left and right. There were no Germans inside the fence; none near enough to overhear him, even if he raised his voice. So he did raise it, and we all heard.

"I come from Berlin!"

"Ah!" said we—as one man. For another minute he stood eying us, waiting to see whether any man would speak.

"We be honest men!" said a trooper who stood not far from me, and several others murmured, so I spoke up.

"He has not come for nothing," said I. "Let us listen first and pass judgment afterward."

"We have heard enough treachery!" said the trooper who had spoken first, but the others growled him down and presently there was silence.

"You have eyes," said Ranjoor Singh, "and ears, and nose, and lips for nothing at all but treachery!" He spoke very slowly, sahib. "You have listened, and smelled for it, and have spoken of nothing else, and what you have sought you think you have found! To argue with men in the dark is like gathering wind into baskets. My business is to lead, and I will lead. Your business is to follow, and you shall follow." Then, "Simpletons!" said he again; and having said that he was silent, as if to judge what effect his words were having.

No man answered him. I can not speak for the others, although there was a wondrous maze of lies put forth that night by way of explanation that I might repeat. All I know is that through my mind kept running against my will self-accusation, self-condemnation, self-contempt! I had permitted my love for Ranjoor Singh to be corrupted by most meager evidence. If I had not been his enemy, I had not been true to him, and who is not true is false. I fought with a sense of shame as I have since then fought with thirst and hunger. All the teachings of our Holy One accused me. Above all, Ranjoor Singh's face accused me. I remembered that for more than twenty years he had stood to all of us for an example of what Sikh honor truly is, and that he had been aware of it.

"I know the thoughts ye think!" said he, beginning again when he had given us time to answer and none had dared. "I will give you a real thought to put in the place of all that foolishness. This is a regiment. I am its last surviving officer. Any regiment can kill its officers. If ye are weary of being a regiment, behold—I am as near you as a man's throat to his hand! Have no fear"—(that was a bitter thrust, sahib!)—"this is a German saber; I will use no German steel on any of you. I will not strike back if any seek to kill me."

There was no movement and no answer, sahib. We did not think; we waited. If he had coaxed us with specious arguments, as surely a liar would have done, that would probably have been his last speech in the world. But there was not one word he said that did not ring true.

"I have been made a certain offer in Berlin," said he, after another long pause. "First it was made to me alone, and I would not accept it. I and my regiment, said I, are one. So the offer was repeated to me as the leader of this regiment. Thus they admitted I am the rightful leader of it, and the outcome of that shall be on their heads. As major of this regiment, I accepted the offer, and as its major I now command your obedience."

"Obedience to whom?" asked I, speaking again as it were against my will, and frightened by my own voice.

"To me," said he.

"Not to the Germans?" I asked. He wore a German uniform, and so for that matter did we all.

"To me," he said again, and he took one step aside that he might see my face better. "You, Hira Singh, you heard Colonel Kirby make over the command!"

Every man in the regiment knew that Colonel Kirby had died across my knees. They looked from Ranjoor Singh to me, and from me to Ranjoor Singh, and I felt my heart grow first faint from dread of their suspicion, and then bold, then proud that I should be judged fit to stand beside him. Then came shame again, for I knew I was not fit. My loyalty to him had not stood the test. All this time I thought I felt his eyes on me like coals that burned; yet when I dared look up he was not regarding me at all, but scanning the two lines of faces, perhaps to see if any other had anything to say.

"If I told you my plan," said he presently, when

he had cleared his throat, "you would tear it in little pieces. The Germans have another plan, and they will tell you as much of it as they think it good for you to know. Mark what my orders are! Listen to this plan of theirs. Pretend to agree. Then you shall be given weapons. Then you shall leave this camp within a week."

That, sahib, was like a shell bursting in the midst of men asleep. What did it mean? Eyes glanced to left and right, looking for understanding and finding none, and no man spoke because none could think of anything to say. It was on my tongue to ask him to explain when he gave us his final word on the matter—and little enough it was, yet sufficient if we obeyed.

"Remember the oath of a Sikh!" said he. "Remember that he who is true in his heart to his oath has Truth to fight for him! Treachery begets treason, treason begets confusion; and who are ye to stay the course of things? Faith begets faith; courage gives birth to opportunity!"

He paused, but we knew he had not finished yet, and he kept us waiting full three minutes wondering what would come. Then:

"As for your doubts," said he. "If the head aches, shall the body cut it off that it may think more clearly? Consider that!" said he. "Dismiss!"

We fell out and he marched away like a king with thoughts of state in mind. I thought his beard was grayer than it had been, but oh, sahib, he strode as an arrow goes, swift and straight, and splendid. Lonely as an arrow that has left the sheaf!

I had to run to catch up with him, and I was out of breath when I touched his sleeve. He turned and waited while I thought of things to say, and then struggled to find words with which to say them.

"Sahib!" said I. "Oh, Major sahib!" And then my throat became full of words each struggling to be first, and I was silent.

"Well?" said he, standing with both arms folded, looking very grave, but not angry nor contemptuous.

"Sahib," I said, "I am a true man. As I stand here, I am a true man. I have been a fool—I have been half-hearted—I was like a man in the dark; I listened and heard voices that deceived me!"

"And am I to listen and hear voices, too?" he asked.

"Nay, sahib!" I said. "Not such voices, but true words!"

"Words?" he said. "Words! Words! There have already been too many words. Truth needs no words to prove it true, Hira Singh. Words are the voice of nothingness!"

"Then, sahib—" said I, stammering.

"Hira Singh," said he, "each man's heart is his own. Let each man keep his own. When the time comes we shall see no true men eating shame," said he.

And with that he acknowledged my salute, turned on his heel, and marched away. And the great gate slammed behind him. And German officers pressing close on either side talked with him earnestly, asking, as plainly as if I heard the words, what he had said, and what we had said, and what the outcome was to be. I could see his lips move as he answered, but no man living could have guessed what he told them. I never did know what he told them. But I have lived to see the fruit of what he did, and of what he made us do; and from that minute I have never faltered for a second in my faithfulness to Ranjoor Singh.

Be attentive, sahib, and learn what a man of men is Risaldar-major Ranjoor Singh bahadur.

CHAPTER III

Shall he who knows not false from true judge treason?—EASTERN PROVERB.

You may well imagine, sahib, in the huts that night there was noise as of bees about to swarm. No man slept. Men flitted like ghosts from hut to hut—not too openly, nor without sufficient evidence of stealth to keep the guards in good conceit of themselves, but freely for all that. What the men of one hut said the men of the next hut knew within five minutes, and so on, back and forth.

I was careful to say nothing. When men questioned me, "Nay," said I. "I am one and ye are many. Choose ye! Could I lead you against your wills?" They murmured at that, but silence is easier to keep than some men think.

Why did I say nothing? In the first place, sahib, because my mind was made at last. With all my heart now, with the oath of a Sikh and the truth of a Sikh I was Ranjoor Singh's man. I believed him true, and I was ready to stand or fall by that belief, in the dark, in the teeth of death, against all odds, anywhere. Therefore there was nothing I could say with wisdom. For if they were to suspect my true thoughts, they would lose all confidence in me, and then I should be of little use to the one man who could help all of us. I judged that what Ranjoor Singh most needed was a silent servant who would watch and obey the first hint. Just as I had watched him in battle and had herded the men for him to lead, so would I do now. There should be deeds, not words, for the foundation of a new beginning.

In the second place, sahib, I knew full well that if Gooja Singh or any of the others could have persuaded me to advance an opinion it would have been pounced on, and changed out of all recognition, yet named my opinion nevertheless. This altered opinion they would presently adopt, yet calling it mine, and when the outcome of it should fail at last to please them they would blame me. For such is the way of the world. So I had two good reasons, and the words I spoke that night could have been counted without aid of pen and paper.

The long and short of it was that morning found them undecided. There was one opinion all held—even Gooja Singh, who otherwise took both sides as to everything—that above all and before all we were all true men, loyal to our friends, the British, and foes of every living German or Austrian or Turk so long as the war should last. The Germans had bragged to us about the Turks being in the war on their side, and we had thought deeply on the subject of their choice of friends. Like and like mingle, sahib. As for us, my grandfather fought for the British in '57, and my father died at Kandahar under Bobs bahadur. On that main issue we were all one, and all ashamed to be prisoners while our friends were facing death. But dawn found almost no two men agreed as to Ranjoor Singh, or in fact on any other point.

Not long after dawn, came the Germans again, with new arguments. And this time they began to let us feel the iron underlying their persuasion. Once, to make talk and gain time before answering a question, I had told them of our labor in the bunkers on the ship that carried us from India. I had boasted of the coal we piled on the fire-room floor. Lo, it is always foolish to give information to the enemy—always, sahib—always! There is no exception.

Said they to us now: "We Germans are devoting all our energy to prosecution of this war. Nearly all our able-bodied men are with the regiments. Every man must do his part, for we are a nation in arms. Even prisoners must do their part. Those who do not fight for us must work to help the men who do fight."

"Work without pay?" said I.

"Aye," said they, "work without pay. There is coal, for instance. We understand that you Sikhs have proved yourselves adept at work with coal. He who can labor in the bunkers of a ship can handle pick and shovel in the mines, and most of our miners have been called up. Yet we need more coal than ever."

So, sahib. So they turned my boast against me. And the men around me, who had heard me tell the tale about our willing labor on the ship, now eyed me furiously; although at the time they had enjoyed the boast and had added details of their own. The Germans went away and left us to talk over this new suggestion among ourselves, and until afternoon I was kept busy speaking in my own defense.

"Who could have foreseen how they would use my words against us?" I demanded. But they answered that any fool could have foreseen it, and that my business was to foresee in any case and to give them good advice. I kept that saying in my heart, and turned it against *them* when the day came.

That afternoon the Germans returned, with knowing smiles that were meant to seem courteous, and with an air of confidence that was meant to appear considerate. Doubtless a cat at meal-time believes men think him generous and unobtrusive. They went to great trouble to prove themselves our wise counselors and disinterested friends.

"We have explained to you," said they, "what hypocrites the British are,—what dust they have thrown in your eyes for more than a century—how they have grown rich at your expense, deliberately keeping India in ignorance and subjection, in poverty and vice, and divided against itself. We have told you what German aims are on the other hand, and how successful our armies are on every front as the result of the consistence of those aims. We have proved to you how half the world already takes our side—how the Turks fight for us, how Persia begins to join the Turks, how Afghanistan already moves, and how India is in rebellion. Now—wouldn't you like to join our side—to throw the weight of Sikh honor and Sikh bravery into the scale with us? That would be better fun than working in the mines," said they.

"Are we offered that alternative?" I asked, but they did not answer that question. They went away again and left us to our thoughts.

And we talked all the rest of that day and most of the next night, arriving at no decision. When they asked me for an opinion, I said, "Ranjoor Singh told us this would be, and he gave us orders what to do." When they asked me ought they to obey him, I answered, "Nay, choose ye! Who can make you obey against your wills?" And when they asked me would I abide by their decision, "Can the foot walk one way," I answered, "while the body walks another? Are we not one?" said I.

"Then," said they, "you bid us consider this proposal to take part against our friends?"

"Nay," said I, "I am a true man. No man can make me fight against the British."

They thought on that for a while, and then surrounded me again, Gooja Singh being spokesman for them all. "Then you counsel us," said he, "to choose the hard labor in the coal mines?"

"Nay," said I. "I counsel nothing."

"But what other course is there?" said he.

"There is Ranjoor Singh," said I.

"But he desired to lead us against the British," said he.

"Nay," said I. "Who said so?"

Gooja Singh answered: "He, Ranjoor Singh himself, said so."

"Nay," said I. "I heard what he said. He said he will lead us, but he said nothing of his plan. He did not say he will lead us against the British."

"Then it was the Germans. They said so," said Gooja Singh. "They said he will lead us against the British."

"The Germans said," said I, "that their armies are outside Paris—that India is in rebellion—that Pertab Singh was hanged in Delhi—that the British rule in India has been altogether selfish—that our wives and children have been butchered by the British in cold blood. The Germans," said I, "have told us very many things."

"Then," said he, "you counsel us to follow Ranjoor Singh?"

"Nay," said I. "I counsel nothing."

"You are a coward!" said he. "You are afraid to give opinion!"

"I am one among many!" I answered him.

They left me alone again and talked in groups, Gooja Singh passing from one group to another like a man collecting tickets. Then, when it was growing dusk, they gathered once more about me and Gooja Singh went through the play of letting them persuade him to be spokesman.

"If we decide to follow Ranjoor Singh," said he, "will you be one with us?"

"If that is the decision of you all," I answered, "then yes. But if it is Gooja Singh's decision with the rest consenting, then no. Is that the decision of you all?" I asked, and they murmured a sort of answer.

"Nay!" said I. "That will not do! Either yes or no. Either ye are willing or ye are unwilling. Let him who is unwilling say so, and I for one will hold no judgment against him."

None answered, though I urged again and again. "Then ye are all willing to give Ranjoor Singh a trial?" said I; and this time they all answered in the affirmative.

"I think your decision well arrived at!" I made bold to tell them. "To me it seems you have all seen wisdom, and although I had thoughts in mind," said I, "of accepting work in the collieries and blowing up a mine perhaps, yet I admit your plan is better and I defer to it."

They were much more pleased with that speech than if I had admitted the truth, that I would never have agreed to any other plan. So that now they were much more ready than they might have been to listen to my next suggestion.

"But," said I, with an air of caution, "shall we not keep any watch on Ranjoor Singh?"

"Let us watch!" said they. "Let us be forehanded!"

"But how?" said I. "He is an officer. He is not bound to lay bare his thoughts to us."

They thought a long time about that. It grew dark, and we were ordered to our huts, and lights were put out, and still they lay awake and talked of it. At last Gooja Singh flitted through the dark and came to me and asked me my opinion on the matter.

"One of you go and offer to be his servant," said I. "Let that servant serve him well. A good servant should know more about his master than the master himself."

"Who shall that one be?" he asked; and he went back to tell the men what I had said.

After midnight he returned. "They say you are the one to keep watch on him," said he.

"Nay, nay!" said I, with my heart leaping against my ribs, but my voice belying it. "If I agree to that, then later you will swear I am his friend and condemn me in one judgment with him!"

"Nay," said he. "Nay truly! On the honor of a Sikh!"

"Mine is also the honor of a Sikh," said I, "and I will cover it with care. Go back to them," I directed, "and let them all come and speak with me at dawn."

"Is my word not enough?" said he.

"Was Ranjoor Singh's enough?" said I, and he went, muttering to himself.

I slept until dawn—the first night I had slept in three—and before breakfast they all clustered about me, urging me to be the one to keep close watch on Ranjoor Singh.

"God forbid that I should be stool pigeon!" said I. "Nay, God forbid! Ranjoor Singh need but give an order that ye have no liking for and ye will shoot me in the back for it!"

They were very earnest in their protestations, urging me more and more; but the more they urged the more I hung back, and we ate before I gave them any answer. "This is a plot," said I, "to get me in trouble. What did I ever do that ye should combine against me?"

"Nay!" said they. "By our Sikh oath, we be true men and your friends. Why do you doubt us?"

Then said I at last, as it were reluctantly, "If ye demand it—if ye insist—I will be the go-between. Yet

I do it because ye compel me by weight of unanimity!" said I.

"It is your place!" said they, but I shook my head, and to this day I have never admitted to them that I undertook the work willingly.

Presently came the Germans to us again, this time accompanied by officers in uniform who stood apart and watched with an air of passing judgment. They asked us now point-blank whether or not we were willing to work in the coal mines and thus make some return for the cost of keeping us; and we answered with one voice that we were not coal-miners and therefore not willing.

"The alternative," said they, "is that you apply to fight on the side of the Central Empires. Men must all either fight or work in these days; there is no room for idlers."

"Is there no other work we could do?" asked Gooja Singh.

"None that we offer you!" said they. "If you apply to be allowed to fight on the side of the Central Empires, then your application will be considered. However, you would be expected to forswear allegiance to Great Britain, and to take the military oath as provided by our law; so that in the event of any lapse of discipline or loyalty to our cause you could be legally dealt with."

"And the alternative is the mines?" said I.

"No, no!" said the chief of them. "You must not misunderstand. Your present destination is the coal mines, where you are to earn your keep. But the suggestion is made to you that you might care to apply for leave to fight on our side. In that case we would not send you to the coal mines until at least your application had been considered. It is practically certain it would be considered favorably."

The conversation was in English as usual and many of the men had not quite understood. Those on the outside had not heard properly. So I bade four men lift me, and I shouted to them in our own tongue all that the German had said. There fell a great silence, and the four men let me drop to the earth between them.

"So is this the trap Ranjoor Singh would lead us into?" said the trooper nearest me, and though he spoke low, so still were we all that fifty men heard him and murmured. So I spoke up.

Said I, "We will answer when we shall have spoken again with Ranjoor Singh. He shall give our answer. It is right that a regiment should answer through its officer, and any other course is lacking discipline!"

Sahib, I have been surprised a thousand times in this war, but not once more surprised than by the instant effect my answer had. It was a random answer, made while I searched for some argument to use; but the German spokesman turned at once and translated to the officers in uniform. Watching them very closely, I saw them laugh, and it seemed to me they approved my answer and disapproved some other matter. I think they disapproved the civilian method of mingling with us in a mob, for a moment later the order was given us in English to fall in, and we fell in two deep. Then the civilian Germans drew aside and one of the officers in uniform strode toward the entrance gate. We waited in utter silence, wondering what next, but the officer had not been gone ten minutes when we caught sight of him returning with Ranjoor Singh striding along beside him.

Ranjoor Singh and he advanced toward us and I saw Ranjoor Singh speak with him more emphatically than his usual custom. Evidently Ranjoor Singh had his way, for the officer spoke in German to the others and they all walked out of the compound in a group, leaving Ranjoor Singh facing us. He waited until the gate clanged shut behind them before he spoke.

"Well?" said he. "I was told the regiment asked for word with me. What is the word?"

"Sahib," said I, standing out alone before the men, not facing him, but near one end of the line, so that I could raise my voice with propriety and all the men might hear. He backed away, to give more effect to that arrangement. "Sahib," I said, "we are in a trap. Either we go to the mines, or we fight for the Germans against the British. What is your word on the matter?"

"Ho!" said he. "Is it as bad as that? As bad as that?" said he. "If ye go to the mines to dig coal, they will use that coal to make ammunition for their guns! That seems a poor alternative! They fight as much with ammunition as with men!"

"Sahib," said I, "it is worse than that! They seek to compel us to sign a paper, forswearing our allegiance to Great Britain and claiming allegiance to them! Should we sign it, that makes us out traitors in the first place, and makes us amenable to their law in the second place. They could shoot us if we disobeyed or demurred."

"They could do that in the mines," said he, "if you failed to dig enough coal to please them. They would call it punishment for malingering—or some such name. If they take it into their heads to have you all shot, doubt not they will shoot!"

"Yet in that case," said I, "we should not be traitors."

"I will tell you a story," said he, and we held our breath to listen, for this was his old manner. This had ever been his way of putting recruits at ease and of making a squadron understand. In that minute, for more than a minute, men forgot they had ever suspected him.

"When I was a little one," said he, "my mother's aunt, who was an old hag, told me this tale. There was a pack of wolves that hunted in a forest near a village. In the village lived a man who wished to be headman. Abdul was his name, and he had six sons. He wished to be headman that he might levy toll among the villagers for the up-keep of his sons, who were hungry and very proud. Now Abdul was a cunning hunter, and his sons were strong. So he took thought, and chose a season carefully, and set his sons to dig a great trap. And so well had Abdul chosen—so craftily the six sons digged—that one night they caught all that wolf-pack in the trap. And they kept them in the trap two days and a night, that they might hunger and thirst and grow amenable.

"Then Abdul leaned above the pit, and peered down at the wolves and began to bargain with them. 'Wolves,' said he, 'your fangs be long and your jaws be strong, and I wish to be headman of this village.' And they answered, 'Speak, Abdul, for these walls be high, and our throats be dry, and we wish to hunt again!' So he bade them promise that if he let them go they would seek and slay the present headman and his sons, so that he might be headman in his place. And the wolves promised. Then when he had made them swear by a hundred oaths in a hundred different ways, and had bound them to keep faith by God and by earth and sky and sea and by all the holy things he could remember, he stood aside and bade his six sons free the wolves.

"The sons obeyed, and helped the wolves out of the trap. And instantly the wolves fell on all six sons, and slew and devoured them. Then they came and stood round Abdul with their jaws dripping with blood.

" 'Oh, wolves,' said he, trembling with fear and anger, 'ye are traitors! Ye are forsworn! Ye are faithless ones!'

"But they answered him, 'Oh, Abdul, shall he who knows not false from true judge treason?' and forthwith they slew him and devoured him, and went about their business.

"Now, which had the right of that—Abdul or the wolves?"

"We are no wolves!" said Gooja Singh in a whining voice. "We be true men!"

"Then I will tell you another story," Ranjoor

Singh answered him. And we listened again, as men listen to the ticking of a clock. "This is a story the same old woman, my mother's aunt, told me when I was very little.

"There was a man—and this man's name also was Abdul—who owned a garden, and in it a fish-pond. But in the fish-pond were no fish. Abdul craved fish to swim hither and thither in his pond, but though he tried times out of number he could catch none. Yet at fowling he had better fortune, and when he was weary one day of fishing and laid his net on land he caught a dozen birds.

"'So-ho!' said Abdul, being a man much given to thought, and he went about to strike a bargain. 'Oh, birds,' said he, 'are ye willing to be fish? For I have no fishes swimming in my pond, yet my heart desires them greatly. So if ye are willing to be fish and will stay in my good pond and swim there, gladdening my eyes, I will abstain from killing you but instead will set you in the pond and let you live.'

"So the birds, who were very terrified, declared themselves willing to be fish, and the birds swore even more oaths than he insisted on, so that he was greatly pleased and very confident. Therefore he used not very much precaution when he came to plunge the birds into the water, and the instant he let go of them the birds with feathers scarcely wet flew away and perched on the trees about him.

"Then Abdul grew very furious. 'Oh, birds,' said he, 'ye are traitors. Ye are forsworn! Ye are liars—breakers of oaths—deceitful ones!' And he shook his fist at them and spat, being greatly enraged and grieved at their deception.

"But the birds answered him, 'Oh, Abdul, a captive's gyves and a captive's oath are one, and he who rivets on the one must keep the other!' And the birds flew away, but Abdul went to seek his advocate to have the law of them! Now, what think ye was the advocate's opinion in the matter, and what remedy had Abdul?"

Has the sahib ever seen three hundred men all at the same time becoming conscious of the same idea? That is quite a spectacle. There was no whispering, nor any movement except a little shifting of the feet. There was nothing on which a watchful man could lay a finger. Yet between one second and the next they were not the same men, and I, who watched Ranjoor Singh's eyes as if he were my opponent in a duel, saw that he was aware of what had happened, although not surprised. But he made no sign except the shadow of one that I detected, and he did not change his voice—as yet.

"As for me," he said, telling a tale again, "I wrote once on the seashore sand and signed my name beneath. A day later I came back to look, but neither name nor words remained. I was what I had been, and stood where the sea had been, but what I had written in sand affected me not, neither the sea nor any man. Thought I, if one had lent me money on such a perishable note the courts would now hold him at fault, not me; they would demand evidence, and all he could show them would be what he had himself bargained for. Now it occurs to me that seashore sand, and the tricks of rogues, and blackmail, and tyranny perhaps are one!"

Eye met eye, all up and down both lines of men. There was swift searching of hearts, and some of the men at my end of the line began talking in low tones. So I spoke up and voiced aloud what troubled them.

"If we sign this paper, sahib," said I, "how do we know they will not find means of bringing it to the notice of the British?"

"We do not know," he answered. "Let us hope. Hope is a great good thing. If they chained us, and we broke the chains, they might send the broken links to London in proof of what thieves we be. Who would gain by that?"

I saw a very little frown now and knew that he judged it time to strike on the heated metal. But Gooja Singh turned his back on Ranjoor Singh.

"Let him sign this thing," said he, "and let us sign our names beneath his name. Then he will be in the same trap with us all, and must lead us out of it or perish with us!"

So Gooja Singh offered himself, all unintentionally, to be the scapegoat for us all and I have seldom seen a man so shocked by what befell him. Only a dozen words spoke Ranjoor Singh—yet it was as if he lashed him and left him naked. Whips and a good man's wrath are one.

"Who gave thee leave to yelp?" said he, and Gooja Singh faced about like a man struck. By order of the Germans he and I stood in the place of captains on parade, he on the left and I on the right.

"To your place!" said Ranjoor Singh.

Gooja Singh stepped back into line with me, but Ranjoor Singh was not satisfied.

"To your place in the rear!" he ordered. And so I have seen a man who lost a lawsuit slink round a corner of the court.

Then I spoke up, being stricken with self-esteem at the sight of Gooja Singh's shame (for I always knew him to be my enemy).

"Sahib," said I, "shall I pass down the line and ask each man whether he will sign what the Germans ask?"

"Aye!" said he, "like the carrion crows at judgment! Halt!" he ordered, for already I had taken the first step. "When I need to send a havildar," said he, "to ask my men's permission, I will call for a havildar! To the rear where you belong!" he ordered. And I went round to the rear, knowing something of Gooja Singh's sensations, but loving him no better for the fellow-feeling. When my footfall had altogether ceased and there was silence in which one could have heard an insect falling to the ground, Ranjoor Singh spoke again. "There has been enough talk," said he. "In pursuance of a plan, I intend to sign whatever the Germans ask. Those who prefer not to sign what **I sign**—fall out! Fall out, I say!"

Not a man fell out, sahib. But that was not enough for Ranjoor Singh.

"Those who intend to sign the paper,—two paces forward,—march!" said he. And as one man we took two paces forward.

"So!" said he. "Right turn!" And we turned to the right. "Forward! Quick march!" he ordered. And he made us march twice in a square about him before he halted us again and turned us to the front to face him. Then he was fussy about our alignment, making us take up our dressing half a dozen times; and when he had us to his satisfaction finally he stood eying us for several minutes before turning his back and striding with great dignity toward the gate.

He talked through the gate and very soon a dozen Germans entered, led by two officers in uniform and followed by three soldiers carrying a table and a chair. The table was set down in their midst, facing us, and the senior German officer—in a uniform with a very high collar—handed a document to Ranjoor Singh. When he had finished reading it to himself he stepped forward and read it aloud to us. It was in Punjabi, excellently rendered, and the gist of it was like this:

We, being weary of British misrule, British hypocrisy, and British arrogance, thereby renounced allegiance to Great Britain, its king and government, and begged earnestly to be permitted to fight on the side of the Central Empires in the cause of freedom. It was expressly mentioned, I remember, that we made this petition of our own initiative and of our own free will, no pressure having been brought to bear on us, and nothing but kindness having been offered us since we were taken prisoners.

"That is what we are all required to sign," said Ranjoor Singh, when he had finished reading, and he licked his lips in a manner I had never seen before.

Without any further speech to us, he sat down at the table and wrote his name with a great flourish on the paper, setting down his rank beside his name. Then he called to me, and I sat and wrote my name below his, adding my rank also. And Gooja Singh followed me. After him, in single file, came every surviving man of Outram's Own. Some men scowled, and some men laughed harshly, and if one of our race had been watching on the German behalf he would have been able to tell them something. But the Germans mistook the scowls for signs of anger at the British, and the laughter they mistook for rising spirits, so that the whole affair passed off without arousing their suspicion.

Nevertheless, my heart warned me that the Germans would not trust a regiment seduced as we were supposed to have been. And, although Ranjoor Singh had had his way with us, the very having had destroyed the reawakening trust in him. The troopers felt that he had led them through the gates of treason. I could feel their thoughts as a man feels the breath of coming winter on his cheek.

When the last man had signed we stood at attention and a wagonload of rifles was brought in, drawn by oxen. They gave a rifle to each of us, and we were made to present arms while the German military oath was read aloud. After that the Germans walked away as if they had no further interest. Only Ranjoor Singh remained, and he gave us no time just then for comment or discontent.

The mauser rifles were not so very much unlike our own, and he set us to drilling with them, giving us patient instruction but very little rest until evening. During the longest pause in the drill he sent for knapsacks and served us one each, filled down to the smallest detail with everything a soldier could need, even to a little cup that hung from a hook beneath one corner. We were utterly worn out when he left us at nightfall, but there was a lot of talking nevertheless before men fell asleep.

"This is the second time he has trapped us in deadly earnest!" was the sum of the general complaint they hurled at me. And I had no answer to give them, knowing well that if I took his part I should share his condemnation—which would not help him; neither would it help them nor me.

"My thought, of going to the mines and being troublesome, was best!" said I. "Ye overruled me. Now ye would condemn me for not preventing you! Ye are wind blowing this way and that!"

They were so busy defending themselves to themselves against that charge that they said no more until sleep fell on them; and at dawn Ranjoor Singh took hold of us again and made us drill until our feet burned on the gravel and our ears were full of the tramp-tramp-tramp, and the *ek-do-tin* of manual exercise.

"Listen!" said he to me, when he had dismissed us for dinner, and I lingered on parade. "Caution the men that any breach of discipline would be treated under German military law by drum-head court martial and sentence of death by shooting.

Advise them to avoid indiscretions of any kind," said he.

So I passed among them, pretending the suggestion was my own, and they resented it, as I knew they would. But I observed from about that time they began to look on Ranjoor Singh as their only possible protector against the Germans, so that their animosity against him was offset by self-interest.

The next day came a staff officer who marched us to the station, where a train was waiting. Impossible though it may seem, sahib, to you who listen, I felt sad when I looked back at the huts that had been our prison, and I think we all did. We had loathed them with all our hearts all summer long, but now they represented what we knew and we were marching away from them to what we knew not, with autumn and winter brooding on our prospects.

Not all our wounded had been returned to us; some had died in the German hospitals. Two hundred-and-three-and-thirty of us all told, including Ranjoor Singh, lined up on the station platform—fit and well and perhaps a little fatter than was seemly.

Having no belongings other than the rifles and knapsacks and what we stood in it took us but a few moments to entrain. Almost at once the engine whistled and we were gone, wondering whither. Some of the troopers shouted to Ranjoor Singh to ask our destination, but he affected not to hear. The German staff officer rode in the front compartment alone, and Ranjoor Singh rode alone in the next behind him; but they conversed often through the window, and at stations where the two of them got out to stretch their legs along the platform they might have been brothers-in-blood relating love-affairs. Our troopers wondered.

"Our fox grows gray," said they, "and his impudence increases."

"Would it help us out of this predicament," said I, "if he smote that German in the teeth and spat on him?"

They laughed at that and passed the remark along from window to window, until I roared at them to keep their heads in. There were seven of us non-commissioned officers, and we rode in one compartment behind the officers' carriage, Gooja Singh making much unpleasantness because there was not enough room for us all to lie full length at once. We were locked into our compartment, and the only chance we had of speaking with Ranjoor Singh was when they brought us food at stations and he strode down the train to see that each man had his share.

"What is our destination?" we asked him then, repeatedly.

"If ye be true men," he answered, "why are ye troubled about destination? Can the truth lead you into error? Do I seem afraid?" said he.

That was answer enough if we had been the true men we claimed to be, and he gave us no other. So we watched the sun and tried to guess roughly, I recalling all the geography I ever knew, yet failing to reach conclusions that satisfied myself or any one. We knew that Turkey was in the war, and we knew that Bulgaria was not. Yet we traveled eastward, and southeastward.

I know now that we traveled over the edge of Germany into Austria, through Austria into Hungary, and through a great part of Hungary to the River Danube, growing so weary of the train that I for one looked back to the Flanders trenches as to long-lost happiness! Every section of line over which we traveled was crowded with traffic, and dozens of German regiments kept passing and repassing us. Some cheered us and some were insulting, but all of them regarded us with more or less astonishment.

The Austrians were more openly curious about us than the Germans had been, and some of them tried to get into conversation, but this was not encouraged; when they climbed on the footboards to peer through the windows and ask us questions officers ordered them away.

Of all the things we wondered at on that long ride, the German regiments impressed us most. Those that passed and repassed us were mostly artillery and infantry, and surely in all the world before there never were such regiments as those—with the paint worn off their cannon, and their clothes soiled, yet with an air about them of successful plunderers, confident to the last degree of arrogance in their own efficiency—not at all like British regiments, nor like any others that I ever saw. It was Ranjoor Singh who drew my attention to the fact that regiments passing us in one direction would often pass us again on their way back, sometimes within the day.

"As shuttles in a loom!" said he. "As long as they can do that they can fight on a dozen fronts."

His words set me wondering so that I did not answer him. He was speaking through our carriage window and I stared out beyond him at a train-load of troops on the far side of the station.

"One comes to us," said I. I was watching a German sergeant, who had dragged his belongings from that train and was crossing toward us.

"Aye!" said Ranjoor Singh, so that I knew now there had been purpose in his visit. "Beware of him." Then he unlocked the carriage door and waited for the German. The German came, and cursed the man who bore his baggage, and halted before Ranjoor Singh, staring into his face with a manner of impudence new to me. Ranjoor Singh spoke about ten words to him in German and the sergeant there and then saluted very respectfully. I noticed that the German staff officer was watching all this from a little distance, and I think the sergeant caught his eye.

At any rate, the sergeant made his man throw the baggage through our compartment door. The man returned to the other train. The sergeant climbed in next to me. Ranjoor Singh locked the door again, and both trains proceeded. When our train was beginning to gain speed the newcomer shoved me in the ribs abruptly with his elbow—thus.

"So much for knowing languages!" said he to me in fairly good Punjabi. "Curse the day I ever saw India, and triple-curse this system of ours that enabled them to lay finger on me in a moving train and transfer me to this funeral procession! Curse you, and curse this train, and curse all Asia!" Then he thrust me in the ribs again, as if that were a method of setting aside formality.

"You know Cawnpore?" said he, and I nodded.

"You know the Kaiser-i-hind Saddle Factory?"

I nodded again, being minded to waste no words because of Ranjoor Singh's warning.

"I took a job as foreman there twenty years ago because the pay was good. I lived there fifteen years until I was full to the throat of India—Indian food, Indian women, Indian drinks, Indian heat, Indian smells, Indian everything. I hated it, and threw up the job in the end. Said I to myself, 'Thank God,' said I, 'to see the last of India.' And I took passage on a German steamer and drank enough German beer on the way to have floated two ships her size! *Aecht Deutches bier,* you understand," said he, nudging me in the ribs with each word. *Aecht* means *real,* as distinguished from the export stuff in bottles. "I drank it by the barrel, straight off ice, and it went to my head!

"That must be why I boasted about knowing Indian languages before I had been two hours in port. I was drunk, and glad to be home, and on the lookout for another job to keep from starving; so I boasted I could speak and write Urdu and Punjabi. That brought me employment in an export house. But who would have guessed it would end in my being dragged away from my regiment to march with a lot of Sikhs? Eh? Who would have guessed it? There goes my regiment one way, and here go I another! What's our destination? God knows! Who are you, and what are you? God neither knows nor cares! What's to be the end of this? The end of me, I expect—and all because I got drunk on the way home! It I get alive out of this," said he, "I'll get drunk once for the glory of God and then never touch beer again!"

And he struck me on the thigh with his open palm. The noise was like powder detonating, and the pain was acute. I cursed him in his teeth and he grinned at me as if he and I were old friends. Little blue eyes he had, sahib—light blue, set in full red cheeks. There were many little red veins crisscrossed under the skin of his face, and his breath smelt of beer and tobacco. I judged he had the physical strength of a buffalo, although doubtless short of wind.

He had very little hair. Such as he had was yellow, but clipped so short that it looked white. His yellow mustache was turned up thus at either corner of his mouth; and the mouth was not unkind, not without good humor.

"What is your name?" said I.

"Tugendheim," said he. "I am Sergeant Fritz Tugendheim, of the 281 (Pappenheim) Regiment of Infantry, and would God I were with my regiment! What do they call you?"

"Hira Singh," said I.

"And your rank?"

"Havildar," said I.

"Oh-ho!" said he. "So you're all non-commissioned in here, are you? Seven of you, eh? Seven is a lucky number! Well——" He looked us each slowly in the face, narrowing his eyes so that we could scarcely see them under the yellow lashes. "Well," said he, "they won't mistake me for any of you, nor any of you for me—not even if I should grow whiskers!"

He laughed at that joke for about two minutes, slapping me on the thigh again and laughing all the louder when I showed my teeth. Then he drew out a flask of some kind of pungent spirits from his pocket, and offered it to me. When I refused he drank the whole of it himself and flung the glass flask through the window. Then he settled himself in the corner from which he had ousted me, put his feet on the edge of the seat opposite, and prepared to sleep. But before very long our German staff officer shouted for him and he went in great haste, a station official opening the door for him and locking us in again afterward. He rode for hours with the staff officer and Gooja Singh examined the whole of his kit, making remarks on each piece, to the great amusement of us all.

He came back before night to sleep in our compartment, but before he came I had taken opportunity to pass word through the window to the troopers in the carriage next behind.

"Ranjoor Singh," said I, "warns us all to be on guard against this German. He is a spy set to overhear our talk."

That word went all down the train from window to window and it had some effect, for during all the days that followed Tugendheim was never once able to get between us and our thoughts, although he tried a thousand times.

Night followed day, and day night. Our train

crawled, and waited, and crawled, and waited, and we in our compartment grew weary to the death of Tugendheim. A thousand times I envied Ranjoor Singh alone with his thoughts in the next compartment; and so far was he from suffering because of solitude that he seemed to keep more and more apart from us, only passing swiftly down the train at meal-times to make sure we all had enough to eat and that there were no sick.

I reached the conclusion myself that we were being sent to fight against the Russians, and I know not what the troopers thought; they were beginning to be like caged madmen. But suddenly we reached a broad river I knew must be the Danube and were allowed at last to leave the train. We were so glad to move about again that any news seemed good news, and when Ranjoor Singh, after much talk with our staff officer and some other Germans, came and told us that Bulgaria had joined the war on the side of the Central Powers, we laughed and applauded.

"That means that our road lies open before us," Ranjoor Singh said darkly.

"Our road whither?" said I.

"To Stamboul!" said he.

"What are we to do at Stamboul?" asked Gooja Singh, and the staff officer, whose name I never knew, heard him and came toward us.

"At Stamboul," said he, in fairly good Punjabi, "you will strike a blow beside our friends, the Turks. Not very far from Stamboul you shall be given opportunity for vengeance on the British. The next-to-the-last stage of your journey lies through Bulgaria, and the beginning of it will be on that steamer."

We saw the steamer, lying with its nose toward the bank. It was no very big one for our number, but they marched us to it, Ranjoor Singh striding at our head as if all the world were unfolding before him, and all were his. We were packed on board and the steamer started at once, Ranjoor Singh and the staff officer sharing the upper part with the steamer's captain, and Tugendheim elbowing us for room on the open deck. So we journeyed for a whole day and part of a night down the Danube, Tugendheim pointing out to me things I should observe along the route, but grumbling vastly at separation from his regiment.

"You bloody Sikhs!" said he. "I would rather march with lice—yet what can I do? I must obey orders. See that castle!" There were many castles, sahib, at bends and on hilltops overlooking the river. "They built that," said he, "in the good old days before men ever heard of Sikhs. Life was worth while in those days, and a man lived a lifetime with his regiment!"

"Ah!" said I, choosing not to take offense; for one fool can make trouble that perhaps a thousand wise men can not still. If he had thought, he must have known that we Sikhs spend a lifetime with our regiments, and therefore know more about such matters than any German reservist. But he was little given to thought, although not ill-humored in intention.

"Behold that building!" said he. "That looks like

a brewery! Consider the sea of beer they brew there once a month, and then think of your oath of abstinence and what you miss!"

So he talked, ever nudging me in the ribs until I grew sore and my very gorge revolted at his foolishness. So we sailed, passing along a river that at another time would have delighted me beyond power of speech. A day and a night we sailed, our little steamer being one of a fleet all going one way. Tugs and tugs and tugs there were, all pulling strings of barges. It was as if all the tugs and barges out of Austria were hurrying with all the plunder of Europe God knew whither.

"Whither are they taking all this stuff?" I asked Ranjoor Singh when he came down among us to inspect our rations. He and I stood together at the stern, and I waved my arm to designate the fleet of floating things. We were almost the only troops, although there were soldiers here and there on the tugs and barges, taking charge and supervising.

"To Stamboul," said he. "Bulgaria is in. The road to Stamboul is open."

"Sahib," said I, "I know you are true to the raj. I know the surrender in Flanders was the only course possible for one to whom the regiment had been entrusted. I know this business of taking the German side is all pretense. Are we on the way to Stamboul?"

"Aye," said he.

"What are we to do at Stamboul?" I asked him.

"If you know all you say you know," said he, "why let the future trouble you?"

"But——" said I.

"Nay," said he, "there can be no 'but.' There is false and true. The one has no part in the other. What say the men?"

"They are true to the raj," said I.

"All of them?" he asked.

"Nay, sahib," said I. "Not quite all of them, but almost all."

He nodded. "We shall discover before long which are false and which are true," said he, and then he left me.

So I told the men that we were truly on our way to Stamboul, and there began new wondering and new conjecturing. The majority decided at once that we were to be sent to Gallipoli to fight beside the Turks in the trenches there, and presently they all grew very determined to put no obstacle in the Germans' way but to go to Gallipoli with good will. Once there, said they all, it should be easy to cross to the British trenches under cover of the darkness.

"We will take Ranjoor Singh with us," they said darkly. "Then he can make explanation of his conduct in the proper time and place!" I saw one man hold his turban end as if it were a bandage over his eyes, and several others snapped their fingers to suggest a firing party. Many of the others laughed. Men in the dark, thought I, are fools to do anything but watch and listen. Outlines change with the dawn, thought I, and I determined to reserve my judgment on all points except one—that I set full faith in Ranjoor Singh. But the men for the most part had passed judgment and decided on a plan; so it came about that there was no trouble in the matter of getting them to Stamboul—or Constantinople, as Europeans call it.

At a place in Bulgaria whose name I have forgotten we disembarked and became escort to a caravan of miscellaneous stores, proceeding by forced marches over an abominable road. And after I forget how many days and nights we reached a railway and were once more packed into a train. Throughout that march, although we traversed wild country where any or all of us might easily have deserted among the mountains, Ranjoor Singh seemed so well to understand our intention that he scarcely troubled himself to call the roll. He sat alone by a little fire at night, and slept beside it wrapped in an overcoat and blanket. And when we boarded a train again he was once more alone in a compartment to himself. Once more I was compelled to sit next to Tugendheim.

I grew no fonder of Tugendheim, although he made many efforts to convince me of his friendship, making many prophetic statements to encourage me. "Soon," said he, "you shall have your bayonet in the belly of an Englishman! You will be revenged on them for '57!" My grandfather fought for the British in '57, sahib, and my father, who was little more than old enough to run, carried food to him where he lay on the Ridge before Delhi, the British having little enough food at that time to share among their friends. But I said nothing, and Tugendheim thought I was impressed—as indeed I was. "You will need to fight like the devil," said he, "for if they catch you they'll skin you!"

Partly he wished to discover what my thoughts were, and partly, I think, his intention was to fill me with fighting courage; and, since it would not have done to keep silence altogether, I began to project the matter further and to talk of what might be after the war should have been won. I made him believe that the hope of all us Sikhs was to seek official employment under the German government; and he made bold to prophesy a good job for every one of us. We spent hours discussing what nature of employment would best be suited to our genius, and he took opportunity at intervals to go to the staff officer and acquaint him with all that I had said. By the time we reached Stamboul at last I was more weary of him than an ill-matched bullock of its yoke.

But we did reach Stamboul in the end, on a rainy morning, and marched wondering through its crooked streets, scarcely noticed by the inhabitants. Men seemed afraid to look long at us, but glanced once swiftly and passed on. German officers were everywhere, many of them driven in motor-cars at great speed through narrow thoroughfares, scattering people to right and left; the Turkish officers appeared to treat them with very great respect—although I noticed here and there a few who looked indifferent, and occasionally others who seemed to me indignant.

The mud, though not so bad as that in Flanders, was nearly as depressing. The rain chilled the air, and shut in the view, and few of us had very much sense of direction that first day in Stamboul. Tugendheim, marching behind us, kept up an incessant growl. Ranjoor Singh, striding in front of us with the staff officer at his side, shook the rain from his shoulders and said nothing.

We were marched to a ferry and taken across what I know now was the Golden Horn; and there was so much mist on the water that at times we could scarcely see the ferry. Many troopers asked me if we were not already on our way to Gallipoli, and I, knowing no more than they, bade them wait and see.

On the other side of the Golden Horn we were marched through narrow streets, uphill, uphill, uphill to a very great barrack and given a section of it to ourselves. Ranjoor Singh was assigned private quarters in a part of the building used by many German officers for their mess. Not knowing our tongue, those officers were obliged to converse with him in English, and I observed many times with what distaste they did so, to my great amusement. I think Ranjoor Singh was also much amused by that, for he grew far better humored and readier to talk.

Sahib, that barrack was like a zoo—like the zoo I saw once at Baroda, with animals of all sorts in it! —a great yellow building within walls, packed with Kurds and Arabs and Syrians of more different tribes than a man would readily believe existed in the whole world. Few among them could talk any tongue that we knew, but they were full of curiosity and crowded round us to ask questions; and when Gooja Singh shouted aloud that we were Sikhs from India they produced a man who seemed to think he knew about Sikhs, for he stood on a step and harangued them for ten minutes, they listening with all their ears.

Then came a Turk from the German officers' mess—we were all standing in the rain in an open court between four walls—and he told them truly who we were. Doubtless he added that we were in revolt against the British, for they began to welcome us, shouting and dancing about us, those who could come near enough taking our hands and saying things we could not understand.

Presently they found a man who knew some English, and, urged by them, he began to fill our ears with information. During our train journey I had amused myself for many weary hours by asking Tugendheim for details of the fighting he had seen and by listening to the strings of lies he thought fit to narrate. But what Tugendheim had told were almost truths compared to this man's stories; in place of Tugendheim's studied vagueness there was detail in such profusion that I can not recall now the hundredth part of it.

He told us the British fleet had long been rusting at the bottom of the sea, and that all the British generals and half the army were prisoners in Berlin. Already the British were sending tribute money to their conquerors, and the principal reason why the war continued was that the British could not find enough donkeys to carry all the gold to Berlin, and to prevent trickery of any kind the fighting must continue until the last coin should have been counted.

The British and French, he told us, were all to be compelled, at the point of the sword, to turn Muhammadan, and France was being scoured that minute for women to grace the harems of the kaiser and his sons and generals, all of whom had long ago accepted Islam. The kaiser, indeed, had become the new chief of Islam.

I asked him about the fighting in Gallipoli, and he said that was a bagatelle. "When we shall have driven the remnants of those there into the sea," said he, "one part of us will march to conquer Egypt and the rest will be sent to garrison England and France."

When he had done and we were all under cover at last I repeated to the men all that this fool had said, and they were very much encouraged; for they reasoned that if the Turks and Germans needed to fill up their men with such lies as those, then they must have a poor case indeed. With our coats off, and a meal before us, and the mud and rain forgotten, we all began to feel almost happy; and while we were in that mood Ranjoor Singh came to us with Tugendheim at his heels.

"The plan now is to keep us here a week," said he. "After that to send us to Gallipoli by steamer."

Sahib, there was uproar! Men could scarcely eat for the joy of getting in sight of British lines again—or rather for joy of the promise of it. They almost forgot to suspect Ranjoor Singh in that minute, but praised him to his face and even made much of Tugendheim.

But I, who followed Ranjoor Singh between the tables in case he should have any orders to give, noticed particularly that he did not say we were going to Gallipoli. He said, "The plan now is to send us to Gallipoli." The trade of a leader of squadrons, thought I, is to confound the laid plans of the enemy and to invent unexpected ones of his own.

"The day we land in Gallipoli behind the Turkish trenches," said I to myself, "is unlikely to be yet if Ranjoor Singh lives."

And I was right, sahib. But if I had been given a thousand years in which to do it, I never could have guessed how Ranjoor Singh would lead us out of the trap. Can the sahib guess?

CHAPTER IV

Fear comes and goes, but a man's love lives with him.—EASTERN PROVERB.

Stamboul was disillusionment—a city of rain and plagues and stinks! The food in barracks was maggoty. We breathed foul air and yearned for the streets; yet, once in the streets, we yearned to be back in barracks. Aye, sahib, we saw more in one day of the streets than we thought good for us, none yet understanding the breadth of Ranjoor Singh's wakefulness. He seemed to us like a man asleep in good opinion of himself—that being doubtless the opinion he wished the German officers to have of him.

Part of the German plan became evident at once, for, noticing our great enthusiasm at the prospect of being sent to Gallipoli, Tugendheim, in the hope of winning praise, told a German officer we ought to be paraded through the streets as evidence that Indian troops really were fighting with the Central Powers. The German officer agreed instantly, Tugendheim making faces thus and brushing his mustache more fiercely upward.

So the very first morning after our arrival we were paraded early and sent out with a negro band, to tramp back and forth through the streets until nearly too weary to desire life. Ranjoor Singh marched at our head looking perfectly contented, for which the men all hated him, and beside him went a

Turk who knew English and who told him the names of streets and places.

It did not escape my observation that Ranjoor Singh was interested more than a little in the water-front. But we all tramped like dumb men, splashed to the waist with street dirt, aware we were being used to make a mental impression on the Turks, but afraid to refuse obedience lest we be not sent to Gallipoli after all. One thought obsessed every single man but me: To get to Gallipoli, and escape to the British trenches during some dark night, or perish in the effort.

As for me, I kept open mind and watched. It is the non-commissioned officer's affair to herd the men for his officer to lead. To have argued with them or have suggested alternative possibilities would have been only to enrage them and make them deaf to wise counsels when the proper time should come. And, besides, I knew no more what Ranjoor Singh had in mind than a dead man knows of the weather. We marched through the streets, and marched, stared at silently, neither cheered nor mocked by the inhabitants; and Ranjoor Singh arrived at his own conclusions. Five several times during that one day he halted us in the mud at a certain place along the water-front, although there was a better place near by; and while we rested he asked peculiar questions, and the Turk boasted to him, explaining many things.

We were exhausted when it fell dark and we climbed up the hill again to barracks. Yet as we entered the barrack gate I heard Ranjoor Singh tell a German officer in English that we had all greatly enjoyed our view of the city and the exercise. I repeated what I had heard while the men were at supper, and they began to wonder greatly.

"Such a lie!" said they.

"That surely was a lie?" I asked, and they answered that the man who truly had enjoyed such tramping to and fro was no soldier but a mud-fish.

"Then, if he lies to them," I said, "perhaps he tells us the truth after all."

They howled at me, calling me a man without understanding. Yet when I went away I left them thinking, each man for himself, and that was good. I went to change the guard, for some of our men were put on sentry-go that night outside the officers' quarters, in spite of our utter weariness. We were smarter than the Kurds, and German officers like smartness.

Weary though Ranjoor Singh must have been, he sat late with the German officers, for the most part keeping silence while they talked. I made excuse to go and speak with him half a dozen times, and the last time I could hardly find him among the wreaths of cigarette smoke.

"Sahib, must we really stay a week in this hole?" I asked.

"So say the Germans," said he.

"Are we to be paraded through the streets each day?" I asked.

"I understand that to be the plan," he answered.

"Then the men will mutiny!" said I.

"Nay!" said he, "let them seek better cause than that!"

"Shall I tell them so?" said I, and he looked into my eyes through the smoke as if he would read down into my very heart.

"Aye!" said he at last. "You may tell them so!"

So I went and shook some of the men awake and told them, and when they had done being angry they laughed at me. Then those awoke the others, and soon they all had the message. On the whole, it bewildered them, even as it did me, so that few dared offer an opinion and each began thinking for himself again. By morning they were in a mood to await developments. They were even willing to tramp the streets; but Ranjoor Singh procured us a day's rest. He himself spent most of the day with the German officers, poring over maps and talking. I went to speak with him as often as I could invent excuse, and I became familiar with the word Wass-muss that they used very frequently. I heard the word so many times that I could not forget it if I tried.

The next day Ranjoor Singh had a surprise for us. At ten in the morning we were all lined up in the rain and given a full month's pay. It was almost midday when the last man had received his money, and when we were dismissed and the men filed in to dinner Ranjoor Singh bade me go among them and ask whether they did not wish opportunity to spend their money.

So I went and asked the question. Only a few said yes. Many preferred to keep their money against contingencies, and some thought the question was a trick and refused to answer it at all. I returned to Ranjoor Singh and told him what they answered.

"Go and ask them again!" said he.

So I went among them again as they lay on the cots after dinner, and most of them jeered at me for my pains. I went and found Ranjoor Singh in the officers' mess and told him.

"Ask them once more!" said he.

This third time, being in no mood to endure mockery, I put the question with an air of mystery. They asked what the hidden meaning might be, but I shook my head and repeated the question with a smile, as if I knew indeed but would not tell.

"Says Ranjoor Singh," said I, "would the men like opportunity to spend their money?"

"No!" said most of them, and Gooja Singh asked how long it well might be before we should see money again.

"Shall I bear him, a third time, such an answer?" I asked, looking more mysterious than ever. And just then it happened that Gooja Singh remembered the advice to seek better cause for mutiny. He drummed on his teeth with his fingernails.

"Very well!" said he. "Tell him we will either spend our money or let blood! Let us see what he says to that!"

"Shall I say," said I, "that Gooja Singh says so?"

"Nay, nay!" said he, growing anxious. "Let that be the regiment's answer. Name no names!"

I thought it a foolish answer, given by a fool, but the men were in the mood to relish it and began to laugh exceedingly.

"Shall I take that answer?" said I, and they answered "Yes!" redoubling their emphasis when I objected. "The Germans do Ranjoor Singh's thinking for him these days," said one man; "take that answer and let us see what the Germans have to say to it through his mouth!"

So I went and told Ranjoor Singh, whispering to him in a corner of the officers' mess. Some Turks had joined the Germans and most of them were bending over maps that a German officer had spread upon a table in their midst; he was lecturing while the others listened. Ranjoor Singh had been listening, too, but he backed into a corner as I entered, and all the while I was whispering to him I kept hearing the word Wassmuss—Wassmuss—Wassmuss. The German who was lecturing explained something about this Wassmuss.

"What is Wassmuss?" I asked, when I had given Ranjoor Singh the men's answer. He smiled into my eyes.

"Wassmuss is the key to the door," said he.

"To which door?" I asked him.

"There is only one," he answered.

"Shall I tell that to the men?" said I.

At that he began scowling at me, stroking his beard with one hand. Then he stepped back and forth a time or two. And when he saw with the corner of his eye that he had the senior German officer's attention he turned on me and glared again. There was sudden silence in the room, and I stood at attention, striving to look like a man of wood.

"It is as I said," said he in English. "It was

most unwise to pay them. Now the ruffians demand liberty to go and spend—and that means license! They have been prisoners of war in close confinement too long. You should have sent them to Gallipoli before they tasted money or anything else but work! Who shall control such men now!"

The German officer stroked his chin, eying Ranjoor Singh sternly, yet I thought irresolutely.

"If they would be safer on board a steamer, that can be managed. A steamer came in to-day, that would do," said he, speaking in English, perhaps lest the Turks understand. "And there is Tugendheim, of course. Tugendheim could keep watch on board."

I think he had more to say, but at that minute Ranjoor Singh chose to turn on me fiercely and order me out of the room.

"Tell them what you have heard!" he said in Punjabi, as if he were biting my head off, and I expect the German officer believed he had cursed me. I saluted and ran, and one of the Turkish officers aimed a kick at me as I passed. It was by the favor of God that the kick missed, for had he touched me I would have torn his throat out, and then doubtless I should not have been here to tell what Ranjoor Singh did. To this day I do not know whether he had every move planned out in his mind, or whether part was thinking and part good fortune. When a good man sets himself to thinking, God puts thoughts into his heart that others can not overcome, and it may be that he simply prayed. I know not—although I know he prayed often, as a true Sikh should.

I told the men exactly what had passed, except that I did not say Ranjoor Singh had bidden me do so. I gave them to understand that I was revealing a secret, and that gave them greater confidence in my loyalty to them. It was important they should not suspect me of allegiance to Ranjoor Singh.

"It is good!" said they all, after a lot of talking and very little thought. "To be sent on board a steamer could only mean Gallipoli. There we will make great show of ferocity and bravery, so that they will send us to the foremost trenches. It should be easy to steal across by night to the British trenches, dragging Ranjoor Singh with us, and when we are among friends again let him give what account of himself he may! What new shame is this, to tell the Germans we will make trouble because we have a little money at last! Let the shame return to roost on him!"

They began to make ready there and then, and while they packed the knapsacks I urged them to shout and laugh as if growing mutinous. Soldiers, unless prevented, load themselves like pack animals with a hundred unnecessary things, but none of us had more than the full kit for each man that the Germans had served out, so that packing took no time at all. An hour after we were ready came Ranjoor Singh, standing in the door of our quarters with that senior German officer beside him, both of them scowling at us, and the German making more than a little show of possessing a repeating pistol. So that Gooja Singh made great to-do about military compliments, rebuking several troopers in loud tones for not standing quickly to attention, and shouting to me to be more strict. I let him have his say.

Angrily as a gathering thunder-storm Ranjoor

Singh ordered us to fall in, and we scrambled out through the doorway like a pack of hunting hounds released. No word was spoken to us by way of explanation, Ranjoor Singh continuing to scowl with folded arms while the German officer went back to look the quarters over, perhaps to see whether we had done damage, or perhaps to make certain nothing had been left. He came out in a minute or two and then we were marched out of the barrack in the dimming light, with Tugendheim in full marching order falling into step behind us and the senior German officer smoking a cigar beside Ranjoor Singh. A Kurdish soldier carried Tugendheim's bag of belongings, and Tugendheim kicked him savagely when he dropped it in a pool of mud. I thought the Kurd would knife him, but he refrained.

I think I have said, sahib, that the weather was vile. We were glad of our overcoats. As we marched along the winding road downhill we kept catching glimpses of the water-front through driving rain, light after light appearing as the twilight gathered. Nobody noticed us. There seemed to be no one in the streets, and small wonder!

Before we were half-way down toward the water there began to be a very great noise of firing, of big and little cannon and rifles. There began to be shouting, and men ran back and forth below us. I asked Tugendheim what it all might mean, and he said probably a British submarine had shown itself. I whispered that to the nearest men and they passed the word along. Great contentment grew among us, none caring after that for rain and mud. That was the nearest we had been to friends in oh how many months—if it truly were a British submarine!

We reached the water-front presently and were brought to a halt in exactly the place where Ranjoor Singh had halted us those five times on the day we tramped the streets. We faced a dock that had been vacant two days ago, but where now a little steamer lay moored with ropes, smoke coming from its funnel. There was no other sign of life, but when the German officer shouted about a dozen times the Turkish captain came ashore, wrapped in a great shawl, and spoke to him.

While they two spoke I asked Ranjoor Singh whether that truly had been a British submarine, and he nodded; but he was not able to tell me whether or not it had been hit by gun-fire. Some of the men overheard, and although we all knew that our course to Gallipoli would be the more hazardous in that event we all prayed that the artillery might have missed. Fear comes and goes, but a man's love lives in him.

When the Turkish captain and the German officer finished speaking, the Turk went back to his steamer without any apparent pleasure, and we were marched up the gangway after him. It was pitch-dark by that time and the only light was that of a lantern by which the German officer stood, eying us one by one as we passed. Tugendheim came last, and he talked with Tugendheim for several minutes. Then he went away, but presently returned with, I should say, half a company of Kurdish soldiers, whom he posted all about the dock. Then he departed finally, with a wave of his cigar, as much as to say that sheet of the ledger had been balanced.

It was a miserable steamer, sahib. We stood about on iron decks and grew hungry. There were no awnings—nothing but the superstructure of the bridge, and, although there were but two-hundred-and-thirty-four of us, including Tugendheim, we could not stow ourselves so that all could be sheltered from the rain and let the mud cake dry on our legs and feet. There was a little cabin that Tugendheim took for himself, but Ranjoor Singh remained with us on deck. He stood in the rain by the gangway, looking first at one thing, then at another. I watched him.

Presently he went to the door of the engine-room, opened it, and looked through. I was about to look, too, but he shut it in my face.

"It is enough that they make steam," said he; and I looked up at the funnel and saw steam mingled with the smoke. In a little wheel-house on the bridge the Turkish captain sat on a shelf, wrapped in his shawl, smoking a great pipe, and his mate, who was also a Turk, sat beside him staring at the sky. I asked Ranjoor Singh whether we might expect to have the whole ship to ourselves. Said I, "It would not be difficult to overpower those two Turks and their small crew and make them do our bidding!" But he answered that a regiment of Kurds was expected to keep us company at dawn. Then he went up to the bridge to have word with the Turkish captain, and I went to the ship's side to stare about. Over my shoulder I told the men about the Kurds who were coming, and they were not pleased.

Peering into the dark and wondering that so great

a city as Stamboul should show so few lights, I observed the Kurdish sentinels posted about the dock.

"Those are to prevent us from going ashore until their friends come!" said I, and they snarled at me like angry wolves.

"We could easily rush ashore and bayonet every one of them!" said Gooja Singh.

But not a man would have gone ashore again for a commission in the German army. Gallipoli was written in their hearts. Yet I could think of a hundred thousand chances still that might prevent our joining our friends the British in Gallipoli. Nor was I sure in my own mind that Ranjoor Singh intended we should try. I was sure only of his good faith, and content to wait developments.

Though the lights of the city were few and very far between, so many search-lights played back and forth above the water that there seemed a hundred of them. I judged it impossible for the smallest boat to pass unseen and I wondered whether it was difficult or easy to shoot with great guns by aid of search-lights, remembering what strange tricks light can play with a gunner's eyes. Mist, too, kept rising off the water to add confusion.

While I reflected in that manner, thinking that the shadow of every wave and the side of every boat might be a submarine, Ranjoor Singh came down from the bridge and stood beside me.

"I have seen what I have seen!" said he. "Listen! Obey! And give me no back answers!"

"Sahib," said I, "I am thy man!" But he answered nothing to that.

"Pick the four most dependable men," he said,

"and bid them enter that cabin and gag and bind Tugendheim. Bid them make no noise and see to it that he makes none, but let them do him no injury, for we shall need him presently! When that is done, come back to me here!"

So I left him at once, he standing as I had done, staring at the water, although I thought perhaps there was more purpose in his gaze than there had been in mine.

I chose four men and led them aside, they greatly wondering.

"There is work to be done," said I, "that calls for true ones!"

"Such men be we!" said all four together.

"That is why I picked you from among the rest!" said I, and they were well pleased at that. Then I gave them their orders.

"Who bids us do this?" they demanded.

"I!" said I. "Bind and gag Tugendheim, and we have Ranjoor Singh committed. He gave the order, and I bid you obey it! How can he be false to us and true to the Germans, with a gagged German prisoner on his hands?"

They saw the point of that. "But what if we are discovered too soon?" said they.

"What if we are sunk before dawn by a British submarine!" said I. "We will swim when we find ourselves in water! For the present, bind and gag Tugendheim!"

So they went and stalked Tugendheim, the German, who had been drinking from a little pocket flask. He was drowsing in a chair in the cabin, with his hands deep down in his overcoat pockets and his helmet over his eyes. Within three minutes I was back at Ranjoor Singh's side.

"The four stand guard over him!" said I.

"Very good!" said he. "That was well done! Now do a greater thing."

My heart burned, sahib, for I had once dared doubt him, yet all he had to say to me was, "Well done! Now do a greater thing!" If he had cursed me a little for my earlier unbelief I might have felt less ashamed!

"Go to the men," said he, "and bid those who wish the British well to put all the money they received this morning into a cloth. Bid those who are no longer true to the British to keep their money. When the money is all in the cloth, bring it here to me."

"But what if they refuse?" said I.

"Do *you* refuse?" he asked.

"Nay!" said I. "Nay, sahib!"

"Then why judge them?" said he. So I went.

Can the sahib imagine it? Two-hundred-and-three-and-thirty men, including non-commissioned officers, wet and muddy in the dark, beginning to be hungry, all asked at once to hand over all their pay if they be true men, but told to keep it if they be traitors!

No man answered a word, although their eyes burned up the darkness. I called for a lantern, and a man brought one from the engine-room door. By its light I spread out a cloth, and laid all my money on it on the deck. The sergeant nearest me followed my example. Gooja Singh laid down only half his money.

"Nay!" said I. "All or none! This is a test for true men! Half-true and false be one and the same to-night!" So Gooja Singh made a wry face and laid down the rest of his money, and the others all followed him, not at all understanding, as indeed I myself did not understand, but coming one at a time to me and laying all their money on the cloth. When the last man had done I tied the four corners of the cloth together (it was all wet with the rain and slush on deck, and heavy with the weight of coin) and carried it to Ranjoor Singh. (I forgot the four who stood guard over Tugendheim; they kept their money.)

"We are all true men!" said I, dumping it beside him.

"Good!" said he. "Come!" And he took the bundle of money and ascended the bridge ladder, bidding me wait at the foot of it for further orders. I stood there two hours without another sign of him, although I heard voices in the wheel-house.

Now the men grew restless. Reflection without action made them begin to doubt the wisdom of surrendering all their money at a word. They began to want to know the why and wherefore of the business, and I was unable to tell them.

"Wait and see!" said I, but that only exasperated them, and some began to raise their voices in anger. So I felt urged to invent a reason, hoping to explain it away afterward should I be wrong. But as it turned out I guessed at least a little part of Ranjoor

Singh's great plan and so achieved great credit that was useful later, although at the time I felt myself losing favor with them.

"Ranjoor Singh will bribe the captain of the ship to steam away before that regiment of Kurds can come on board," said I. "So we shall have the ship at our mercy, provided we make no mistakes."

That did not satisfy them, but it gave them something new to think about, and they settled down to wait in silence, as many as could crowding their backs against the deck-house and the rest suffering in the rain. I would rather have heard them whispering, because I judged the silence to be due to low spirits. I knew of nothing more to say to encourage them, and after a time their depression began to affect me also. Rather than watch them, I watched the water, and more than once I saw something I did not recognize, that nevertheless caused my skin to tingle and my breath to come in jerks. Sikh eyes are keen.

It was perhaps two hours before midnight when the long spell of firing along the water-front began and I knew that my eyes and the dark had not deceived me. All the search-lights suddenly swept together to one point and shone on the top-side of a submarine—or at least on the water thrown up by its top-side. Only two masts and a thing like a tower were visible, and the plunging shells threw water over those obscuring them every second. There was a great explosion, whether before or after the beginning of the gun-fire I do not remember, and a ship anchored out on the water no great distance from us heeled over and began to sink. One search-light was turned on the sinking ship, so that I could see hundreds of men on her running to and fro and jumping; but all the rest of the water was now left in darkness.

The guards who had been set to prevent our landing all ran to another wharf to watch the gun-fire and the sinking ship, and it was at the moment when their backs were turned that two Turkish seamen came down from the bridge and loosed the ropes that held us to the shore. Then our ship began to move out slowly into the darkness without showing lights or sounding whistle. There was still no sign of Ranjoor Singh, nor had I time to look for him; I was busy making the men be still, urging, coaxing, cursing—even striking them.

"Are we off to Gallipoli?" they asked.

"We are off to where a true man may remember the salt!" said I, knowing no more than they.

I know of nothing more confusing to a landsman, sahib, than a crowded harbor at night. The many search-lights all quivering and shifting in the one direction only made confusion worse and we had not been moving two minutes when I no longer knew north from south or east from west. I looked up, to try to judge by the stars. I had actually forgotten it was raining. The rain came down in sheets and overhead the sky began at little more than arm's length! Judge, then, my excitement.

We passed very close to several small steamers that may have been war-ships, but I think they were merchant ships converted into gunboats to hunt submarines. I think, too, that in the darkness they mistook us for another of the same sort, for, although we almost collided with two of them, they neither fired on us nor challenged. We steamed straight past them, beginning to gain speed as the last one fell away behind.

Does the sahib remember whether the passage from Stamboul into the Sea of Marmora runs south or east or west? Neither could I remember, although at another time I could have drawn a map of it, having studied such things. But memory plays us strange tricks, and cavalrymen were never intended to maneuver in a ship! Ranjoor Singh, up in the wheel-house, had a map—a good map, that he had stolen from the German officers—but I did not know that until later. I stood with both hands holding the rails of the bridge ladder wondering whether gunfire or submarine would sink us and urging the men to keep their heads below the bulwark lest a searchlight find us and the number of heads cause suspicion.

I have often tried to remember just how many hours we steamed from Stamboul, yet I have no idea to this day beyond that the voyage was ended before dawn. It was all unexpected—we were too excited, and too fearful for our skins to recall the passage of hours. It was darker than I have ever known night to be, and the short waves that made our ship pitch unevenly were growing steeper every minute, when Ranjoor Singh came at last to the head of the ladder and shouted for me. I went to him up the steps, holding to each rail for dear life.

"Take twenty men," he ordered, "and uncover the forward hatch. Throw the hatch coverings overboard. The hold is full of cartridges. Bring up some boxes and break them open. Distribute two hundred rounds to every man, and throw the empty boxes overboard. Then get up twenty more boxes and place them close together, in readiness to take with us when we leave the ship. Let me know when that is all done."

So I took twenty men and we obeyed him. Two hundred rounds of cartridges a man made a heavy extra load and the troopers grumbled.

"Can we swim with these?" they demanded.

"Who knows until he has tried?" said I.

"How far may we have to march with such an extra weight?" said they.

"Who knows!" said I, counting out two hundred more to another man. "But the man," I said, "who lacks one cartridge of the full count when I come to inspect shall be put to the test whether he can swim at all!"

Some of them had begun to throw half of their two hundred into the water, but after I said that they discontinued, and I noticed that those who had so done came back for more cartridges, pretending that my count had been short. So I served them out more and said nothing. There were hundreds of thousands of rounds in the hold of the ship, and I judged we could afford to overlook the waste.

At last we set the extra twenty boxes in one place together, slipping and falling in the process because the deck was wet and the ship unsteady; and then I went and reported to Ranjoor Singh.

"Very good," said he. "Make the men fall in along the deck, and bid them be ready for whatever may befall!"

"Are we near land, sahib?" said I.

"Very near!" said he.

I ran to obey him, peering into the blackness to discover land, but I could see nothing more than the white tops of waves, and clouds that seemed to meet the sea within a rope's length of us. Once or twice I thought I heard surf, but the noise of the rain and of the engines and of the waves pounding against the ship confused my ears, so that I could not be certain.

When the men were all fallen in I went and leaned over the bulwark to try to see better; and as I did that we ran in under a cliff, for the darkness grew suddenly much darker. Then I surely heard surf. Then another sound startled me, and a shock nearly threw me off my feet. I faced about, to find twenty or thirty men sprawling their length upon the deck, and when I had urged and helped them up the engines had stopped turning, and steam was roaring savagely through the funnel. The motion of the ship was different now; the front part seemed almost still, but the behind part rose and fell jerkily.

I busied myself with the men, bullying them into silence, for I judged it most important to be able to hear the first order that Ranjoor Singh might give; but he gave none just yet, although I heard a lot of talking on the bridge.

"Is this Gallipoli?" the men kept asking me in whispers.

"If it were," said I, "we should have been blown to

little pieces by the guns of both sides before now!" If I had been offered all the world for a reward I could not have guessed our whereabouts, nor what we were likely to do next, but I was very sure we had not reached Gallipoli.

Presently the Turkish seamen began lowering the boats. There were but four boats, and they made clumsy work of it, but at last all four boats were in the water; and then Ranjoor Singh began at last to give his orders, in a voice and with an air that brought reassurance. No man could command as he did who had the least little doubt in his heart of eventual success. There is even more conviction in a true man's voice than in his eye.

He ordered us overside eight at a time, and me in the first boat with the first eight.

"Fall them in along the first flat place you find on shore, and wait there for me!" said he. And I said, "Ha, sahib!" wondering as I swung myself down a swaying rope whether my feet could ever find the boat. But the sailors pulled the rope's lower end, and I found myself in a moment wedged into a space into which not one more man could have been crowded.

The waves broke over us, and there was a very evil surf, but the distance to the shore was short and the sailors proved skilful. We landed safely on a gravelly beach, not so very much wetter than we had been, except for our legs (for we waded the last few yards), and I hunted at once for a piece of level ground. Just thereabouts it was all nearly level, so I fell my eight men in within twenty yards of the surf, and waited. I felt tempted to throw out pickets, yet afraid not to obey implicitly. Ranjoor Singh had given no order about pickets.

I judge it took more than an hour, and it may have been two hours, to bring all the men and the twenty boxes of cartridges ashore. At last in three boats came the captain of the ship, and the mate, and the engineer, and nearly all the crew. Then I grew suddenly afraid and hot sweat burst out all over me, for by the one lantern that had been hung from the ship's bridge rail to guide the rowers I could see that the ship was moving! The ship's captain had climbed out of the last boat and was standing close to it. I went up to him and seized his shoulder.

"What dog's work is this?" said I. "Speak!" I said, shaking him, although he could not talk any tongue that I knew—but I shook him none-the-less until his teeth chattered, and, his arms being wrapped in that great shawl of his, there was little he could do to prevent me.

As I live, sahib, on the word of a Sikh I swear that not even in that instant did I doubt Ranjoor Singh. I believed that the Turkish captain might have stabbed him, or that Tugendheim might have played some trick. But not so the men. They saw the lantern receding and receding, dancing with the motion of the ship, and they believed themselves deserted.

"Quick! Fire on him!" shouted some one. "Let him not escape! Kill him before he is out of range!"

I never knew which trooper it was who raised that cry, although I went to some trouble to discover afterward. But I heard Gooja Singh laugh like a hyena; and I heard the click of cartridges being thrust into magazines. I was half minded to let them shoot, hoping they might hit Tugendheim. But the Turk freed his arms at last, and began struggling.

"Look!" he said to me in English. *"Voilà!"* said he in French. *"Regardez!* Look—see!"

I did look, and I saw enough to make me make swift decision. The light was nearer to the water—quite a lot nearer. I flung myself on the nearest trooper, whose rifle was already raised, and taken by surprise he loosed his weapon. With it I beat the next ten men's rifles down, and they clattered on the beach. That made the others pause and look at me.

"The man who fires the first shot dies!" said I, striving to make the breath come evenly between my teeth for sake of dignity, yet with none too great success. But in the principal matter I was successful, for they left their alignment and clustered round to argue with me. At that I refused to have speech with them until they should have fallen in again, as befitted soldiers. Falling in took time, especially as they did it sulkily; and when the noise of shifting feet was finished I heard oars thumping in the oarlocks.

A boat grounded amid the surf, and Ranjoor Singh jumped out of it, followed by Tugendheim and his four guards. The boat's crew leaped into the water and hauled the boat high and dry, and as they did that I saw the ship's lantern disappear altogether.

Ranjoor Singh went straight to the Turkish captain. "Your money," said he, speaking in English slowly—I wonder, sahib, oh, I have wondered a thousand times in what medley of tongues strange to all of them they had done their bargaining!—"Your money," said he, "is in the boat in which I came. Take it, and take your men, and go!"

The captain and his crew said nothing, but got into the boats and pushed away. One of the boats was overturned in the surf, and there they left it, the sailors scrambling into the other boats. They were out of sight and sound in two minutes. Then Ranjoor Singh turned to me.

"Send and gather fire-wood!" he ordered.

"Where shall dry wood be in all this rain?" said I.

"Search!" said he.

"Sahib," said I, "a fire would only betray our whereabouts."

"Are you deaf?" said he.

"Nay!" I said.

"Then obey!" said he. So I took twenty men, and we went stumbling through rain and darkness, hunting for what none of us believed was anywhere. Yet within fifteen minutes we found a hut whose roof was intact, and therefore whose floor and inner parts were dry enough. It was a little hut, of the length of perhaps the height of four men, and the breadth of the height of three—a man and a half high from floor to roof-beam. It was unoccupied, but there was straw at one end—dry straw, on which doubtless guards had slept. I left the men standing there and went and told Ranjoor Singh.

I found him talking to the lined up men in no gentle manner. As I drew nearer I heard him say the word "Wassmuss." Then I heard a trooper ask him, "Where are we?" And he answered, "Ye stand on Asia!" That was the first intimation I received that we were in Asia, and I felt suddenly lonely, for Asia is wondrously big, sahib.

Whatever Ranjoor Singh had been saying to the men he had them back under his thumb for the time being; for when I told him of my discovery of the hut he called them to attention, turned them to the right, and marched them off as obedient as a machine, Tugendheim following like a man in a dream between his four guards and struggling now and then to loose the wet thongs that were beginning to cut into his wrists. He had not been trussed over-tenderly, but I noticed that Ranjoor Singh had ordered the gag removed.

The hut stood alone, clear on all four sides, and after he had looked at it, Ranjoor Singh made the men line up facing the door, with himself and me and Tugendheim between them and the hut. Presently he pushed Tugendheim into the hut, and he bade me stand in the door to watch him.

"Now the man who wishes to ask questions may," he said then, and there was a long silence, for I suppose none wished to be accused of impudence and perhaps made an example for the rest. Besides, they were too curious to know what his next intention might be to care to offend him. So I, seeing that he wished them to speak, and conceiving that to be part of his plan for establishing good feeling, asked the first question—the first that came into my head.

"What shall we do with this Tugendheim?" said I.

"That I will show you presently," said he. "Who else has a question to ask?" And again there was silence, save for the rain and the grinding and pounding on the beach.

Then Gooja Singh made bold, as he usually did when he judged the risk not too great. He was behind the men, which gave him greater courage; and it suited him well to have to raise his voice, because the men might suppose that to be due to insolence, whereas Ranjoor Singh must ascribe it to necessity. Well I knew the method of Gooja Singh's reasoning, and I knitted my fists in a frenzy of fear lest he say the wrong word and start trouble. Yet I need not have worried. I observed that Ranjoor Singh seemed not disturbed at all, and he knew Gooja Singh as well as I.

"It seems for the time being that we have given the slip to both Turks and Germans," said Gooja Singh; and Ranjoor Singh said, "Aye! For the time being!"

"And we truly stand on Asia?" he asked.

"Aye!" said Ranjoor Singh.

"Then why did we not put those Turks ashore, and steam away in their ship toward Gallipoli to join our friends?" said he.

"Partly because of submarines," said Ranjoor Singh, "and partly because of gun-fire. Partly because of mines floating in the water, and partly again from lack of coal. The bunkers were about empty. It was because there was so little coal that the Germans trusted us alone on board."

"Yet, why let the Turks have the steamer?" asked

Gooja Singh, bound, now that he was started, to prove himself in the right. "They will float about until daylight and then send signals. Then will come Turks and Germans!"

"Nay!" said Ranjoor Singh. "No so, for I sank the steamer! I myself let the sea into her hold!"

Gooja Singh was silent for about a minute, and although it was dark and I could not see him I knew exactly the expression of his face—wrinkled thus, and with the lower lip thrust out, so!

"Any more questions?" asked Ranjoor Singh, and by that time Gooja Singh had thought again. This time he seemed to think he had an unanswerable one, for his voice was full of insolence.

"Then how comes it," said he, "that you turned those Turks loose in their small boats when we might have kept them with us for hostages? Now they will row to the land and set their masters on our tracks! Within an hour or two we shall all be prisoners again! Tell us why!"

"For one thing," said Ranjoor Singh, without any resentment in his voice that I could detect (although *that* was no sign!), "I had to make some sort of bargain with them, and having made it I must keep it. The money with which I bribed the captain and his mate would have been of little use to them unless I allowed them life and liberty as well."

"But they will give the alarm and cause us to be followed!" shouted Gooja Singh, his voice rising louder with each word.

"Nay, I think not!" said Ranjoor Singh, as calmly as ever. "In the first place, I have a written receipt from captain and mate for our money, stating the reason for which it was paid; if we were made prisoners again, that paper would be found in my possession and it might go ill with those Turks. In the second place, they will wish to save their faces. In the third place, they must explain the loss of their steamer. So they will say the steamer was sunk by a submarine, and that they got away in the boats and watched us drown. The crew will bear out what the captain and the mate say, partly from fear, partly because that is the custom of the country, but chiefly because they will receive a small share of the bribe. Let us hope they get back safely—for their story will prevent pursuit!"

For about two minutes again there was silence, and then Gooja Singh called out: "Why did you not make them take us to Gallipoli?"

"There was not enough coal!" said I, but Ranjoor Singh made a gesture to me of impatience.

"The Germans wished us to go to Gallipoli," said he, "and I have noticed that whatever they may desire is expressly intended for their advantage and not ours. In Gallipoli they would have kept us out of range at the rear, and presently they would have caused a picture of us to be taken serving among the Turkish army. That they would have published broadcast. After that I have no idea what would have happened to us, except that I am sure we should never have got near enough to the British lines to make good our escape. We must find another way than that!"

"We might have made the attempt!" said Gooja Singh, and a dozen men murmured approval.

"Simpletons!" came the answer. "The Germans laid their plans for the first for photographs to lend color to lies about the Sikh troops fighting for them! Ye would have played into their hands!"

"What then?" said I, after a minute, for at that answer they had all grown dumb.

"What then?" said he. "Why, this: We are in Asia, but still on Turkish soil. We need food. We shall need shelter before many hours. And we need discipline, to aid our will to overcome! Therefore there never was a regiment more fiercely disciplined than this shall be! From now until we bring up in a British camp—and God knows when or where that may happen!—the man who as much as thinks of disobedience plays with death! Death—ye be as good as dead men now!" said he.

He shook himself. A sense of loneliness had come on me since he told us we were in Asia, and I think the men felt as I did. There had been nothing to eat on the steamer, and there was nothing now. Hunger and cold and rain were doing their work. But Ranjoor Singh stood and shook himself, and moved slowly along the line to look in each man's face, and I took new courage from his bearing. If I could have known what he had in store for us, I would have leaped and shouted. Yet, no, sahib; that is not true. If he had told me what was coming, I would never have believed. Can the sahib imagine, for instance, what was to happen next?

"Ye are as good as dead men!" he said, coming back to the center and facing all the men. "Consider!" said he. "Our ship is sunk and the Turks, to save their own skins, will swear they saw us drown. Who, then, will come and hunt for dead men?"

I could see the eyes of the nearest men opening wider as new possibilities began to dawn. As for me—my two hands shook.

"And we have with us," said he, "a hostage who might prove useful—a hostage who might prove amenable to reason. Bring out the prisoner!" said he.

So I bade Tugendheim come forth. He was sitting on the straw where the guards had pushed him, still working sullenly to free his hands. He came and peered through the doorway into darkness, and Ranjoor Singh stood aside to let the men see him. They can not have seen much, for it was now that utter gloom that precedes dawn. Nor can Tugendheim have seen much.

"Do you wish to live or die?" asked Ranjoor Singh, and the German gaped at him.

"That is a strange question!" he said.

"Is it strange," asked Ranjoor Singh, "that a prisoner should be asked for information?"

"I am not afraid to die," said Tugendheim.

"You mean by rifle-fire?" asked Ranjoor Singh, and Tugendheim nodded.

"But there are other kinds of fire," said Ranjoor Singh.

"What do you mean?" asked Tugendheim.

"Why," said Ranjoor Singh, "if we were to fire this hut to warm ourselves, and you should happen to be inside it—what then?"

"If you intend to kill me," said Tugendheim, "why not be merciful and shoot me?" His voice was brave enough, but it seemed to me I detected a strain of terror in it.

"Few Germans are afraid to be shot to death," said Ranjoor Singh.

"But what have I done to any of you that you should want to burn me alive?" asked Tugendheim; and that time I was positive his voice was forced.

"Haven't you been told by your officers," said Ranjoor Singh, "that the custom of us Sikhs is to burn all our prisoners alive?"

"Yes," said Tugendheim. "They told us that. But that was only a tale to encourage the first-year men. Having lived in India, I knew better."

"Did you trouble yourself to tell anybody better?" asked Ranjoor Singh, but Tugendheim did not answer.

"Then can you give me any reason why you should not be burned alive here, now?" asked Ranjoor Singh.

"Yes!" said Tugendheim. "It would be cruel. It would be devil's work!" He was growing very uneasy, although trying hard not to show it.

"Then give me a name for the tales you have been party to against us Sikhs!" said Ranjoor Singh; but once more the German refrained from answering. The men were growing very attentive, breathing all in unison and careful to make no sound to disturb the talking. At that instant a great burst of firing broke out over the water, so far away that I could only see one or two flashes, and, although that was none too reassuring to us, it seemed to Tugendheim like his death knell. He set his lips and drew back half a step.

"Can you wish to live with the shame of all those lies against us on your heart—you, who have lived in India and know so much better?" asked Ranjoor Singh.

"Of course I wish to live!" said Tugendheim.

"Have you any price to offer for your life?" asked Ranjoor Singh, and stepping back two paces he ordered a havildar with a loud voice to take six men and hunt for dry kindling. "For there is not enough here," said he.

"Price?" said Tugendheim. "I have a handful of coins, and my uniform, and a sword. You left my baggage on the steamer——"

"Nay!" said Ranjoor Singh. "Your baggage came ashore in one of the boats. Where is it? Who has it?"

A man stepped forward and pointed to it, lying in the shadow of the hut with the rain from the roof dripping down on it.

"Who brought it ashore?" asked Ranjoor Singh.

"I," said the trooper.

"Then, for leaving it there in the rain, you shall carry it three days without assistance or relief!" said Ranjoor Singh. "Get back to your place in the ranks!" And the man got back, saying nothing. Ranjoor Singh picked up the baggage and tossed it past Tugendheim into the hut.

"That is all I have!" said Tugendheim.

"If you decide to burn, it shall burn with you," said Ranjoor Singh, "and that trooper shall carry a good big stone instead to teach him manners!"

"Gott in Himmel!" exclaimed Tugendheim, losing

his self-control at last. "Can I offer what I have not got?"

"Is there nothing you can do?" asked Ranjoor Singh.

"In what way? How?" asked the German.

"In the way of making amends to us Sikhs for all those lies you have been party to," said Ranjoor Singh. "If you were willing to offer to make amends, I would listen to you."

"I will do anything in reason," said Tugendheim, looking him full in the eye and growing more at ease.

"I am a reasonable man," said Ranjoor Singh.

"Then, speak!" said Tugendheim.

"Nay, nay!" said Ranjoor Singh, "it is for you to make proposals, and not for me. It is not I who stand waiting to be burned alive! Let me make you a suggestion, however. What had we Sikhs to offer when we were prisoners in Germany?"

"Oh, I see!" said Tugendheim. "You mean you wish me to join you—to be one of you?"

"I mean," said Ranjoor Singh, "that if you were to apply to be allowed to join this regiment for a while, and to be allowed to serve us in a certain manner, we would consider the proposal. Otherwise—is my meaning clear?"

"Yes!" said Tugendheim.

"Then——?" said Ranjoor Singh.

"I apply!" said Tugendheim; and at that moment the havildar and his men returned with some straw they had found in another tumble-down hut. They had it stuffed under their overcoats to keep it dry.

"Too late!" said Tugendheim with a grimace, but

Ranjoor Singh bade them throw the straw inside for all that.

"In Germany we were required to set our names to paper," he said, and Tugendheim looked him in the eyes again for a full half minute. "Do you expect better conditions than were offered us?" asked Ranjoor Singh.

"I will sign!" said Tugendheim.

"What will you sign?" asked Ranjoor Singh.

"Anything in reason," answered Tugendheim.

"Let me tell you what I have here, then," said Ranjoor Singh, and he groped in his inner pocket for a paper, that he brought out very neatly folded, sheltering it from the rain under his cape. "This," said he, "is signed by the Turkish captain and mate of that sunken steamer. It is a receipt for all our money, to be taken and divided equally between you—mentioned by name—and them—mentioned also by name, on condition that the ship be sunk and we be let go. If you will sign the paper—here—above their signatures—it will entitle you to one-third of all that money. They would neither of them dare to refuse to share with you!"

"What if I refuse to sign?" asked Tugendheim, making a great savage wrench to free his wrists, but failing.

"The suggestion is yours," said Ranjoor Singh. "You have only your own judgment for a guide."

"If I sign it, will you let me go?" he asked.

"No," said Ranjoor Singh, "but we will not burn you alive if you sign. Here is a fountain-pen. Your hands shall be loosed when you are ready."

Tugendheim nodded, so I went and cut his hands loose; and when I had chafed his wrists for a minute or two he was able to write on my shoulder, I bending forward and Ranjoor Singh watching like a hawk lest he tear the paper. But he made no effort to play tricks.

When Ranjoor Singh had folded the paper again he said: "Those two Turks quite understood that you were to be asked to sign as well. In fact, if there is any mishap they intend to lay all the blame on you. But it is to their interest as much as yours to keep us from being captured."

"You mean I'm to help you escape?" asked Tugendheim.

"Exactly!" said Ranjoor Singh. "Now that you have signed that, I am willing to bargain with you. We intend to find Wassmuss."

Tugendheim pricked up his ears and began to look almost willing.

"We have heard of this Wassmuss, and have taken quite a fancy to him. Your friends proposed to send us to the trenches, but we have already had too much of that work and we intend to find Wassmuss and take part with him. Let your business be to obey me implicitly and to help us reach Wassmuss, and on the day we reach our goal you shall go free with this paper given back to you. Disobey me, and you shall sample unheard-of methods of repentance! Do we understand each other?"

"I understand you!" said Tugendheim.

"I, too, wish to understand," said Ranjoor Singh.

"It is a bargain," said Tugendheim. But I noticed

they did not shake hands after European fashion, although I think Tugendheim would have been willing. He was a hearty man in his way, given to bullying, but also to quick forgetfulness; and I will say this much for him, that although he was ever on the lookout for some way of breaking his agreement, he kept it loyally enough while a way was lacking. I have met men I liked less.

It was growing by that time to be very nearly dawn, and the weather did not improve. The rain came down in squalls and sheets and the wind screamed through it, and we were famished as well as wet to the skin—all, that is to say, except Tugendheim, who had enjoyed the shelter of the hut. The teeth of many of the men were chattering. Yet we stood about for an hour more, because it was too dark and too dangerous to march over unknown ground. I suspect Ranjoor Singh did not dare squander what little spirit the men had left; if they had suspected him of losing them in the dark they might have lost heart altogether.

But at last there grew a little cold color in the sky and the sea took on a shade of gray. Then Ranjoor Singh told off the same four men who had first arrested him to guard our prisoner by day and night, taking turns to pretend to be his servant, with orders to give instant alarm should his movements seem suspicious. After that Tugendheim was searched, but, nothing of interest being found on him, his money and various little things were given back.

"Had he no pistol?" asked Ranjoor Singh.

"Yes," said I, "but I took it when we bound and gagged him on the steamer." And I drew it out and showed it, feeling proud, never having had such a weapon—for the law of British India is strict.

"Why did you not tell me?" he asked, and I was silent. "Give it here!" said he, and I gave it up. He examined it, drew out the cartridges, and passed it to Tugendheim, who pocketed it with a laugh. It was three days before he spoke to Tugendheim and caused him to give me the pistol back. I think the men were impressed, and I was glad of it, although at the time I felt ashamed.

Presently Ranjoor Singh himself chose an advance guard of twenty men and put me in command of it.

"March eastward," he ordered me. "According to my map, you should find a road within a mile or two running about northeast and southwest; turn to the left along it. Halt if you see armed men, and send back word. Keep a lookout for food, for the men are starving, but loot nothing without my order! March!" said he.

"May I ask a question, sahib," said I, still lingering.

"Ask," said he.

"Would you truly have burned the German alive?" said I, and he laughed.

"That would have been a big fire," said he. "Do you think none would have come to investigate?"

"That is what I was thinking," said I.

"Do such thoughts burn your brain?" said he. "A threat to a bully—to a fool, folly—to a drunkard, drink—to each, his own! Be going now!"

So I saluted him and led away, wondering in my heart, the weather growing worse, if that were possible, but my spirits rising. I knew now that my back was toward Gallipoli, where the nearest British were, yet my heart felt bold with love for Ranjoor Singh and I did not doubt we would strike a good blow yet for our friends, although I had no least idea who Wassmuss was, nor whither we were marching. If I had known—eh, but listen, sahib—this is a tale of tales!

CHAPTER V

If a man stole my dinner, I might let him run; but if he stole my horse, he and I and death would play hide-and-seek!—RANJOOR SINGH.

That dawn, sahib, instead of lessening, the rainstorm grew into a deluge that saved us from being seen. As I led my twenty men forward I looked back a time or two, and once I could dimly see steamers and some smaller boats tossing on the sea. Then the fiercest gust of rain of all swept by like a curtain, and it was as if Europe had been shut off forever—so that I recalled Gooja Singh's saying on the transport in the Red Sea, about a curtain being drawn and our not returning that way. My twenty men marched numbly, some seeming half-asleep.

By and by, with heels sucking in the mud, we came to the road of which Ranjoor Singh had spoken and I turned along it. It had been worn into ruts and holes by heavy traffic and now the rain made matters worse, so we made slow progress. But before long I was able to make out dimly through the storm what looked like a railway station. There was a line of telegraph poles, and where it crossed our road there were buildings enough to have contained two regiments. I could see no sign of men, but in that light, with rain swirling hither and thither, it was difficult to judge. I halted, and sent a man back to warn Ranjoor Singh.

We blew on our fingers and stamped to keep life

in ourselves, until at the end of ten minutes he came striding out of the rain like a king on his way to be crowned. My twenty were already speechless with unhappiness and hunger, but he had instilled some of his own spirit into the rest of the regiment, for they marched with a swing in good order. He had Tugendheim close beside him and had inspired him, too. It may be the man was grinning in hope of our capture within an hour, and in that case he was doomed to disappointment. He was destined also to see the day when he should hope for our escape. But from subsequent acquaintance with him I think he was appreciating the risk we ran and Ranjoor Singh's great daring. I say this for Tugendheim, that he knew and respected resolution when he saw it.

When I had pointed out what I could see of the lay of the land, Ranjoor Singh left me in charge and marched away with Tugendheim and Tugendheim's four guards. I looked about for shelter, but there was none. We stood shivering, the rain making pools at our feet that spread and became one. So I made the men mark time and abused them roundly for being slack about it, they grumbling greatly because our prisoner was marched away to shelter, whereas we must stand without. I bullied them as much as I dared, and we stamped the road into a veritable quagmire, as builders tread mud for making sun-dried bricks, so that when three-quarters of an hour had passed and a man came running back with a message from Ranjoor Singh there was a little warmth in us. I did not need to use force to get the column started.

"Come!" said the trooper. "There is food, and shelter, and who knows what else!"

So we went best foot first along the road, feeling less than half as hungry and not weak at all, now that we knew food was almost within reach. Truly a man's desires are the vainest part of him. Less hungry we were at once, less weary, and vastly less afraid; yet, too much in a hurry to ask questions of the messenger!

Ranjoor Singh came out of a building to meet us, holding up his hand, so I made the men halt and began to look about. It was certainly a railway station, with a long platform, and part of the platform was covered by a roof. Parallel to that was a great shed with closed sides, and through its half-open door I could smell hay—a very good smell, sahib, warming to the heart. To our right, across what might be called a yard—thus—were many low sheds, and in one there were horses feeding; in others I could see Turkish soldiers sprawling on the straw, but they took no notice of us. Three of the low sheds were empty, and Ranjoor Singh pointed to them.

"Let all except twenty men," said he, "go and rest in those sheds. If any one asks questions, say only 'Allah!' So they will think you are Muhammadans. If that should not seem sufficient, say 'Wassmuss!' But unless questioned many times, say nothing! As you value your lives, say nothing more than those two words to any one at all! Rather be thought fools than be hanged before breakfast!"

So all but twenty of the men went and lay down on straw in the three empty sheds, and I took the twenty and followed him into the great shed with closed sides. Therein, besides many other things, we beheld great baskets filled with loaves of bread,—not very good bread, nor at all fresh, but staff of life itself to hungry men. He bade the men count out four loaves for each and every one of us, and then at last, he gave me a little information.

"The Germans in Stamboul," he said, "talked too loud of this place in my hearing." I stood gnawing a loaf already, and I urged him to take one, but he would eat nothing until all the men should have been fed. "They detrain Dervish troops at this point," said he, "and march them to the shore to be shipped to Gallipoli, because they riot and make trouble if kept in barracks in Skutari or Stamboul. This bread was intended for two train-loads of them."

"Then the Dervishes will riot after all!" said I, and he laughed—a thing he does seldom.

"The sooner the better!" said he. "A riot might cover up our tracks even better than this rain."

"Is there no officer in charge here?" I asked him.

"Aye, a Turkish officer," said he. "I heard the Germans complain about his inefficiency. A day or two later and we might have found a German in his place. He mistakes us for friends. What else could we be?" And he laughed again.

"But the telegraph wire?" said I.

"Is down," he said, "both between here and Skutari, and between here and Inismid. God sent this storm to favor us, and we will praise God by making use of it."

"Where is Tugendheim?" said I, but it was some

minutes before he answered me, for, since the loaves were counted he went to see them distributed, and I followed him.

"Tugendheim," he said at last, "has driven the Turkish officer to seek refuge in seclusion! I used the word 'Wassmuss,' and that had effect; but Tugendheim's insolence was our real passport. Nobody here doubts that we are in full favor at Stamboul. Wassmuss can keep for later on."

"Sahib," said I, seeing he was in good humor now, "tell me of this Wassmuss."

"All in good time!" he answered. And when he has decided it is not yet time to answer, it is wisest to be still. After fifteen or twenty minutes with the men, I followed him across the yard and entered the station waiting-room—a pretentious place, with fancy bronze handles on the doors and windows.

Lo, there sat Tugendheim, with his hands deep in his pockets and a great cigar between his teeth. His four guards stood with bayonets fixed, making believe to wait on him, but in truth watching him as caged wolves eye their dinner. Ranjoor Singh was behaving almost respectfully toward him, which filled me with disgust; but presently I saw and understood. There was a little window through which to sell tickets, and down in one corner of it the frosting had been rubbed from off the glass.

"There is an eye," said I in an undertone, "that I could send a bullet through without difficulty!" But Ranjoor Singh called me a person without judgment and turned his back.

"When do we start?" asked Tugendheim.

"When the men have finished eating," he answered, and at that I stared again, for I knew the men's mood and did not believe it possible to get them away without a long rest, nor even in that case without argument.

"What if they refuse?" said I, and Ranjoor Singh faced about to look at me.

"Do you refuse?" he asked. "Go and warn them to finish eating and be ready to march in twenty minutes!"

So I went, and delivered the message, and it was as I had expected, only worse.

"So those are his words? What are words!" said they. "Ask him whither he would lead us!" shouted Gooja Singh. He had been talking in whispers with a dozen men at the rear of the middle hut.

"If I take him such dogs' answers," said I, "he will dismiss me and there will be no more a go-between."

"Go, take him this message," shouted Gooja Singh. "But for his sinking of our ship we should now be among friends in Gallipoli! Could we not have seized another ship and plundered coal? Tell him, therefore, if he wishes to lead us he must use good judgment. Are we leaves blown hither and thither for his amusement? Nay! We belong to the British Army! Tell him we will march toward Gallipoli or nowhither! We will march until opposite Gallipoli, and search for some means of crossing."

"I will take that as Gooja Singh's message, then," said I.

"Nay, nay!" said he. "That is the regiment's

message!" And the dozen men with whom he had been whispering nodded acquiescence.

"Is Gooja Singh the regiment?" I asked.

"No," said he, "but I am *of* the regiment. I am not a man running back and forth, false to both sides!"

I was not taken by surprise. Something of that sort sooner or later I knew must come, but I would have preferred another time and place.

"Be thou go-between then, Gooja Singh!" said I. "I accepted only under strong persuasion. Gladly I relinquish! Go thou, and carry thy message to Ranjoor Singh!" And I sat down in the entrance of the middle hut, as if greatly relieved of heavy burdens. "I have finished!" I said. "I am not even havildar! I will request reduction to the ranks!"

For about a minute I sat while the men stared in astonishment. Then they began to rail at me, but I shook my head. They coaxed me, but I refused. Presently they begged me, but I took no notice.

"Let Gooja Singh be your messenger!" said I. And at that they turned on Gooja Singh, and some of them went and dragged him forward, he resisting with arms and feet. They set him down before me.

"Say the word," said they, "and he shall be beaten!"

So I got on my feet again and asked whether they were soldiers or monkey-folk, to fall thus suddenly on one of their number, and he a superior. I bade them loose Gooja Singh, and I laid my hand on his shoulder, helping him to his feet.

"Are we many men with many troubles, or one regiment?" said I.

At that most of them grew ashamed, and those who had assaulted Gooja Singh began to make excuses, but he went back to the rear to the men who had whispered with him. They drew away, and he sat in silence apart, I rejoicing secretly at his discomfiture but fearful nevertheless.

"Now!" said I. "Appoint another man to wait on Ranjoor Singh!"

But they cried out, "Nay! We will have none but you. You have done well—we trust you—we are content!"

I made much play of unwillingness, but allowed them to persuade me in the end, yielding a little at a time and gaining from them ever new protestations of their loyalty until at last I let them think they had convinced me.

"Nevertheless," said they, "tell Ranjoor Singh he must lead us toward Gallipoli!" They were firm on that point.

So I went back to the waiting-room and told Ranjoor Singh all that had happened, omitting nothing, and he stood breaking pieces from a loaf of bread, with his fingers, not burying his teeth into the loaf as most of us had done. He asked me the names of the men who had so spoken and I told him, he repeating them and considering each name for a moment or two.

"Have they finished eating?" he asked at last, and I told him they had as good as finished. So he ate his own bread faster.

"Come," he ordered presently, beckoning to Tugendheim and the four guards to follow.

It was raining as hard as ever as we crossed the station yard, and the men had excuse enough for disliking to turn out. Yet they scented development, I think, and none refused, although they fell in just not sullenly enough to call for reprimand. Ranjoor Singh drew the roll from his inner pocket and they all answered to their names. Then, without referring to the list again, he named those who I had told him used high words to me, beginning at Gooja Singh and omitting none.

"Fall out!" he ordered. And when they had obeyed, "Fall in again over there on the left!"

There were three-and-twenty of them, Gooja Singh included, and they glared at me. So did others, and I wondered grimly how many enemies I had made. But then Ranjoor Singh cleared his throat and we recognized again the old manner that had made a squadron love him to the death at home in India—the manner of a man with good legs under him and no fear in his heart. All but the three-and-twenty forgot forthwith my part in the matter.

"Am I to be herdsman, then?" said he, pitching his voice against wind and rain. "Are ye men—or animals? Hunted animals would have known enough to eat and hurry on. Hunted animals would be wise enough to run in the direction least expected. Hunted animals would take advantage of ill weather to put distance between them and their foe. Some of you, then, must be less than animals! Men I can lead. Animals I can drive. But what shall be done with such less-than-animals as can neither be led nor driven?"

Then he turned about half-left to face the three-and-twenty, and stood as it were waiting for their answer, with one hand holding the other wrist behind his back. And they stood shifting feet and looking back at him, extremely ill-at-ease.

"What is the specific charge against us?" asked Gooja Singh, for the men began to thrust him forward. But Ranjoor Singh let no man draw him from the main point to a lesser one.

"You have leave," said he, "to take one box of cartridges and go! Gallipoli lies that way!" And he pointed through the rain.

Then the two-and-twenty forgot me and began at once abusing Gooja Singh, he trying to refute them, and Ranjoor Singh watching them all with a feeling, I thought, of pity. Tugendheim, trying to make the ends of his mustaches stand upright in the rain, laughed as if he thought it a very great joke; but the rest of the men looked doubtful. I knew they were unwilling to turn their backs on any of our number, yet afraid to force an issue, for Ranjoor Singh had them in a quandary. I thought perhaps I might mediate.

"Sahib," said I.

"Silence!" he ordered. So I stepped back to my place, and a dozen men laughed at me, for which I vowed vengeance. Later when my wrath had cooled I knew the reprimand and laughter wiped out suspicion of me, and when my chance came to take vengeance on them I refrained, although careful to reassert my dignity.

After much argument, Gooja Singh turned his back at last on the two-and-twenty and saluted Ranjoor Singh with great abasement.

"Sahib," said he, "we have no wish to go one way and you another. We be of the regiment."

"Ye have set yourselves up to be dictators. Ye have used wild words. Ye have tried to seduce the rest. Ye have my leave to go!" said Ranjoor Singh.

"Nay!" said Gooja Singh. "We will not go! We follow the regiment!"

"Will ye follow like dogs that pick up offal, then?" he asked, and Gooja Singh said, "Nay! We be no dogs, but true men! We be faithful to the salt, sahib," said he. "We be sorry we offended. We be true men—true to the salt."

Now, that was the truth. Their fault had lain in not believing their officer at least as faithful as they and ten times wiser. Every man in the regiment knew it was truth, and for all that the rain poured down in torrents, obscuring vision, I could see that the general feeling was swinging all one way. If I had dared, I would have touched Ranjoor Singh's elbow, and have whispered to him. But I did not dare. Nor was there need. The instant he spoke again I knew he saw clearer than I.

"Ye speak of the salt," said he.

"Aye!" said Gooja Singh. "Aye, sahib! In the name of God be good to us! Whom else shall we follow?"

"Aye, sahib!" said the others. "Put us to the test!"

The lined-up regiment, that had been standing rigid, not at attention, but with muscles tense, now stood easier, and it might have been a sigh that passed among them.

"Then, until I release you for good behavior, you three-and-twenty shall be ammunition bearers," said Ranjoor Singh. "Give over your rifles for other men to carry. Each two men take a box of cartridges. Swiftly now!" said he.

So they gave up their rifles, which in itself was proof enough that they never intended harm, but were only misled by Gooja Singh and the foolishness of their own words. And they picked up the cartridge boxes, leaving Gooja Singh standing alone by the last one. He made a wry face. "Who shall carry this?" said he, and Ranjoor Singh laughed.

"My rank is havildar!" said Gooja Singh.

Ranjoor Singh laughed again. "I will hold court-martial and reduce you to the ranks whenever I see the need!" said he. "For the present, you shall teach a new kind of lesson to the men you have misled. They toil with ammunition boxes. You shall stride free!"

Gooja Singh had handed his rifle to me, and I passed it to a trooper. He stepped forward now to regain it with something of a smirk on his fat lips.

"Nay, nay!" said Ranjoor Singh, with another laugh. "No rifle, Gooja Singh! Be herdsman without honor! If one man is lost on the road you shall be sent back alone to look for him! Herd them, then; drive them, as you value peace!"

There being then one box to be provided for, he chose eight strong men to take turns with it, each two to carry for half an hour; and that these might know there was no disgrace attached to their task, they were placed in front, to march as if they were the band. Nor was Gooja Singh allowed to march last, as I expect he had hoped; he and his twenty-two were set in the midst, where they could eat shame, always under the eyes of half of us. Then Ranjoor Singh raised his voice again.

"To try to reach Gallipoli," he said, "would be as wise as to try to reach Berlin! Both shores are held by Turkish troops under German officers. We found the one spot where it was possible to slip through undetected. We must make the most of that. Moreover, if they refuse to believe we were drownd last night, they will look for us in the direction of Gallipoli, for all the German officers in Stamboul knew how your hearts burned to go thither. It was a joke among them! Let it be our business to turn the joke on them! There will be forced marches now—long hungry ones— Form fours!" he ordered. "By the right—Quick march!" And we wheeled away into the rain, he marching on the flank. I ran and overtook him.

"Take a horse, sahib!" I urged. "See them in that shed! Take one and ride, for it is more fitting!"

"Better plunder and burn!" said he. "If a man stole my dinner I might let him run; but if he stole my horse, he and I and death would play hide-and-seek! We need forgetfulness, not angry memories, behind us! Keep thou a good eye on Tugendheim!"

So I fell to the rear, where I could see all the men, Tugendheim included. In a very few minutes we had lost the station buildings in the rain behind us and then Ranjoor Singh began to lead in a wide semicircle, so that before long I judged we were marching about southeastward. At the end of an hour or so he changed direction to due east, and presently we saw another telegraph line. I overtook him again and suggested that we cut it.

"Nay!" said he. "If that line works and we are not believed drowned, too many telegrams will have been sent already! To cut it would give them our exact position! Otherwise—why make trouble and perhaps cause pursuit?"

So we marched under the telegraph wire and took a course about parallel to it. At noon it ceased raining and we rested, eating the bread, of which every man had brought away three loaves. After that, what with marching and the wind and sun our clothes began to dry and we became more cheerful—all, that is to say, except the ammunition bearers, who abused Gooja Singh with growing fervency. Yet he was compelled to drive them lest he himself be court martialed and reduced to the ranks.

Cheerfulness and selfishness are often one, sahib, for it was not what we could see that raised our spirits. We marched by village after village that had been combed by the foragers for Turkish armies, and saw only destitution to right and left, behind and before. The only animals we saw were dead ones except the dogs hunting for bones that might have marrow in them still.

We saw no men of military age. Only very old men were left, and but few of those; they and the women and children ran away at sight of us, except a very few who seemed careless from too much misery. One such man had a horse, covered from head to foot with sores, that he offered to sell to Ranjoor Singh.

I did not overhear what price he asked, but I heard the men scoffing at such avarice as would rob the vultures. He went away saying nothing, like a man in stupor, leaving the horse to die. Nay, sahib, he had not understood the words.

We slept that first night in a village whose one street was a quagmire and a cesspool. There was no difficulty in finding shelter because so many of the houses were deserted; but the few inhabitants of the other houses could not be persuaded to produce food. Ranjoor Singh took their money away from the four men whom I had overlooked when we all gave up our money on the steamer, and with that, and Tugendheim for extra argument, he went from house to house. Tugendheim used no tenderness, such being not his manner of approach, but nothing came of it. They may have had food hidden, but we ate stale bread and gave them some of it, although Ranjoor Singh forbade us when he saw what we were doing. He thought I had not been looking when he gave some of his own to a little one.

We were up and away at dawn, with all the dogs in Asia at our heels. They smelled our stale bread and yearned for it. It was more than an hour before the last one gave up hope and fell behind. They are hard times, sahib, when the street dogs are as hungry as those were.

Hunger! We met hunger day after day for eight days—hunger and nothing else, although it was good enough land—better than any I have seen in the Punjab. There was water everywhere. The air, too, was good to breathe, tempting us to fill our lungs and march like new men, yet causing appetite we could not assuage. We avoided towns, and all large villages, Ranjoor Singh consulting his map whenever we halted and marching by the little compass the Germans had given him. We should have seen sheep or goats or cattle had there been any; but there was none. Utterly not one! And we Sikhs are farmers, not easily deceived on such matters; we knew that to be grazing land we crossed. It was a land of fruit, too, in the proper season. There had been cattle by the thousand, but they were all gone—plundered by the Turks to feed their armies.

Ranjoor Singh did his best to make us husband our stale loaves, but we ate the last of them and became like famished wolves. Some of us grew footsore, for we had German boots, to which our feet were not yet thoroughly accustomed, but he gave us no more rest than he needed for his own refreshment—and that was wonderfully little. We had to nurse and bandage our feet as best we could, and march—march—march! He had a definite plan, for he led unhesitatingly, but he would not tell us the plan. He was stern when we begged for longer rests, merciless toward the ammunition bearers, silent at all times unless compelled to give orders or correct us. Most of the time he kept Tugendheim marching beside him, and Tugendheim, I think, began to regard him with quite peculiar respect; for he admired resolution.

Most of us felt that our last day of marching was upon us, for we were ready to drop when we skirted a village at about noon on the eighth day and saw in the distance a citadel perched on a rocky hill above the sky-line. We were on flat land, but there was a knoll near, and to that Ranjoor Singh led us, and there he let us lie. He, weary as we but better able to overcome, drew out his map and spread it, weighting the four corners with stones; and he studied it chin on hand for about five minutes, we watching him in silence.

"That," said he, standing at last and pointing toward the distant citadel, "is Angora. Yonder" (he made a sweeping motion) "runs the railway whose terminus is at Angora. There are many long roads hereabouts, so that the place has become a depot for food and stores that the Turks plunder and the Germans despatch over the railway to the coast. The railway has been taken over by the Germans."

"Are we to storm the town?" asked a trooper, and fifty men mocked him. But Ranjoor Singh looked down kindly at him and gave him a word of praise.

"No, my son," he said. "Yet if all had been stout enough to ask that, I would have dared attempt it. No, we are perhaps a little desperate, but not yet so desperate as that."

He began sweeping the horizon with his eyes, quartering the countryside mile by mile, overlooking nothing. I saw him watch the wheeling kites and look below them, and twice I saw him fix his gaze for minutes at a time on one place.

"We will eat to-night!" he said at last. "Sleep," he ordered. "Lie down and sleep until I summon you!" But he called me to his side and kept me wakeful for a while yet.

"Look yonder," said he, and when I had gazed for

about two minutes I was aware of a column of men and animals moving toward the city. A little enough column.

"How fast are they moving?" he asked me, and I gazed for several minutes, reaching no decision. I said they were too far away, and coming too much toward us for their speed to be accurately judged. Yet I thought they moved slowly.

Said he, "Do you see that hollow—one, two, three miles this side of them?" And I answered yes. "That is a bend of the river that flows by the city," said he. "There is water there, and fire-wood. They have come far and are heading toward it. They are too far spent to reach Angora before night. They will not try. That is where they will camp."

"Sahib," I said, considering his words as a cook tastes curry, "our men be overweary to have fight in them."

"Who spoke of fighting?" said he. So I went and lay down, and fell asleep wondering. When he came and roused me it was already growing late. By the time I had roused the men and they were all lined up we could no longer see Angora for the darkness; which worked both ways—those in Angora could not see us.

"If any catch sight of us," said Ranjoor Singh, speaking in a loud voice to us all, "let us hope they mistake us for friends. What Turk or German looks for an enemy hereabouts? The chances are all ours, but beware! Be silent as ye know how! Forward!"

It was a pitiable effort, for our bellies yearned and our feet were sore and stiff. We stumbled from weariness, and men fell and were helped up again. Gooja Singh and his ammunition bearers made more noise than a squadron of mounted cavalry, and the way proved twice as long as the most hopeless had expected. Yet we made the circuit unseen and, as far as we knew, unheard—certainly unchallenged. Doubtless, as Ranjoor Singh said afterward, the Turks were too overriden by Germans and the Germans too overconfident to suspect the presence of an enemy.

At any rate, although we made more noise than was expedient, we halted at last among low bushes and beheld nine or ten Turkish sentries posted along the rim of a rise, all unaware of us. Two were fast asleep. Some sat. The others drowsed, leaning on their rifles. Ranjoor Singh gave us whispered orders and we rushed them, only one catching sight of us in time to raise an alarm. He fired his rifle, but hit nobody, and in another second they were all surrounded and disarmed.

Then, down in the hollow we saw many little campfires, each one reflected in the water. Some Turks and about fifty men of another nation sat up and rubbed their eyes, and a Turkish captain—an upstanding flabby man, came out from the only tent to learn what the trouble might be. Ranjoor Singh strode down into the hollow and enlightened him, we standing around the rim of the rise with our bayonets fixed and rifles at the "ready." I did not hear what Ranjoor Singh said to the Turkish captain because he left me to prevent the men from stampeding toward the smell of food—no easy task.

After five minutes he shouted for Tugendheim,

and the German went down the slope visibly annoyed by the four guards who kept their bayonets within a yard of his back. It was a fortunate circumstance for us, not only then but very many times, that Tugendheim would have thought himself disgraced by appealing to a Turk. Seeing there was no German officer in the hollow, he adopted his arrogant manner, and the Turkish officer drew back from him like a man stung. After that the Turkish captain appeared to resign himself to impotence, for he ordered his men to pile arms and retired into his tent.

Then Ranjoor Singh came up the slope and picked the twenty men who seemed least ready to drop with weariness, of whom I regretted to be one. He set us on guard where the Turkish sentries had been, and the Turks were sent below, where presently they fell asleep among their brethren, as weary, no doubt, from plundering as we were from marching on empty bellies. None of them seemed annoyed to be disarmed. Strange people! Fierce, yet strangely tolerant!

Then all the rest of the men, havildars no whit behind the rest, swooped down on the camp-fires, and presently the smell of toasting corn began to rise, until my mouth watered and my belly yearned. Fifteen or twenty minutes later (it seemed like twenty hours, sahib!) hot corn was brought to us and we on guard began to be new men. Nevertheless, food made the guard more sleepy, and I was hard put to it walking from one to another keeping them awake.

All that night I knew nothing of what passed in the camp below, but I learned later on that Ranjoor Singh found among the Syrians whose business was to load and drive carts a man named Abraham. All in the camp who were not Turks were Syrians, and these Syrians had been dragged away from their homes scores of leagues away and made to labor without remuneration. This Abraham was a gifted man, who had been in America, and knew English, as well as several dialects of Kurdish, and Turkish and Arabic and German. He knew better German than English, and had frequently been made to act interpreter. Later, when we marched together, he and I became good friends, and he told me many things.

Well, sahib, after he had eaten a little corn, Ranjoor Singh questioned this man Abraham, and then went with him through the camp, examining the plunder the Turks had seen fit to requisition. It was plain that this particular Turkish officer was no paragon of all the virtues, and Ranjoor Singh finally entered his tent unannounced, taking Abraham with him. So it was that I learned the details later, for Abraham told me all I asked.

On a box beside the bed Ranjoor Singh found writing-paper, envelopes, and requisition forms not yet filled out, but already signed with a seal and a Turkish signature. There was a map, and a list of routes and villages. But best of all was a letter of instructions signed by a German officer. There were also other priceless things, of some of which I may chance to speak later.

I was told by Abraham that during the conversation following Ranjoor Singh's seizure of the papers the word Wassmuss was bandied back and forth a thousand times, the Turk growing rather more amenable each time the word was used. Finally the Turk resigned himself with a shrug of the shoulders, and was left in his tent with a guard of our men at each corner.

Then, for all that the night was black dark and there were very few lanterns, the camp began to be turned upside down, Ranjoor Singh ordering everything thrown aside that could not be immediately useful to us. There were forty carts, burdened to the breaking point, and twenty of them Ranjoor Singh abandoned as too heavy for our purpose. Most of the carts had been drawn by teams of six mules each, but ten of them had been drawn by horses, and besides the Turkish captain's horse there were four other spare ones. There were also about a hundred sheep and some goats.

Ranjoor Singh ordered all the corn repacked into fourteen of the carts, sheep and goats into four carts, and ammunition into the remaining two, leaving room in each cart for two men so that the guard who had stood awake all night might ride and sleep. That left him with sixty-four spare horses. Leaving the Turkish officer his own horse, but taking the saddle for himself, he gave Tugendheim one, me another, the third to Gooja Singh—he being next non-commissioned officer to me in order of seniority, and having had punishment enough—and the fourth horse, that was much the best one, he himself took. Then he chose sixty men to cease from being infantry and become a sort of cavalry again—cavalry without saddles as yet, or stirrups—cavalry with rifles—cavalry with aching feet—but cavalry none the less. He picked the sixty with great wisdom, choosing for the most part men who had given no trouble, but he included ten or twelve grumblers, although for a day or two I did not understand why. There was forethought in everything he did.

The sheep that could not be crowded into the carts he ordered butchered there and then, and the meat distributed among the men; and all the plunder that he decided not to take he ordered heaped in one place where it would not be visible unless deliberately looked for. The plundered money that he found in the Turk's tent he hid under the corn in the foremost cart, and we found it very useful later on. The few of our men who had not fallen asleep were for burning the piled-up plunder, but he threatened to shoot whoever dared set match to it.

"Shall we light a beacon to warn the countryside?" said he.

A little after midnight there began to be attempts by Turkish soldiers to break through and run for Angora. But I had kept my twenty guards awake with threats of being made to carry ammunition—even letting the butt of my rifle do work not set down in the regulations. So it came about that we captured every single fugitive. They were five all told, and I sent them, tied together, down to Ranjoor Singh. Thereupon he went to the Turk, and promised him personal violence if another of his men should attempt to break away. So the Turk gave orders that were obeyed.

Then, when all the plunder in the camp had been rearranged, and the mules and horses reapportioned, four hours yet before dawn, Ranjoor Singh took out his fountain-pen and executed the stroke of genius that made what followed possible. Without Abraham I do not know what he would have done. I can not imagine. Yet I feel sure he would have contrived something. He made use of Abraham as the best tool available, and that is no proof he could not have done as well by other means. I have learned this: that Ranjoor Singh, with that faith of his in God, can do anything. Anything. He is a true man, and God puts thoughts into his heart.

Among the Turk's documents were big sheets of paper for official correspondence, similar to that on which his orders were written. Ranjoor Singh ascertained from Abraham that he who had signed those orders was the German officer highest in command in all that region, who had left Angora a month previously to superintend the requisitioning.

So Ranjoor Singh sent for Tugendheim, whose writing would have the proper clerical appearance, and by a lantern in the tent dictated to him a letter in German to the effect that this Turkish officer, by name Nazim, with all his men and carts and animals, had been diverted to the aid of Wassmuss. The letter went on to say that on his way back to Angora this same high German officer would himself cover the territory thus left uncared for, so that nothing need be done about it in the meanwhile. (He wrote that to prevent investigation and perhaps pursuit by the men in Angora who waited Nazim and his plunder.)

At the foot of the letter Abraham cleverly copied the signature of the very high German officer, after making many experiments first on another sheet of paper.

Tugendheim of course protested vehemently that he would do no such thing, when ordered to write. But Ranjoor Singh ordered the barrel of a Turkish soldier's rifle thrust in the fire, and the German did not protest to the point of permitting his feet to be singed. He wrote a very careful letter, even suggesting better phraseology—his reason for that being that, since he was thus far committed, our total escape would be the best thing possible for him. The Germans, who are so fond of terrifying others, are merciless to their own who happen to be guilty of weak conduct, and to have said he was compelled to write that letter would have been no excuse if we were caught. Henceforward it was strictly to his interest to help us.

Finally, when the letter had been sealed in its envelope, there came the problem of addressing it, and the Turk seemed ignorant on that point, or else stupid. Perhaps he was wilfully ignorant, hoping that the peculiar form of the address might cause suspicion and investigation. But what with Tugendheim's familiarity with German military custom, and Ranjoor Singh's swift thought, an address was devised that served the purpose, judging by results.

Then came the problem of delivering the letter. To have sent one of the Turkish soldiers with it would have been the same thing as marching to Angora and surrendering; for of course the Turk would have told of what happened in the night, and where it happened, and all about it. To have sent one of the half-starved Syrians would probably have amounted to the same thing; for the sake of a belly-ful, or from fear of ill-treatment the wretched man would very likely tell too much. But Abraham was different. Abraham was an educated man, who well understood the value to us of silence, and who seemed to hate both Turks and Germans equally.

So Ranjoor Singh took Abraham aside and talked with him five minutes. And the end of that was that a Turkish soldier was compelled to strip himself and change clothes with Abraham, the Turk taking no pleasure at all in the exchange. Then Abraham was given a horse, and on the outside of the envelope in one corner was written in German, "Bearer should be supplied with saddle for his horse and sent back at once with acknowledgment of receipt of this."

There and then Ranjoor Singh gave Abraham the letter, shook hands with him, helped him on the horse, and sent him on his way—three hours before dawn. Then promptly he gave orders to all the other Syrians to strike camp and resume their regular occupation of driving mules.

The Turkish officer, although not deprived of his horse, was not permitted to ride until after daybreak, because of the difficulty otherwise of guarding him in the dark. The same with Tugendheim; although there was little reason for suspecting him of wanting to escape, with that letter fresh in his memory, he was nevertheless compelled to walk until daylight should make escape impossible.

The Turkish officer was made to march in front with his four-and-forty soldiers, who were given back their rifles but no bayonets or ammunition. Gooja Singh, whose two-and-twenty were ready by that time to pull his beard out hair by hair, was given fifty men who hated him less fiercely and set to march next behind the Turks. Then came the carts in single column, and after them Tugendheim and the remainder of our infantry. Behind the infantry rode the cavalry, and very last of all rode Ranjoor Singh, since that was for the present the post of chiefest danger.

As for me, I tumbled into a cart and fell asleep at once, scarcely hearing the order shouted to the Turk to go forward. The men who had been on guard with me all did the same, falling asleep like I almost before their bodies touched the corn.

When I awoke it was already midday. We had halted near some trees and food was being served out. I got under the cart to keep the sun off me, and lay there musing until a trooper had brought my meal. The meal was good, and my thoughts were good—excellent! For had we not been a little troop of lean ghosts, looking for graves to lie in? The talk along the way had been of who should bury us, or who should bury the last man, supposing we all died one by one! Had we not been famished until the very wind was a wall too heavy to prevail against? And were we not now what the drill-book calls a composite force, with full bellies, carts, horses and equipment? Who thought about graves any longer? I lay and laughed, sahib, until a trooper brought me dinner—laughed for contempt of the Germans we had left behind, and for the Turks whose plunder we had stolen,—laughed like a fool, like a man without brain or experience or judgment.

Not until I had eaten my fill did I bethink me of Ranjoor Singh. Then I rose lazily, and was astonished at the stiffness in my ankles. Nevertheless I contrived to stride with military manner, in order that any Turk or Syrian beholding me might know me for a man to be reckoned with, the added pain and effort being well worth while.

Nor did I have far to look for Ranjoor Singh. The instant I raised my eyes I saw him sitting on a great rock beneath the shadow of a tree, with his horse tied below him eating corn from a cloth spread on the ground. In order to reach him with least inconvenience, I made a circuit and approached from the rear, because in that direction the rock sloped away gradually and I was in no mood to climb, nor in condition to climb with dignity.

So it happened that I came on him unaware. Nevertheless, I was surprised that his ears should not detect my footfall. The horse, six feet below us, was aware of me first and snorted, yet Ranjoor Singh did not turn his head.

"Sahib!" said I; but he did not move.

"Sahib!" I said, going a step nearer and speaking louder. But he neither moved nor answered. Now I knew there was no laughing matter, and my hand trembled as I held it out to touch his shoulder. His arms were folded above his knees and his chin rested on them. I shook him slightly, and his chin fell down between his knees; but he did not answer. Now I knew beyond doubt he was not asleep, for however weary he would ever awake at a touch or the lightest whisper. I began to fear he was dead, and a feeling of sickness swept over me as that grim fear took hold.

"Sahib!" I said again, taking his shoulders with both hands. And he toppled over toward me, thus, like a dead man. Yet he breathed. I made certain he was breathing.

I shook him twice or thrice, with no result. Then I took him in my arms, thus, one arm under the knees and one under his armpits, and lifted him. He is a heavy man, all bone and sinew, and my stiff ankles caused me agony; but I contrived to lay him gently full length in the shadow of the tree-trunk, and then I covered him with his overcoat, to keep away flies. I had scarcely finished that when Gooja Singh came, and I cursed under my breath; but openly I appeared pleased to see him.

"It is well you came!" said I. "Thus I am saved the necessity of sending one to bring you. Our sahib is asleep," I said, "and has made over the command to me until he shall awake again."

"He sleeps very suddenly!" said Gooja Singh, and he stood eying me with suspicion.

"Well he may!" said I, thinking furiously—as a man in a burning house—yet outwardly all calm. "He has done all our thinking for us all these days; he has borne alone the burden of responsibility. He has enforced the discipline," said I with a deliberate stare that made Gooja Singh look sullen, "and God knows how necessary that has been! He has let no littlest detail of the march escape him. He has eaten no more than we; he has marched as far and as fast as we; he has slept less than any of us. And now," said I, "he is weary. He kept awake until I came, and fell asleep in my arms when he had given me his orders."

Gooja Singh looked as if he did not believe me. But my words had been but a mask behind which I was thinking. As I spoke I stepped sidewise, as if to prevent our voices from disturbing the sleeper, for it seemed wise to draw Gooja Singh to safer distance. Now I sat down at last on the summit of the rock exactly where Ranjoor Singh was sitting when I spied him first, hoping that perhaps in his place his thoughts would come to me. And whether the place had anything to do with it or not I do not know, but certainly wise thoughts did come. I reached a decision in that instant that was the saving of us, and for which Ranjoor Singh greatly commended me later on. Because of it, in the days to come, he placed greater confidence in my ability and faithfulness and judgment.

"What were his orders?" asked Gooja Singh. "Or were they secret orders known only to him and thee?"

"If you had not come," said I, "I would have sent for you to hear the orders. When he wakes," I added, "I shall tell him who obeyed the swiftest."

I was thinking still. Thinking furiously. I knew nothing at all yet about Abraham, and that was good, for otherwise I might have decided to wait there for him to overtake us.

"Have the men finished eating?" I asked, and he answered he was come because they had finished eating.

"Then the order is to proceed at once!" said I. "Send a cart here under the rock and eight good men, that we may lower our sahib into it. With the exception of that one cart let the column proceed in the same order as before, the Turk and his men leading."

"Leading whither?" asked Gooja Singh.

"Let us hope," said I, "to a place where orders are obeyed in military manner without question! Have you heard the order?" I asked, and I made as if to go and wake our officer.

Without another word Gooja Singh climbed down from the rock and went about shouting his commands as if he himself were their originator. Meanwhile I thought busily, with an eye for the wide horizon, wondering whether we were being pursued, or whether telegrams had not perhaps been sent to places far ahead, ordering Turkish regiments to form a cordon and cut us off. I wondered more than ever who Wassmuss might be, and whether Ranjoor Singh had had at any time the least idea of our eventual destination. I had no idea which direction to take. There was no track I could see, except that made by our own cart-wheels. On what did I base my decision, then? I will tell you, sahib.

I saw that not only Ranjoor Singh's horse, but all the cattle had been given liberal amounts of corn. It seemed to me that unless he intended to continue by forced marches Ranjoor Singh would have begun by economizing food. Moreover, I judged that if he had intended resting many hours in that spot he would have had me summoned and have gone to sleep himself. The very fact that he had let me sleep on seemed to me proof that he intended going forward. Doubtless, he would depend on me to stand guard during the night. So I reasoned it. And I also thought it probable he had told the Turk in which direction to lead, seeing that the Turk doubtless knew more of that countryside than any. Ahead of us was all Asia and behind us was the sea. Who was I that I should know the way? But by telling the Turk to lead on, I could impose on him responsibility for possible error, and myself gain more time to think. And for that decision, too, Ranjoor Singh saw fit to praise me later.

They brought the cart, and with the help of eight men, I laid Ranjoor Singh very comfortably on the corn, and covered him. Then I bade those eight be bodyguard, letting none approach too close on pain of violence, saying that Ranjoor Singh needed a long deep sleep to restore his energy. Also, I bade them keep that cart at the rear of the column, and I myself chose the rear place of all so as to keep control, prevent straggling, and watch against pursuit.

Pursued? Nay, sahib. Not at that time. Nevertheless, that thought of mine, to choose the last place, was the very gift of God. We had been traveling about three parts of an hour when I perceived a very long way off the head of a camel caravan advancing at swift pace toward us—or almost toward us. It seemed to me to be coming from Angora. And it so happened that at the moment when I saw it first the front half of our column had already dipped beyond a rise and was descending a rather gentle slope.

I hurried the tail of the column over the rise by

twisting it, as a man twists bullocks' tails. And then I bade the whole line halt and lie down, except those in charge of horses; them I ordered into the shelter of some trees, and the carts I hurried behind a low ridge—all except Ranjoor Singh's cart; that I ordered backed into a hollow near me. So we were invisible unless the camels should approach too close.

The Turks and Tugendheim I saw placed in the midst of all the other unmounted men, and ordered them guarded like felons; and I bade those in charge of mules and horses stand by, ready to muzzle their beasts with coats or what-not, to prevent neighing and braying. Then I returned to the top of the rise and lay down, praying to God, with a trooper beside me who might run and try to shake Ranjoor Singh back to life in case of direst need.

I lay and heard my heart beat like a drum against the ground, praying one moment, and with the next breath cursing some hoof-beat from behind me and the muffled reprimand that was certain to follow it. The men were as afraid as I, and the thing I feared most of all was panic. Yet what more could I do than I had done? I lay and watched the camels, and every step that brought them nearer felt like a link in a chain that bound us all.

One thing became perfectly evident before long. There were not more than two hundred camels, therefore in a fight we should be able to beat them off easily. But unless we could ambuscade them (and there was no time to prepare that now) it would be impossible to kill or capture them all. Some would get away and those would carry the alarm to the nearest military post. Then gone would be all hope for us of evading capture or destruction. But it was also obvious to me that no such caravan would come straight on toward us at such speed if it knew of our existence or our whereabouts. They expected us as little as we expected them.

So I lay still, trembling, wondering what Ranjoor Singh would say to me, supposing he did not die in the cart there—wondering what the matter might be with Ranjoor Singh—wondering what I should do supposing he did die and we escaped from this present predicament. I knew there was little hope of my maintaining discipline without Ranjoor Singh's aid. And I had not the least notion whither to lead, unless toward Russia.

Such thoughts made me physically sick, so that it was relief to turn away from them and watch the oncoming caravan, especially as I began to suspect it would not come within a mile of us. Presently I began to be certain that it would cross our track rather less than a mile away. I began to whisper to myself excitedly. Then at last "Yes!" said I, aloud.

"Yes!" said a voice beside me, and I nearly jumped out of my skin, "unless they suspect the track of our cart-wheels and follow it up, we are all right!"

I looked round into the eyes of Ranjoor Singh, and felt my whole skin creep like a snake's at sloughing time!

"Sahib!" said I.

"You have done well enough," said he, "except that if attacked you would have hard work to gather your forces and control them. But never mind, you did quite well enough for this first time!" said Ranjoor Singh.

"Sahib!" I said. "But I thought you were in a cart, dying!"

"In a cart, yes!" he said. "Dying, no—although that was no fault of somebody's!"

I begged him to explain, and while we watched the camels cross our track—(God knows, sahib, why they did not grow suspicious and follow along it)—he told me how he had sat on the great rock, not very sleepy, but thinking, chin on knee, when suddenly some man crawled up from behind and struck him a heavy blow.

"Feel my head," said he, and I felt under his turban. There was a bruise the size of my folded fist. I swore—as who would not? "Is it deep?" I said, still watching the camels, and before he answered me he sent the trooper to go and find his horse.

"Superficial," he said then. "By the favor of God but a water bruise. My head must have yielded beneath the blow."

"Who struck it?" said I, scarcely thinking what I said, for my mind was full of the camels, now flank toward us, that would have served our purpose like the gift of God could we only have contrived to capture them.

"How should I know?" he answered. "See—they pass within a half-mile of where I sat. Is not that the rock?" And I said yes.

"Had you lingered there," he said, "word about us would have gone back to Angora at top camel speed. What possessed you to come away?"

"God!" said I, and he nodded, so that I began to preen myself. He noticed my gathering self-esteem.

"Nevertheless," he said, aloud, but as if talking to himself, yet careful that I should hear, "had this not happened to me I should have seen those camels on the sky-line. Did you count the camels?"

"Two hundred and eight," said I.

"How many armed men with them?" he asked. "My eyes are yet dim from the blow."

"One hundred and four," said I, "and an officer or two."

He nodded. "The prisoners would have been a nuisance," he said, "yet we might have used them later. What with camels and what with horses—and there is a good spot for an ambuscade through which they must pass presently—I went and surveyed it while they cooked my dinner—never mind, never mind!" said he. "If you had made a mistake it would have been disastrous. Yet—two hundred and eight camels would have been an acquisition—a great acquisition!"

So my self-esteem departed—like water from a leaky goatskin, and I lay beside him watching the last dozen camels cross our trail, the nose of one tied to the tail of another, one man to every two. I lay conjecturing what might have been our fate had I had cunning enough to capture that whole caravan, and not another word was spoken between us until the last two camels disappeared beyond a ridge. Then:

"Was there any man close by, when you found me?" asked Ranjoor Singh.

"Nay, sahib," said I.

"Was there any man whose actions, or whose words, gave ground for suspicion?" he asked.

"Nay, sahib," I began; but I checked myself, and he noticed it.

"Except—?" said he.

"Except that when Gooja Singh came," I said, "he seemed unwilling to believe you were asleep."

"How long was it before Gooja Singh came?" he asked.

"He came almost before I had laid you under the tree and covered you," said I.

"And you told him I was asleep?" he said.

"Yes," said I; and at that he laughed silently, although I could tell well enough that his head ached, and merriment must have been a long way from him.

"Has Gooja Singh any very firm friend with us?" he asked, and I answered I did not know of one. "The ammunition bearers who were his friends now curse him to his face," I said.

"Then he would have to do his own dirty work?" said he.

"He has to clean his own rifle," I answered. And Ranjoor Singh nodded.

Then suddenly his meaning dawned on me. "You think it was Gooja Singh who struck the blow?" I asked. We were sitting up by that time. The camels were out of sight. He rose to his feet and beckoned for his horse before he answered.

"I wished to know who else might properly be suspected," he said, taking his horse's bridle. So I beckoned for my horse, and ordering the cart in which he had lain to be brought along after us, I rode at a walk beside him to where our infantry were left in hiding.

"Sahib," I said, "it is better after all to shoot this Gooja Singh. Shoot him on suspicion!" I urged. "He makes only trouble and ill-will. He puts false construction on every word you or I utter. He misleads the men. And now you suspect him of having tried to kill you! Bid me shoot him, sahib, and I obey!"

"Who says I suspect him?" he answered. "Nay, nay, nay! I will have no murder done—no drumhead tyranny, fathered by the lees of fear! Let Gooja Singh alone!"

"Does your head not ache?" I asked him.

"More than you guess!" said he. "But my heart does not ache. Two aches would be worse than one. Come silently!"

So I rode beside him silently, and making a circuit and signaling to the watchers not to betray our presence, we came on our hiding infantry unsuspected by them. We dismounted, and going close on foot were almost among them before they knew. Gooja Singh was on his feet in their midst, giving them information and advice.

"I tell you Ranjoor Singh is dead!" said he. "Hira Singh swears he is only asleep, but Hira Singh lies! Ranjoor Singh lies dead on top of the corn in the cart in yonder gully, and Hira Singh—"

I know not what more he would have said, but Ranjoor Singh stopped him. He stepped forward, smiling.

"Ranjoor Singh, as you see, is alive," he said, "and

if I am dead, then I must be the ghost of Ranjoor Singh come among you to enforce his orders! Rise!" he ordered. "Rise and fall in! Havildars, make all ready to resume the march!"

"Shoot him, sahib!" I urged, taking out my pistol, that had once been Tugendheim's. "Shoot him, or let me do it!"

"Nay, nay!" he said, laughing in my face, though not unkindly. "I am not afraid of him."

"But I, sahib," I said. "I fear him greatly!"

"Yet thou and I be two men, and I command," he answered gently. "Let Gooja Singh alone."

So I went and grew very busy ordering the column. In twenty minutes we were under way, with a screen of horsemen several hundred yards ahead and another little mounted rear-guard. But when the order had been given to resume the march and the carts were squeaking along in single file, I rode to his side again with a question. I had been thinking deeply, and it seemed to me I had the only answer to my thoughts.

"Tell me, sahib," I said, "our nearest friends must be the Russians. How many hundred miles is it to Russia?"

But he shook his head and laughed again. "Between us and Russia lies the strongest of all the Turkish armies," he said. "We could never get through."

"I am a true man!" I said. "Tell me the plan!" But he only nodded, and rode on.

"God loves all true men," said he.

CHAPTER VI

Where the weakest joint is, smite.—RANJOOR SINGH.

Well, sahib, Abraham caught up with us on the evening of the third day after leaving with that letter to the Germans in Angora, having ridden moderately to spare his horse. He said there were only two German officers there when he reached the place, and they seemed worried. They gave him the new saddle asked for, and a new horse under it; also a letter to carry back. Ranjoor Singh gave me the horse and saddle, letting Abraham take my sorry beast, that was beginning to recover somewhat under better treatment.

Ranjoor Singh smiled grimly as he read the letter. He translated parts of it to me—mainly complaints about lack of this and that and the other thing, and very grave complaints against the Turks, who, it seemed, would not cooperate. You would say that was good news to all of us, that should have inspired us with new spirit. But as I said in the beginning, sahib, there are reasons why the British must rule India yet a while. We Sikhs, who would rule it otherwise, are all divided.

We were seven non-commissioned officers. If we seven had stood united behind Ranjoor Singh there was nothing we could not have done, for the men would then have had no example of disunity. You may say that Ranjoor Singh was our rightful officer and we had only to obey him, but I tell you, sahib, obedience that is worth anything must come from the heart and understanding. Ranjoor Singh was as much dependent on good-will as if we had had the choosing of him. So he had to create it, and that which has once been lost, for whatever reason, is doubly and redoubly hard to make again. He did what he did in spite of us, although I tried to help.

Of us seven, first in seniority came I; and as I have tried already to make clear I was Ranjoor Singh's man (not that he believed it altogether yet). If he had ordered me to make black white, I would have perished in the effort to obey; but I had yet to prove that.

Next in order to me was Gooja Singh, and although I have spared the regiment's shame as much as possible, I doubt not that man's spirit has crept out here and there between my words—as a smell creeps from under coverings. He hated me, being jealous. He hated Ranjoor Singh, because of merited rebuke and punishment. He was all for himself, and if one said one thing, he must say another, lest the first man get too much credit. Furthermore, he was a *badmash,** born of a money-lender's niece to a man mean enough to marry such. Other true charges I could lay against him, but my tale is of Ranjoor Singh and why should I sully it with mean accounts; Gooja Singh must trespass in among it, but let that be all.

Third of us daffadars in order of seniority was

* Low ruffian.

Anim Singh, a big man, born in the village next my father's. He was a naik in the Tirah in '97 when he came to the rescue of an officer, splitting the skull of an Orakzai, wounding three others, and making prisoner a fourth who sought to interfere. Thus he won promotion, and he held it after somewhat the same manner. A blunt man. A fairly good man. A very good man with the saber. A gambler, it is true—but whose affair is that? A ready eye for rustling curtains and footholds near open windows, but that is his affair again—until the woman's husband intervenes. And they say he can look after himself in such cases. At least, he lives. Behold him, sahib. Aye, that is he yonder, swaggering as if India can scarcely hold him—that one with his arm in a sling. A Sikh, sahib, with a soldier's heart and ears too big for his head—excellent things on outpost, where the little noises often mean so much, but all too easy for Gooja Singh to whisper into.

Of the other four, the next was Ramnarain Singh, the shortest as to inches of us all, but perhaps the most active on his feet. A man with a great wealth of beard and too much dignity due to his father's *thalukdari*.* His father pockets the rent of three fat villages, so the son believes himself a wisehead. A great talker. Brave in battle, as one must be to be daffadar of Outram's Own, but too assertive of his own opinion. He and Gooja Singh were ever at outs, resentful of each other's claim to wisdom.

Next was Chatar Singh, like me, son and grandson

* Landed estate.

of a soldier of the raj—a bold man, something heavy on his horse, but able to sever a sheep in two with one blow of his saber—very well regarded by the troopers because of physical strength and willingness to overlook offenses. Chatar Singh's chief weakness was respect for cunning. Having only a great bull's heart in him and ability to go forward and endure, he regarded cunning as very admirable; and so Gooja Singh had one daffadar to work on from the outset (although I did what I could to make trouble between them).

The remaining two non-commissioned officers were naiks—corporals, as you would say—Surath Singh and Mirath Singh, both rather recently promoted from the ranks and therefore likely to see both sides to a question (whereas a naik should rightly see but one). Very early I had taken those two naiks in hand, showing them friendship, harping on the honor and pleasure of being daffadar and on the chance of quick promotion.

Given a British commanding officer—just one British officer—even a little young one—one would have been enough—it would have been hard to find better backing for him. Even Gooja Singh would scarcely have failed a British leader. But not only was the feeling still strong against Ranjoor Singh; there was another cloud in the sky. Did the sahib ever lay his hands on loot? No? Ah! Love of that runs in the blood, and crops out generation after generation!

Until the British came and overthrew our Sikh kingdom—and that was not long ago—loot was the staff of life of all Sikh armies. In those days when an army needed pay there was a war. Now, except for one month's pay that, as I have told, the Germans had given us, we had seen no money since the day when we surrendered in that Flanders trench; and what the Germans gave us Ranjoor Singh took away, in order to bribe the captain of a Turkish ship. And Gooja Singh swore morning, noon and night that as prisoners of war we should not be entitled to pay from the British in any event, even supposing we could ever contrive to find the British and rejoin them.

"Let us loot, then, and pay ourselves!" was the unanimous verdict, I being about the only one who did not voice it. I claim no credit. I saw no loot, so what was the use of talking? We were crossing a desert where a crow could have found small plunder. But being by common consent official go-between I rode to Ranjoor Singh's side and told him what the men were saying.

"Aye," he nodded, not so much as looking sidewise, "any one would know they are saying that. What say the Turk and Tugendheim?"

"Loot, too!" said I, and he grunted.

It was this way, sahib. Our Turkish officer prisoner was always put with his forty men to march in front—behind our advance guard but in front of the carts and infantry. Thus there was no risk of his escaping, because for one thing he had no saddle and rode with much discomfort and so unsafely that he preferred to march on foot more often than not; and for another, that arrangement left him never out of sight of nearly all of us. One of us daffadars would generally march beside him, and some of the Syrian muleteers had learned English either in Egypt or the Levant ports, so that there was no lack of interpreters. I myself have marched beside the Turk for miles and miles on end, with Abraham translating for us.

"Why not loot? Who can prevent you? Who shall call you to account?" was the burden of the Turk's song.

And Tugendheim, who spoke our tongue fluently, marched as a rule among the men, or rode with the mounted men, watched day and night by the four troopers who had charge of him—better mounted than he, and very mindful of their honor in the matter. He made himself as agreeable as he could, telling tales about his life in India—not proper tales to tell to a sahib, but such as to make the troopers laugh; so that finally the things he said began to carry the weight that goes with friendliness. He soon discovered what the feeling was toward Ranjoor Singh, and somehow or other he found out what the Turk was talking about. After that he took the Turk's cue (although he sincerely despised Turks) and began with hint and jest to propagate lust for loot in the men's minds. Partly, I think, he planned to enrich himself and buy his way to safety—(although God knows in which direction he thought safety lay!). Partly, I think, he hoped to bring us to destruction, and so perhaps offset his offense of having yielded to our threats, hoping in that way to rehabilitate himself. So goes a lawyer to court, sure of a fee if his client wins, yet sure, too, of a fee if his client loses, enjoying profit and entertainment in any event. Yet who shall blame Tugendheim? Unlike a lawyer, he stood to take the consequences if both forks of the stick should fail. I told Ranjoor Singh all that Tugendheim and the Turk were saying to the men, and his brow darkened, although he made no comment. He did not trust me yet any more than he felt compelled to.

"Send Abraham to me," he said at last. So I went and sent Abraham, feeling jealous that the Syrian should hear what I might not.

Ranjoor Singh had been forcing the pace, and by the time I speak of now we had nearly crossed that desert, for a rim of hills was in front of us and all about. It was not true desert, such as we have in our Punjab, but a great plain already showing promise of the spring, with the buds of countless flowers getting ready to burst open; when we lay at rest it amused us to pluck them and try to determine what they would look like when their time should come. And besides flowers there were roots, remarkably good to eat, that the Syrians called "daughters of thunder," saying that was the local name. Tugendheim called them truffles. A little water and that desert would be fertile farm-land, or I never saw corn grow!

Ranjoor Singh conversed with Abraham until we entered a defile between the hills; and that night we camped in a little valley with our outposts in a ring around us, Ranjoor Singh sitting by a bright fire halfway up the side of a slope where he could overlook us all and be alone. We had seen mounted men two or three times that day, they mistaking us perhaps for Turkish troops, for they vanished after the first glimpse. Nevertheless, we tethered our horses close in the valley bottom, and lay around them, ready for all contingencies.

I remember that night well, for it was the first since we started eastward in the least to resemble our Indian nights. It made us feel homesick, and some of the men were crooning love-songs. The stars swung low, looking as if a man could almost reach them, and the smoke of our fires hung sweet on the night air. I was listening to Abraham's tales about Turks—tales to make a man bite his beard—when Ranjoor Singh called me in a voice that carried far without making much noise. (I have never known him to raise his voice so high or loud that it lost dignity.) "Hira Singh!" he called, and I answered "Ha, sahib!" and went clambering up the hill.

He let me stand three minutes, reading my eyes through the darkness, before he motioned me to sit. So then we sat facing, I on one side of the fire and he the other.

"I have watched you, Hira Singh," he said at last. "Now and again I have seemed to see a proper spirit in you. Nay, words are but fragments of the wind!" said he. (I had begun to make him protestations.) "There are words tossing back and forth below," he said, looking past me down into the hollow, where shadows of men were, and now and then the eye of a horse would glint in firelight. Then he said quietly, "The spirit of a Sikh requires deeds of us."

"Deeds in the dark?" said I, for I hoped to learn more of what was in his mind.

"Should a Sikh's heart fail him in the dark?" he asked.

"Have I failed you," said I, "since you came to us in the prison camp?"

"Who am I?" said he, and I did not answer, for I wondered what he meant. He said no more for a minute or two, but listened to our pickets calling their numbers one to another in the dark above us.

"If you serve me," he said at last, "how are you better than the stable-helper in cantonments who groomed my horse well for his own belly's sake? I can give you a full belly, but your honor is your own. How shall I know your heart?"

I thought for a long while, looking up at the stars. He was not impatient, so I took time and considered well, understanding him now, but pained that he should care nothing for my admiration.

"Sahib," I said finally, "by this oath you shall know my heart. Should I ever doubt you, I will tear out your heart and lay it on a dung-hill."

"Good!" said he. But I remember he made me no threat in return, so that even to this day I wonder how my words sounded in his ears. I am left wondering whether I was man enough to dare swear such an oath. If he had sworn me a threat in return I should have felt more at ease—more like his equal. But who would have gained by that? My heart and my belly are not one. Self-satisfaction would not have helped.

"Soon," he said, looking into my eyes beside the

fire, "we shall meet opportunities for looting. Yet we have food enough for men and mules and horses for many a day to come; and as the corn grows less more men can ride in the carts, so that we shall move the swifter. But now this map of mine grows vague and our road leads more and more into the unknown. We need eyes ahead of us. I can control the men if I stay with them, but in that case who shall ride on and procure intelligence?"

In a flash I saw his meaning. There was none but he wise enough to ride ahead. But who else could control the men—men who believed they had sloughed the regiment's honor in a Flanders trench and a German prison camp? They were sloughing their personal honor that minute, fraternizing with Turkish prisoners. With their sense of honor gone, could even Ranjoor Singh control them? Perhaps! But if Ranjoor Singh rode forward, who should stay behind and stand in his shoes?

I looked at the stars, that had the color of jewels in them. I listened to the night birds. I heard the wind soughing—the mules and horses stamping—the murmur of men's voices. My tongue itched to say some foolish word, that would have proved me unfit to be trusted out of sight. But the thought came to me to be still and listen. And still I remained until he began again.

"If I told the men what the true position is they would grow desperate," he said. "They would believe the case hopeless."

"They almost believe that now!" said I.

"Have the Turk and Tugendheim been kept apart?" said he.

"Aye," I answered. "They have not had ten words together."

"Good," said he. "Neither Turk nor Tugendheim knows the whole truth, but if they get together they might concoct a very plausible, misleading tale."

"They would better have been bound and gagged," said I.

"No," he answered. "If I had bound and gagged them it would have established sympathy between them, and they would have found some way of talking nevertheless. Kept apart and let talk, the Turk will say one thing, Tugendheim another."

"True," said I. "For now the Turk advises plunder to right and left, and settlement afterward among Armenian villages. He says there are women to be had for the taking. 'Be a new nation!' says he."

"And what says Tugendheim?" asked Ranjoor Singh.

" 'Plunder!' " said I. " 'Plunder and push northward into Russia! The Russians will welcome you,' says he, 'and perhaps accept me into their secret service!—Plunder the Turks!' says Tugendheim. 'Plunder the Armenians!' says the Turk."

"I, too, would be all for Russia," he answered, "but it isn't possible. The coast of the Black Sea, and from the Black Sea down to the Persian frontier, is held by a very great Turkish army. The main caravan routes lie to the north of us, and every inch of them is watched."

"I am glad then that it must be Egypt," said I. "A long march, but friends at the other end. Who but doubts Russians?"

He shook his head. "Syria and Palestine," he said, "are full of an army gathering to invade Egypt. It eats up the land like locusts. An elephant could march easier unseen into a house than we into Syria!"

"So we must double back?" said I. "Good! By now they must have ceased looking for us, supposing they ever thought us anything but drowned. Somewhere we can surely find a ship in which to cross to Gallipoli!"

He laughed and shook his head again. "We slipped through the one unguarded place," he said. "If we had come one day later that place, too, would have been held by some watchful one, instead of by the fool we found in charge."

Then at last I thought surely I knew what his objective *must* me. It had been common talk in Flanders how an expedition marched from Basra up the Tigris.

"Bagdad!" I said. "We march to Bagdad to join the British there! Bagdad is good!"

But he answered, "Bagdad is not yet taken—not yet nearly taken. Between us and Bagdad lies a Turkish army of fifty or sixty thousand men at least."

I sat silent. I can draw a map of the world and set the rivers and cities and boundaries down; so I knew that if we could go neither north- nor south- nor westward, there remained only eastward, straightforward into Persia. He read my thoughts, and nodded.

"Persia is neutral," he said, with a wave of his hand that might mean anything. "The Turks have spared no army for one section of the Persian frontier, choosing to depend on savage tribes. And the Germans have given them Wassmuss to help out."

"Ah!" said I, making ready to learn at last who Wassmuss might be. "When we have found this Wassmuss, are we to make him march with us like Tugendheim?"

"If what the Germans in Stamboul said of him is only half-true," he answered, "we shall find him hard to catch. Wassmuss is a remarkable man. Before the war he was consul in Bagdad or somewhere, and he must have improved his time, for he knows enough now to keep all the tribes stirred up against Russians and British. The Germans send him money, and he scatters it like corn among the hens; but the money would be little use without brains. The Germans admire him greatly, and he certainly seems a man to be wondered at. But he is the one weak point, nevertheless—the only key that can open a door for us."

"But if he is too wary to be caught?" said I.

"Who knows?" he answered with another of those short gruff laughs. "But I know this," said he, "that from afar hills look like a blank wall, yet come closer and the ends of valleys open. Moreover, where the weakest joint is, smite! So I shall ride ahead and hunt for that weakest joint, and you shall shepherd the men along behind me. Go and bring Abraham and the Turk!"

I went and found them. Abraham was already asleep, no longer wearing the Turkish private soldier's uniform but his own old clothes again (because, the Turkish soldier having done nothing meriting punishment, Ranjoor Singh had ordered him his uniform returned). I awoke him and together we went and found the Turk sitting between a Syrian and Gooja Singh; and although I did not overhear one word of what they were saying, I saw that Gooja Singh believed I had been listening. It seemed good to me to let him deceive himself, so I smiled as I touched the Turk's shoulder.

"Lo! Here is our second-in-command!" sneered Gooja Singh, but I affected not to notice.

"Come!" said I, showing the Turk slight courtesy, and, getting up clumsily like a buffalo out of the mud, he followed Abraham and me. Some of the men made as if to come, too, out of curiosity, but Gooja Singh recalled them and they clustered round him.

When I had brought the Turk uphill to the fireside, Ranjoor Singh had only one word to say to him.

"Strip!" he ordered.

Aye, sahib! There and then, without excuse or explanation, he made the Turkish officer remove his clothes and change with Abraham; and I never saw a man more unwilling or resentful! Abraham had told me all about Turkish treatment of Syrians, and it is the way of the world that men most despise those whom they most ill-treat. So that although Turks have no caste distinctions that I know of, that one felt like a high-caste Brahman ordered to change garments with a sweeper. He looked as if he would infinitely rather die.

"Hurry!" Ranjoor Singh ordered him in English.

"*Hurriet?*" said the Turk. *Hurriet* is their Turkish for *liberty*. All the troops in Stamboul used it constantly, and Ranjoor Singh told me it means much the same as the French cry of "Liberty, Equality, Fraternity!" The Turk seemed bewildered, and opened his eyes wider than ever; but whatever his thoughts were about "*hurriet,*" he rightly interpreted the look in Ranjoor Singh's eye and obeyed, grimacing like a monkey as he drew on Abraham's dirty garments.

"You shall wear the rags of a driver of mules if you talk any more about loot to your men or mine!" said Ranjoor Singh. "If I proposed to loot, I would bury you for a beginning, lest there be nothing for the rest of us!"

He made Abraham translate that into Turkish, lest the full gist of it be lost, and I sat comparing the two men. It was strange to see what a change the uniform made in Abraham's appearance—what a change, too, came over the Turk. Had I not known, I could never have guessed the positions had once been reversed. Abraham looked like an officer. The Turk looked like a peasant. He was a big up-standing man, although with pouches under his eyes that gave the lie to his look of strength. Now for the first time Ranjoor Singh set a picked guard over him, calling out the names of four troopers who came hurrying uphill through the dark.

"Let your honor and this man's ward be one!" said he, and they answered "Our honor be it!"

He could not have chosen better if he had lined up the regiment and taken half a day. Those four were troopers whom I myself had singled out as men to be depended on when a pinch should come, and I wondered that Ranjoor Singh should so surely know them, too.

"Take him and keep him!" he ordered, and they went off, not at all sorry to be excused from other duties, as now of course they must be. Counting the four who guarded Tugendheim, that made a total of eight troopers probably incorruptible, for there is nothing, sahib, that can compare with imposing a trust when it comes to making sure of men's good faith. Hedge them about with precautions and they will revolt or be half-hearted; impose open trust in them, and if they be well-chosen they will die true.

"Now," said he to me when they were out of hearing, "I shall take with me one daffadar, one naik, and forty mounted men. Sometimes I shall take Abraham, sometimes Tugendheim, sometimes the Turk. This time I shall take the Turk, and before dawn I shall be gone. Let it be known that the best behaved of those I leave with you shall be promoted to ride with me—just as my unworthy ones shall be degraded to march on foot with you. That will help a little."

"Aye," said I, "a little. Which daffadar will you take? That will help more!" said I.

"Gooja Singh," he answered, and I marveled.

"Sahib," I said, "take him out of sight and bury his body! Make an end!" I urged. "In Flanders they shot men against a wall for far less than he has talked about!"

"Flanders is one place and this another," he answered. "Should I make those good men more distrustful than they are? Should I shoot Gooja Singh unless I am afraid of him?"

I said no more because I knew he was right. If he should shoot Gooja Singh the troopers would ascribe it to nothing else than fear. A British officer might do it and they would say, "Behold how he scorns to shirk responsibility!" Yet of Ranjoor Singh they would have said, "He fears us, and behold the butchery begins! Who shall be next?" Nevertheless, had I stood in his shoes, I would have shot and buried Gooja Singh to forestall trouble. I would have shot Gooja Singh and the Turk and Tugendheim all three with one volley. And the Turk's forty men would have met a like fate at the first excuse. But that is because I was afraid, whereas Ranjoor Singh was not. I greatly feared being left behind to bring the men along, and the more I thought of it, the worse the prospect seemed; so I began to tell of things I had heard Gooja Singh say against him, and which of the men I had heard and seen to agree, for there is no good sense in a man who is afraid.

"Is it my affair to take vengeance on them, or to lead them into safety?" he asked. And what could I answer?

After some silence he spread out his map where firelight shone on it and showed Abraham and me where the Tigris River runs by Diarbekr. "Thus," he said, "we must go," pointing with his finger, "and thus—and thus—by Diarbekr, down by the Tigris, by Mosul, into Kurdistan, to Sulimanieh, and thence into Persia—a very long march through very wild country. Outside the cities I am told no Turk dare show himself with less than four hundred men at his back, so we will keep to the open. If the Turks mistake us for Turks, the better for us. If the tribes mistake us for Turks, the worse for us; for they say the tribes hate Turks worse than smallpox. If they think we are Turks they will attack us. We need ride warily."

"It would take more Turks than there are," I said, "to keep our ruffians from trying to plunder the first city they see! And as for tribes—they are in a mood to join with any one who will help make trouble!"

"Then it may be," he answered quietly, "that they will not lack exercise! Follow me and lend a hand!" And he led down toward the camp-fires, where very few men slept and voices rose upward like the noise of a quarrelsome waterfall.

Just as on that night when we captured the carts and Turks and Syrians, he now used the cover of darkness to reorganize; and the very first thing he did was to make the forty Turkish prisoners change clothes with Syrians—the Turks objecting with much bad language and the Syrians not seeming to relish it much, for fear, I suppose, of reprisals. But he made the Turks hand over their rifles, as well, to the Syrians; and then, of all unlikely people he chose Tugendheim to command the Syrians and to drill them and teach them discipline! He set him to drilling them there and then, with a row of fires to see by.

In the flash of an eye, as you might say, we had thus fifty extra infantry, ten of them neither uniformed nor armed as yet, but all of them at least afraid to run away. Tugendheim looked doubtful for a minute, but he was given his choice of that, or death, or of wearing a Syrian's cast-off clothes and driving mules. He well understood (for I could tell by his manner of consenting) that Ranjoor Singh would send him into action against the first Turks we could find, thus committing him to further treason against the Central Powers; but he had gone too far already to turn back.

And as for the Syrians—they had had a lifetime's experience of Turkish treatment, and had recently been taught to associate Germans with Turks; so if Tugendheim should meditate treachery it was unlikely his Syrians would join him in it. It was promotion to a new life for them—occupation for Tugendheim, who had been growing bored and perhaps dangerous on that account—and not so dreadfully distressing to the Turkish soldiers, who could now ride on the carts instead of marching on weary feet. They had utterly no ambition, those Turkish soldiers; they cared neither for their officer (which was small wonder) nor for the rifles that we took away, which surprised us greatly (for in the absence of lance or saber, we regarded our rifles as evidence of manhood). They objected to the dirty garments they received in exchange for the uniforms, and they despised us Sikhs for men without religion (so they said!); but it did not seem to trouble them whether they fought on one side or the other, or whether they fought at all, so long as they had cigarettes and food. Yet I did not receive the impression they were cowards—brutes, perhaps, but not cowards. When they came under fire later on they made no effort to desert with the carts to their own side; and when we asked them why, they said because we fed them! They added they had not been paid for more than eighteen months.

Why did not Ranjoor Singh make this arrangement sooner, you ask. Why did he wait so long, and then choose the night of all times? Not all thoughts are instantaneous, sahib; some seem to develop out of patience and silence and attention. Moreover, it takes time for captured men to readjust their attitude—as the Germans, for instance, well knew when they gave us time for thought in the prison camp at Oescherleben. When we first took the Syrians prisoner they were so tired and timid as to be worthless for anything but driving carts, whereas now we had fed them and befriended them. On the other hand, in the beginning, the Turks, if given a chance, would have stampeded with the carts toward Angora.

Now that both Turks and Syrians had grown used to being prisoners and to obeying us, they were less likely to think independently—in the same way that a new-caught elephant in the keddah is frenzied and dangerous, but after a week or two is learning tricks.

And as for choosing the night-time for the change, every soldier knows that the darkness is on the side of him whose plans are laid. He who is taken unawares must then contend with both ignorance and darkness. Thieves prefer the dark. Wolves hunt in the dark. Fishermen fish in the dark. And the wise commander who would change his dispositions makes use of darkness, too. Men who might disobey by daylight are like lambs when they can not see beyond the light a camp-fire throws.

But such things are mental, sahib, and not to be explained like the fire of heavy guns or the shock tactics of cavalry—although not one atom less effective. If Ranjoor Singh had lined up the men and argued with them, there might have been mutiny. Instead, when he judged the second ripe, he made sudden new dispositions in the night and gave them something else to think about without suggesting to their minds that he might be worried about them or suspicious of them. On the contrary, he took opportunity to praise some individuals and distribute merited rewards.

For instance, he promoted the two naiks, Surath Singh and Mirath Singh, to be daffadars on probation, to their very great surprise and absolute contentment. The four who guarded Tugendheim he raised to the rank of naik, bidding them help Tugendheim drill the Syrians without relaxing vigilance over him. Then he chose six more troopers to be naiks. And of the eighty mounted men he degraded eighteen to march on foot again, replacing them with more obedient ones. Then at last I understood why he had chosen some grumblers to ride in the first instance—simply in order that he might make room for promotion of others at the proper time, offsetting discontent with emulation.

Then of the eighty mounted men he picked the forty best. He gave Abraham's saddle to Gooja Singh, set one of the new naiks over the left wing, and Gooja Singh over the right wing of the forty, under himself, and ordered rations for three days to be cooked and served out to the forty, including corn for their horses. They had to carry it all in the knapsacks on their own backs, since no one of them yet had saddles.

Gooja Singh eyed me by firelight while this was going on, with his tongue in his cheek, as much as to say I had been superseded and would know it soon. When I affected not to notice he said aloud in my hearing that men who sat on both sides of a fence were never on the right side when the doings happen. And when I took no notice of that he asked me in a very loud voice whether my heart quailed at the prospect of being left a mile or two behind. But I let him have his say. Neither he, nor any of the men, had the slightest idea yet of Ranjoor Singh's real plan.

After another talk with me Ranjoor Singh was to horse and away with his forty an hour before daybreak, the Turkish officer riding bareback in Syrian clothes between the four who had been set to guard him. And the sound of the departing hooves had scarcely ceased drumming down the valley when the men left behind with me began to put me to a test. Abraham was near me, and I saw him tremble and change color. Sikh troopers are not little baa-lambs, sahib, to be driven this and that way with a twig! Tugendheim, too, ready to preach mutiny and plunder, was afraid to begin lest they turn and tear him first. He listened with both ears, and watched with both eyes, but kept among his Syrians.

"Whither has he gone?" the men demanded, gathering round me where I stooped to feel my horse's forelegs. And I satisfied myself the puffiness was due to neither splint nor ring-bone before I answered. There was just a little glimmer of the false dawn, and what with that and the dying fires we could all see well enough. I could see trouble—out of both eyes.

"Whither rides Ranjoor Singh?" they demanded.

"Whither we follow!" said I, binding a strip from a Syrian's loin-cloth round the horse's leg. (What use had the Syrian for it now that he wore uniform? And it served the horse well.)

A trooper took me by the shoulder and drew me upright. At another time he should have been shot for impudence, but I had learned a lesson from Ranjoor Singh too recently to let temper get the better of me.

"Thou art afraid!" said I. "Thy hand on my shoulder trembles!"

The man let his hand fall and laughed to show himself unafraid. Before he could think of an answer, twenty others had thrust him aside and confronted me.

"Whither rides Ranjoor Singh? Whither does he ride?" they asked. "Make haste and tell us!"

"Would ye bring him back?" said I, wondering what to say. Ranjoor Singh had told me little more than that we were drawing near the neighborhood of danger, and that I was to follow warily along his track. "God will put true thoughts in your heart," he told me, "if you are a true man, and are silent, and listen." His words were true. I did not speak until I was compelled. Consider the sequel, sahib.

"Ye have talked these days past," said I, "of nothing but loot—loot—loot! Ye have lusted like wolves for lowing cattle! Yet now ye ask me whither rides Ranjoor Singh! Whither *should* he ride? He rides to find bees for you whose stings have all been drawn, that ye may suck honey without harm! He rides to find you victims that can not strike back! Sergeant Tugendheim," said I, "see that your Syrians do not fall over one another's rifles! March in front with them," I ordered, "that we may all see how well you drill them! Fall in, all!" said I, "and he who wishes to be camp guard when the looting begins, let him be slow about obeying!"

Well, sahib, some laughed and some did not. The most dangerous said nothing. But they all obeyed, and that was the main thing. Not more than an hour and a half after Ranjoor Singh had ridden off our carts were squeaking and bumping along behind us. And within an hour after that we were in action! Aye, sahib, I should say it was less than an hour after the start when I halted to serve out ten cartridges apiece to the Syrians, that Tugendheim might blood them and get himself into deeper water at the same time. He was angry that I would not give him more cartridges, but I told him his men would waste those few, so why should I not be frugal? When the time came I don't think the Syrians hit anything, but they filled a gap and served a double purpose; for after Tugendheim had let them blaze away those ten rounds a piece there was less fear than ever of his daring to attempt escape. Thenceforward his prospects and colours were one. But my tale goes faster than the column did, that could travel no faster than the slowest man and the weakest mule.

We were far in among the hills now—little low hills with broad open spaces between, in which thousands of cattle could have grazed. Only there were no cattle. I rode, as Ranjoor Singh usually did, twenty or thirty horses' length away on the right flank, well forward, where I could see the whole column with one quick turn of the head. I had ten troopers riding a quarter of a mile in front, and a rear-guard of ten more, but none riding on the flanks because to our left the hills were steep and impracticable and to our right I could generally see for miles, although not always.

We dipped into a hollow, and I thought I heard rifle shots. I urged my horse uphill, and sent him up a steep place from the top of which I had a fine view. Then I heard many shots, and looked, and lo a battle was before my eyes. Not a great battle—really only a skirmish, although to my excited mind it seemed much more at first. And the first one I recognized taking his part in it was Ranjoor Singh.

I could see no infantry at all. About a hundred Turkish cavalry were being furiously attacked by sixty or seventy mounted men who looked like Kurds, and who turned out later really to be Kurds. The Kurds were well mounted, riding recklessly, firing from horseback at full gallop and wasting great quantities of ammunition.

The shooting must have been extremely bad, for I could see neither dead bodies nor empty saddles, but nevertheless the Turks appeared anxious to escape—the more so because Ranjoor Singh with his forty men was heading them off. As I watched, one of them blew a trumpet and they all retreated helter-skelter toward us—straight toward us. There was nothing else they could do, now that they had given way. It was like the letter Y—thus, sahib,—see, I draw in the dust—the Kurds coming this way at an angle—Ranjoor Singh and his forty coming this way—and we advancing toward them all along the bottom stroke of the Y, with hills around forming an arena. The best the Turks could do would have been to take the higher ground where we were and there reform, except for the fact that we had come on the scene unknown to them. Now that we had arrived, they were caught in a trap.

There was plenty of time, especially as we were hidden from view, but I worked swiftly, the men obeying readily enough now that a fight seemed certain. I posted Tugendheim with his Syrians in the center, with the rest of us in equal halves to right and left, keeping Abraham by me and giving Anim Singh, as next to me in seniority, command of our left wing. We were in a rough new moon formation, all well under cover, with the carts in a hollow to our rear. By the time I was ready, the oncoming Turks were not much more than a quarter of a mile away; and now I could see empty saddles at last, for some of the Kurds had dismounted and were firing from the ground with good effect.

I gave no order to open fire until they came within three hundred yards of us. Then I ordered volleys, and the Syrians forthwith made a very great noise at high speed, our own troopers taking their time, and aiming low as ordered. We cavalrymen are not good shots as a rule, rather given, in fact, to despising all weapons except the lance and saber, and perhaps a pistol on occasion. But the practise in Flanders had worked wonders, and at our first volley seven or eight men rolled out of the saddles, the horses continuing to gallop on toward us.

The surprise was so great that the Turks drew rein, and we gave them three more volleys while they considered matters, bringing down a number of them. They seemed to have no officer, and were much confused. Not knowing who we were, they turned away from us and made as if to surrender to the enemy they did know, but the Kurds rode in on them and in less than five minutes there was not one Turk left alive. My men were for rushing down to secure the loot, but it seemed likely to me that the Kurds might mistake that for hostility and I prevailed on the men to keep still until Ranjoor Singh should come. And presently I saw Ranjoor Singh ride up to the leader of the Kurds and talk with him, using our Turkish officer prisoner as interpreter. Presently he and the Kurdish chief rode together toward us, and the Kurd looked us over, saying nothing. (Ranjoor Singh told me afterward that the Kurd wished to be convinced that we were many enough to enforce fair play.)

The long and the short of it was that we received half the captured horses—that is, thirty-five, for some had been killed—and all the saddles, no less than ninety of them, besides mauser rifles and uniforms for our ten unarmed Syrians. The Kurds took all the remainder, watching to make sure that the Syrians, whom we sent to help themselves to uniforms, took nothing else. When the Kurds had finished looting, they rode away toward the south without so much as a backward glance at us.

I asked Ranjoor Singh how Turkish cavalry had

come to let themselves get caught thus unsupported, and he said he did not know.

"Yet I have learned something," he said. "I shot the Turkish commander's horse myself, and my men pounced on him. That demoralized his men and made the rest easy. Now, I have questioned the Turk, and between him and the Kurdish chief I have discovered good reason to hurry forward."

"I would weigh that Kurd's information twice!" said I. "He cut those Turks down in cold blood. What is he but a cutthroat robber?"

"Let him weigh what I told him, then, three times!" he answered with a laugh. "Have you any men hurt?"

"No," said I.

"Then give me a mile start, and follow!" he ordered. And in another minute he was riding away at the head of his forty, slowly for sake of the horses, but far faster than I could go with all those laden carts. And I had to give a start of much more than a mile because of the trouble we had in fitting the saddles to our mounts. I wished he had left the captured Turkish officer behind to explain his nation's cursed saddle straps!

We rode on presently over the battle-ground; and although I have seen looting on more than one battlefield I have never seen anything so thorough as the work those Kurds had done. They had left the dead naked, without a boot, or a sock, or a rag of cloth among them. Here and there fingers had been hacked off, for the sake of rings, I suppose. There were vultures on the wing toward the dead, some looking already half-gorged, which made me wonder. I wondered, too, whither the Kurds had ridden off in such a hurry. What could be happening to the southward? Ranjoor Singh had gone due east.

It was not long before Ranjoor Singh rode out of sight in a cloud of dust, disappearing between two low hills that seemed to guard the rim of the hollow we were crossing. At midday I let the column rest in the cleft between those hills, not troubling to climb and look beyond because the men were turbulent and kept me watchful, and also because I knew well Ranjoor Singh would send back word of any danger ahead. And so he did. I was sitting eating my own meal when his messenger came galloping through the gap with a little slip of twisted paper in his teeth.

"Bring them along," said the message. "Don't halt again until you overtake me."

So I made every one of the mounted men take up a man behind, and the rest of the unmounted men I ordered into the carts, including Tugendheim's Syrians, judging it better to overtax the animals than to be too long on the road. And the long and short of that was that we overtook Ranjoor Singh at about four that afternoon. Our animals were weary, but the men were fit to fight.

Ranjoor Singh ordered Abraham to take the Syrians and all the carts and horses down into a hollow where there was a water-hole, and to wait there for further orders. Tugendheim was bidden come with us on foot; and without any explanation he led us all toward a low ridge that faced us, rising here and there into an insignificant hill. It looked like blown sand over which coarse grass had grown, and such it proved to be, for it was on the edge of another desert. It was fifty or sixty feet high, and rather difficult to climb, but he led us straight up it, cautioning us to be silent and not to show ourselves on the far side. On the top we crawled forward eighteen or twenty yards on our bellies, until we lay at last gazing downward. It was plain then whence those half-gorged vultures came.

Who shall describe what we saw? Did the sahib ever hear of Armenian massacres? This was worse. If this had been a massacre we would have known what to do, for our Sikh creed bids us ever take the part of the oppressed. But this was something that we did not understand, that held us speechless, each man searching his own heart for explanation, and Ranjoor Singh standing a little behind us watching us all.

There were hundreds of men, women and little children being herded by Turks toward the desert—southward. The line was long drawn out, for the Armenians were weary. They had no food with them, no tents, and scarcely any clothing. Here and there, in parties at intervals along the line, rode Turkish soldiers; and when an Armenian, man or woman or child, would seek to rest, a Turk would spur down on him and prick him back into line with his lance—man, woman or child, as the case might be. Some of the Turks cracked whips, and when they did that the Armenians who were not too far spent would shudder as if the very sound had cut their flesh. How did I know they were Armenians? I did not know. I learned that afterward.

Some wept. Some moaned. But the most were silent and dry-eyed, moving slowly forward like people in a dream. Oh, sahib, I have had bad dreams in my day, and other men have told me theirs, but never one like that!

There was a little water-hole below where we lay—the merest cupful fed by a trickle from below the hill. Some of them gathered there to scoop the water in their hands and drink, and I saw a Turk ride among them, spurring his horse back and forward until the water was all foul mud. Nevertheless, they continued drinking until he and another Turk flogged them forward.

"Sahib!" said I, calling to Ranjoor Singh. "A favor, sahib!"

He came and lay beside me with his chin on his hand. "What is it?" said he.

"The life of that Turk who trod the water into mud!" said I. "Let me have the winding up of his career!"

"Wait a while!" said he. "Let the men watch. Watch thou the men!"

So I did watch the men, and I saw cold anger grow among them, like an anodyne, making them forget their own affairs. I began to wonder how long Ranjoor Singh would dare let them lie there, unless perhaps he deliberately planned to stir them into uncontrol. But he was wiser than to do that. Just so far he meant their wrath should urge them—so far and no further. He watched as one might watch a fuse.

"Those Kurds of this morning," he told me (never taking his eyes off the men) "hurried off to the southward expecting to meet this very procession. Kurds hate Turks, and Turks fear Kurds, but in this they are playing to and fro, each into the other's hands. The Turks drive Armenians out into the desert, where the Kurds come down on them and plunder. The Turks return for more Armenians, and so the game goes on. I learned all that from our Turkish officer we took this morning."

While he spoke a little child died not a hundred yards away from where I lay. Its mother lay by it and wept, but a Turk spurred down and skewered the child's body on his lance, tossing it into the midst of a score of others who went forward dumbly. Another Turk riding along behind him thrashed the woman to her feet.

"That ought to do," said Ranjoor Singh, crawling backward out of sight and then getting to his feet. Then he called us, and we all crawled backward to the rear edge of the ridge. And there at last we stood facing him. I saw Gooja Singh whispering in Anim Singh's great ear. Ranjoor Singh saw it too.

"Stand forth, Gooja Singh!" he ordered. And Gooja Singh stood a little forward from the others, half-truculent and half-afraid.

"What do you want?" asked Ranjoor Singh. "Of what were you whispering?" But Gooja Singh did not answer.

"No need to tell me!" said Ranjoor Singh. "I know! Ye all seek leave to loot! As sons of *thalukdars**—as trusted soldiers of the raj—as brave men—honorable men—ye seek to prove yourselves!"

---

* Land holder.

They gasped at him—all of them, Tugendheim included. I tell you he was a brave man to stand and throw that charge in the teeth of such a regiment, not one man of whom reckoned himself less than gentleman. I looked to my pistol and made ready to go and die beside him, for I saw that he had chosen his own ground and intended there and then to overcome or fail.

"Lately but one thought has burned in all your hearts," he told them. "Loot! Loot! Loot! Me ye have misnamed friend of Germany—friend of Turkey—enemy of Britain! Yourselves ye call honorable men!"

"Why not?" asked Gooja Singh, greatly daring because the men were looking to him to answer for them. "Hitherto we have done no shameful thing!"

"No shameful thing?" said Ranjoor Singh. "Ye have called me traitor behind my back, yet to my face ye have obeyed me these weeks past. Ye have used me while it served your purpose, planning to toss me aside at the first excuse. Is that not shameful? Now we reach the place where ye must do instead of talk. Below is the plunder ye have yearned for, and here stand I, between it and you!"

"We have yearned for no such plunder as that!" said Gooja Singh, for the men would have answered unless he did, and he, too, was minded to make his bid for the ascendency.

"No?" said Ranjoor Singh. "'No carrion for me!' said the jackal. 'I only eat what a tiger killed!' "

He folded his arms and stood quite patiently. None could mistake his meaning. There was to be, one way or the other, a decision reached on that spot as to who sought honor and who sought shame. He himself submitted to no judgment. It was the regiment that stood on trial! A weak man would have stood and explained himself.

Presently Ramnarain Singh, seeing that Gooja Singh was likely to get too much credit with the men, took up the cudgels and stood forward.

"Tell us truly, sahib," he piped up. "Are you truly for the raj, or is this some hunt of your own on which you lead us?"

"Ye might have asked me that before!" said Ranjoor Singh. "Now ye shall answer me my question first! When I have your answer, I will give you mine swiftly enough, in deeds not words! What is the outcome of all your talk? Below there is the loot, and, as I said, here stand I between it and you! Now decide, what will ye!"

He turned his back, and that was bravery again; for under his eye the men were used to showing him respect, whereas behind his back they had grown used to maligning him. Yet he had thrown their shame in their very teeth because he knew their hearts were men's hearts. Turning his back on jackals would have stung them to worse dishonor. He would not have turned his back on jackals, he would have driven them before him.

It began to occur to the men that they once made me go-between, and that it was my business to speak up for them now. Many of them looked toward me. They began to urge me. Yet I feared to speak up lest I say the wrong thing. Once it had not been difficult to pretend I took the men's part against Ranjoor Singh, but that was no longer so easy.

"What is your will?" said I at last, for Ranjoor Singh continued to keep his back turned, and Gooja Singh and Ramnarain were seeking to forestall each other. Anim Singh and Chatar Singh both strode up to me.

"Tell him we will have none of such plunder as that!" they both said.

"Is that your will?" I asked the nearest men, and they said "Aye!" So I went along the line quickly, repeating the question, and they all agreed. I even asked Tugendheim, and he was more emphatic than the rest.

"Sahib!" I called to Ranjoor Singh. "We are one in this matter. We will have none of such plunder as that below!"

He turned himself about, not quickly, but as one who is far from satisfied.

"So-ho! None of *such* plunder!" said he. "What kind of plunder, then? What is the difference between the sorts of plunder in a stricken land?"

Gooja Singh answered him, and I was content that he should, for not only did I not know the answer myself but I was sure that the question was a trap for the unwary.

"We will plunder Turks, not wretches such as these!" said Gooja Singh.

"Aha!" said Ranjoor Singh, unfolding his arms and folding them again, beginning to stand truculently, as if his patience were wearing thin. "Ye will let the Turks rob the weak ones, in order that ye may rob the Turks! That is a fine point of honor! Ye poor lost fools! Have ye no better wisdom than that? Can ye draw no finer hairs? And yet ye dare offer to dictate to me, and to tell me whether I am true or not! The raj is well served if ye are its best soldiers!"

He spat once, and turned his back again.

"Ye have said we will have no such plunder!" shouted Gooja Singh, but he did not so much as acknowledge the words even by a movement of the head. Then Gooja Singh went whispering with certain of the men, those who from the first had been most partial to him, and presently I saw they were agreed on a course. He stood forward with a new question.

"Tell us whither you are leading?" he demanded. "Tell us the plan?"

Ranjoor Singh faced about. "In order that Gooja Singh may interfere and spoil the plan?" he asked, and Ramnarain Singh laughed very loud at that, many of the troopers joining. That made Gooja Singh angry, and he grew rash.

"How shall we know," he asked, "whither you lead or whether you be true or not?"

"As to whither I lead," said Ranjoor Singh, "God knows that better than I. At least I have led you into no traps yet. And as to whether I am true or not, it is enough that each should know his own heart. I am for the raj!" And he drew his saber swiftly, came to the salute, and kissed the hilt.

Then I spoke up, for I saw my opportunity. "So are we for the raj!" said I. "We too, sahib!" And it was with difficulty then that I restrained the men from bursting into cheers. Ranjoor Singh held his hand up, and we daffadars flung ourselves along the line commanding silence. A voice or two—even a dozen men talking—were inaudible, but the Turks would have heard a cheer.

"Ye?" said Ranjoor Singh. "Ye for the raj? I thought ye were all for loot?"

"Nay!" said Gooja Singh, for he saw his position undermined and began to grow fearful for consequences. "We are all for the raj, and all were for the raj from the first. It is you who are doubtful!"

He thought to arouse feeling again, but the contrast between the one man and the other had been too strong and none gave him any backing. Ranjoor Singh laughed.

"Have a care, Gooja Singh!" he warned. "I promised you court martial and reduction to the ranks should I see fit! To your place in the rear!"

So Gooja Singh slunk back to his place behind the men and I judged him more likely than ever to be dangerous, although for the moment overcome. But Ranjoor Singh had not finished yet.

"Then, on one point we are agreed," he said. "We will make the most of that. Let us salute our own loyalty to India, and the British and the Allies, with determination to give one another credit at least for that in future! Pre—sent arms!"

So we presented arms, he kissing the hilt of his saber again; and it was not until three days afterward that I overheard one of the troopers saying that Gooja Singh had called attention to the fact of its being a German saber. For the moment there was no more doubt among us; and if Gooja Singh had not begun to be so fearful lest Ranjoor Singh take vengeance on him there never would have been doubt again. We felt warm, like men who had come in under cover from the cold.

It was growing dusk by that time, and Ranjoor

Singh bade us at once to return to where the horses and Syrians waited in the hollow, he himself continuing to sit alone on the summit of the ridge, considering matters. We had no idea what he would do next, and none dared ask him, although many of the men urged me to go and ask. But at nightfall he came striding down to us and left us no longer in doubt, for he ordered girths tightened and ammunition inspected.

The Syrians had no part in that night's doings. They were bidden wait in the shadow of the ridge; with mules inspanned, and with Tugendheim in charge we trusted them to guard our Turkish prisoners. Tugendheim bit his nails and made as if to pull his mustache out by the roots, but we suffered no anxiety on his account; his safety and ours were one. He had no alternative but to obey.

Before the moon rose we sent our unmounted men to the top of the ridge under Chatar Singh, and the rest of us rode in a circuit, through a gap that Ranjoor Singh had found, to the plain on the far side.

The Turks had driven their convoy into the desert and had camped behind them, nearly three hundred strong. They had made one big fire and many little ones, and looked extremely cheerful, what with the smell of cooking and the dancing flame. Their horses were picketed together in five lines with only a few guards, so that their capture was an easy matter.

We caught them entirely by surprise and fell on them from three sides at once, our foot-men from the ridge delivering such a hot fire that some of us were hit. I looked long for the Turk who had fouled the water, and for the other one who had lanced the child's body, but failed to identify either of them. I found two who looked like them, crawling out from under a heap of slain, and shot them through the head; but as to whether I slew the right ones or not I do not know.

Three officers we made prisoner, making five that we had to care for. The other officers were slain. We never knew how few or how many Turks escaped under cover of darkness, but I suspect not more than a dozen or two at the most. Whatever tale they told when they got home again, it is pretty certain they gave the Kurds the blame, for how should they suppose us to be anything except Kurds?

We took no loot except the horses and rifles. We stacked the rifles in a cart, picked the best horses, taking twenty-five spare ones with us, and gave our worst horses to the Armenians to eat. We sent a few Syrians in a hurry to warn the Armenians in the desert against those Kurds who had ridden to the south to intercept them, and tipped out two cartsful of corn that we could ill spare, putting our wounded in the empty carts. We had one-and-twenty wounded, many of them by our own riflemen.

Then we rode on into the night, Ranjoor Singh urging us to utmost speed. The Armenians begged us to remain with them, or to take them with us. Some clung to our stirrups, but we had to shake them loose. For what could we do more than we had done for them? Should we die with them in the desert, serving neither them nor us? We gave them the best advice we could and rode away. We bade them eat, and scatter, and hide. And I hope they did.

We rode on, laughing to think that Kurds would be blamed for our doings, and wondering whether the Armenians had enough spirit left to make use of the loot we did not touch. Some of us had lances now; a few had sabers; all had good mounts and saddles. We were likely to miss the corn we had given away; but to offset that we had a new confidence in Ranjoor Singh that was beyond price, and I sang as I rode. I sang the *Anand,* our Sikh hymn of joy. I knew we were a regiment again at last.

CHAPTER VII

Since when did God take sides against the brave?
—RANJOOR SINGH.

Did the sahib ever chance to hear that Persian proverb—"*Duzd ne giriftah padshah ast*"? No? It means "The uncaught thief is king." Ho! but thenceforward that was a campaign that suited us! None could catch us, for we could come and go like the night wind, and the Turks are heavy on their feet. We helped ourselves to what we needed. And a reputation began to hurry ahead of us that made matters easier, for our numbers multiplied in men's imagination.

The Turks whom we had recently defeated gave Kurds the credit for it, and after the survivors had crawled back home whole Turkish regiments were ordered out by telegraph to hunt for raiding Kurds, not us! We cut all the wires we could find uncut, real Kurds having attended to the business already in most instances, and now, instead of slipping unseen through the land we began to leave our signature, and do deliberate damage.

None can beat Sikhs at such warfare as we waged across the breadth of Asiatic Turkey, and none could beat Ranjoor Singh as leader of it. We could outride the Turks, outwit them, outfight them, and outdare them. As the spring advanced the weather improved and our spirits rose; and as we began to take the offensive more and more our confidence increased in Ranjoor Singh until there might never have been any doubt of him, except that Gooja Singh was too conscious of his own faults to dare let matters be. He was ever on the watch for a chance to make himself safe at Ranjoor Singh's expense. He was a good enough soldier when so minded. All of us daffadars were developing into very excellent troop commanders, and he not least of us; but the more efficient he grew the more dangerous he was, for the very good reason that Ranjoor Singh scorned to take notice of his hate and only praised him for efficiency. Whereas he watched all the time for faults in Ranjoor Singh to take advantage of them.

So I took thought, and used discretion, and chose twelve troopers whom I drafted into Gooja Singh's command by twos and threes, he not suspecting. By ones and twos and threes I took them apart and tested them, saying much the same to each.

Said I, "Who mistrusts our sahib any longer?" And because I had chosen them well they each made the same answer. "Nay," said they, "we were fools. He was always truer than any of us. He surrendered in that trench that we might live for some such work as this!"

"If he were to be slain," said I, "what would now become of us?"

"He must not be slain!" said they.

"But what if he *is* slain?" I answered. "Who knows his plans for the future?"

"Ask him to tell his plans," said they. "He trusts you more than any of us. Ask and he will tell."

"Nay," said I, "I have asked and he will not tell. He knows, as well as you or I, that not all the men of this regiment have always believed in him. He knows that none dare kill him unless they know his plans first, for until they have his plans how can they dispense with his leadership?"

"Who are these who wish to kill him?" said they. "Let there be court martial and a hanging!"

"Nay," said I, "let there be a silence and forgetting, lest too many be involved!"

They nodded, knowing well that not one man of us all would escape condemnation if inquiry could be carried back far enough.

"Let there be much watchfulness!" said I.

"Who shall watch Ranjoor Singh?" said they. "He is here, there and everywhere! He is gone before dawn, and perhaps we see him again at noon, but probably not until night. And half the night he spends in the saddle as often as not. Who shall watch him?"

"True!" said I. "But if we took thought, and decided who might—perhaps—most desire to kill him for evil recollection's sake, then we might watch and prevent the deed."

"Aye!" said they, and they understood. So I arranged with Ranjoor Singh to have them transferred to Gooja Singh's troop, making this excuse and that and telling everything except the truth about it. If I had told him the truth, Ranjoor Singh would have laughed and my precaution would have been wasted, but having lied I was able to ride on with easier mind —such sometimes being the case.

We had little trouble in keeping on the horizon

whenever we sighted Turks in force; and then probably the distance deceived them into thinking us Turks, too, for we rode now with no less than five Turkish officers as well as a German sergeant. And in the rear of large bodies of Turks there was generally a defenseless town or village whose Armenians had all been butchered, and whose other inhabitants were mostly too gorged with plunder to show any fight. We helped ourselves to food, clothing, horses, saddlery, horse-feed, and anything else that Ranjoor Singh considered we might need, but he threatened to hang the man who plundered anything of personal value to himself, and none of us wished to die by that means.

We soon began to need medicines and a doctor badly, for we lost no less than eight-and-twenty men between the avenging of those Armenians in the desert and reaching the Kurdish mountains, and once we had more than forty wounded at one time. But finally we captured a Greek doctor, attached to the Turkish army, and he had along with him two mule-loads of medicines. Ranjoor Singh promised him seven deaths for every one of our wounded men who should die of neglect, and most of them began to recover very quickly.

If we had tried merely to plunder; or had raided the same place twice; or, if we had rested merely because we were weary; or, if we had once done what might have been expected of us, I should not now sit beneath this tree talking to you, sahib, because my bones would be lying in Asiatic Turkey. But we rode zigzag-wise, very often doubling on our tracks, Ranjoor Singh often keeping half a day's march ahead of us gathering information.

When we raided a town or village we used to tie our Turkish officers hand and foot and cover them up in a cart, for we wished them to be mistaken for Kurds, not Turks. And in almost the first bazaar we plundered were strange hats such as Kurds wear, that gave us when we wore them in the dark the appearance, perhaps, of Kurds who had stolen strange garments (for the Kurds wear quite distinctive clothes, of which we did not succeed in plundering sufficient to disguise us all).

In more than one town we had to fight for what we took, for there were Turkish soldiers that we did not know about, for all Ranjoor Singh's good scouting. Sometimes we beat them off with very little trouble; sometimes we had about enough fighting to warm our hearts and terrify the inhabitants. But in one town we were caught plundering the bazaar by several hundred Turkish infantry who entered from the far side unexpectedly; and if we had not burned the bazaar I doubt that we should have won clear of that trap. But the smoke and flame served us for a screen, and we got to the rear of the Turks and killed a number of them before galloping off into the dark.

But who shall tell in a day what took weeks in the doing? I do not remember the tenth part of it! We rode, and we skirmished, and we plundered, growing daily more proud of Ranjoor Singh, and most of us forgetting we had ever doubted him. Once we rode for ten miles side by side in the darkness with a

Turkish column that had been sent to hunt for us! Perhaps they mistook our squeaky old carts for their cannon; that had camped for the night unknown to them! Next day we told some Kurds where to find the cannon, and doubtless the Kurds made trouble. We let the column alone, for it was too big for us—about two regiments, I think. They camped at midnight, and we rode on.

We gave our horses all the care we could, but that was none too much, and we had to procure new mounts very frequently. Often we picked up a dozen at a time in the towns and villages, slaying those we left behind lest they be of use to the enemy. Once we wrought a miracle, being nearly at a standstill from hard marching, and almost surrounded by regiments sent out to cut us off. We raided the horse-lines of a Turkish regiment that had camped beside a stream, securing all the horses we needed and stampeding the remainder! Thus we escaped through the gap that regiment had been supposed to close. We got away with their baked bread, too, enough to last us at least three days! That was not far from Diarbekr.

By the time we reached the Tigris and crossed it near Diarbekr we were happy men; for we were not in search of idleness; all most of us asked was a chance to serve our friends, and making trouble for the Turks was surely service! One way and another we made more trouble than ten times our number could have made in Flanders. Every one of us but Gooja Singh was happy.

We crossed the Tigris in the dark, and some of us were nearly drowned, owing to the horses being frightened. We had to abandon our carts, so we burned them; and by the light of that fire we saw great mounds of Turkish supplies that they intended to float down the river to Bagdad on strange rafts made of goatskins. The sentries guarding the stores put up a little fight, and five more of us were wounded, but finally we burned the stores, and the flames were so bright and high that we had to gallop for two miles before we could be safe again in darkness. So we crossed at a rather bad place, and there was something like panic for ten minutes, but we got over safely in the end, wounded and all. We floated the wounded men and ammunition and rations for men and horses across on some of those strange goatskin rafts that go round and round and any way but forward. We found them in the long grass by the river-bank.

At a town on the far side we seized new carts, far better than our old ones. And then, because we might have been expected to continue eastward, we turned to the south and followed the course of the Tigris, straight into Kurdish country, where it did us no good to resemble either Turks or Kurds; for we could not hope to deceive the Kurds into thinking we were of their tribe, and Turks and Kurds are open enemies wherever the Turks are not strong enough to overawe. They were all Kurds in these parts, and no Turks at all, so that our problem became quite different. After two days' riding over what was little else than wilderness, Ranjoor Singh made new dispositions, and we put the Kurdish headgear in our knapsacks.

In the first place, the wounded had been suffering severely from the long forced marches and the jolting of the springless carts. Some of them had died, and the Greek doctor had grown very anxious for his own skin. Ranjoor Singh summoned him and listened to great explanations and excuses, finally gravely permitting him to live, but adding solemn words of caution. Then he ordered the carts abandoned, for there was now no road at all. The forty Turkish soldiers (in their Syrian clothes) were made to carry the wounded in stretchers we improvised, until some got well and some died; those who did not carry wounded were made to carry ammunition, and some of our own men who had tried to disregard Ranjoor Singh's strict orders regarding women of the country were made to help them. That arrangement lasted until we came to a village where the Kurds were willing to exchange mules against the rifles we had taken from the Kurds, one mule for one rifle, we refusing to part with any cartridges.

After that the wounded had to ride on mules, some of them two to a mule, holding each other on, and the cartridge boxes were packed on the backs of other mules, except that men who tried to make free with native women were invariably ordered to relieve a mule. Then we had no further use for the forty Turks, so we turned them loose with enough food to enable them to reach Diarbekr if they were economical. They went off none too eagerly in their Syrian clothes, and I have often wondered whether they ever reached their destination, for the Kurds of those parts are a fierce people, and it is doubtful which they would rather ill-treat and kill, a Turk or a Syrian. The Turks have taught them to despise Armenians and

Syrians, but they despise Turks naturally. (All this I learned from Abraham, who often marched beside me.)

"Those Turks we have released will go back and set their people on our trail," said Gooja Singh, overlooking no chance to throw discredit.

"If they ever get safely back, that is what I hope they will do!" Ranjoor Singh answered. "We will disturb hornets and pray that Turks get stung!"

He would give no explanation, but it was not long before we all understood. Little by little, he was admitting us to confidence in those days, never telling at a time more than enough to arouse interest and hope.

Rather than have him look like a Turk any longer, we had dressed up Abraham in the uniform of one of our dead troopers; and when at last a Kurdish chief rode up with a hundred men at his back and demanded to know our business, Ranjoor Singh called Abraham to interpret. We could easily have beaten a mere hundred Kurds, but to have won a skirmish just then would have helped us almost as little as to lose one. What we wanted was free leave to ride forward.

"Where are ye, and whither are ye bound? What seek ye?" the Kurd demanded, but Ranjoor Singh proved equal to the occasion.

"We be troops from India," said he. "We have been fighting in Europe on the side of France and England, and the Germans and Turks have been so badly beaten that you see for yourself what is happening. Behold us! We are an advance party. These Turkish officers you see are prisoners we have taken on our way. Behold, we have also a German prisoner!

You will find all the Turks between here and Syria in a state of panic, and if plunder is what you desire you would better make haste and get what you can before the great armies come eating the land like locusts! Plunder the Turks and prove yourselves the friends of French and English!"

Sahib, those Kurds would rather loot than go to heaven, and, like all wild people, they are very credulous. There are Kurds and Kurds and Kurds, nations within a nation, speaking many dialects of one tongue. Some of them are half-tame and live on the plains; those the Turks are able to draft into their armies to some extent. Some of the plainsmen, like those I speak of now, are altogether wild and will not serve the Turks on any terms. And most of the hillmen prefer to shoot a Turk on sight. I would rather fight a pig with bare hands than try to stand between a Kurd and Turkish plunder, and it only needed just those few words of Ranjoor Singh's to set that part of the world alight!

We rode for very many days after that, following the course of the Tigris unmolested. The tale Ranjoor Singh told had gone ahead of us. The village Kurds waited to have one look, saw our Turkish prisoners and our Sikh turbans, judged for themselves, and were off! I believe we cost the Turkish garrisons in those parts some grim fighting; and if any Turks were on our trail I dare wager they met a swarm or two of hornets more than they bargained for!

Instead of having to fight our way through that country, we were well received. Wherever we found Kurds, either in tents or in villages, the unveiled women would give us *du*, as they call their curds and whey, and barley for our horses, and now and then a little bread. When other persuasion failed, we could buy almost anything they had with a handful or two of cartridges. They were a savage people,. but not altogether unpleasing.

Once, where the Tigris curved and our road brought us near the banks, by a high cliff past which the river swept at very great speed, we took part in a sport that cost us some cartridges, but no risk, and gave us great amusement. The Kurds of those parts, having heard in advance of our tale of victory, had decided to take the nearest loot to hand; so they had made an ambuscade down near the river level, and when we came on the scene we lent a hand from higher up.

Rushing down the river at enormous speed (for the stream was narrow there) forced between rocks with a roar and much white foam the goatskin rafts kept coming on their way to Mosul and Bagdad, some loaded with soldiers, some with officers, and all with goods on which the passengers must sit to keep their legs dry. The rafts were each managed by two men, who worked long oars to keep them in mid-current, they turning slowly round and round.

The mode of procedure was to volley at them, shooting, if possible, the men with oars, but not despising a burst goatskin bag. In case the men with oars were shot, the others would try to take their place, and, being unskilful, would very swifly run the raft against a rock, when it would break up and drown its passengers, the goods drifting ashore at the bend in the river in due time.

On the other hand, when a few goatskin bags were

pierced the raft would begin to topple over and the men with oars would themselves direct the raft toward the shore, preferring to take their chance among Kurds than with the rocks that stuck up like fangs out of the raging water. No, sahib, I could not see what happened to them after they reached shore. That is a savage country.

One of our first volleys struck a raft so evenly and all together that it blew up as if it had been torpedoed! We tried again and again to repeat that performance, until Ranjoor Singh checked us for wasting ammunition. It was very good sport. There were rafts and rafts and rafts—*kyaks,* I think they call them—and the amount of plunder those Kurds collected on the beach must have been astonishing.

We gave the city of Mosul a very wide berth, for that is the largest city of those parts, with a very large Turkish garrison. Twenty miles to the north of it we captured a good convoy of mules, together with their drivers, headed toward Mosul, and the mules' loads turned out to consist of good things to eat, including butter in large quantities. We came on them in the gathering dusk, when their escort of fifty Turkish infantry had piled arms, we being totally unexpected. So we captured the fifty rifles as well as the mules; and, although the mule-drivers gave us the slip next day, and no doubt gave information about us in Mosul, that did not worry us much. We cut two telegraph wires leading toward Mosul that same night; we cut out two miles of wire in sections, riding away with it, and burned the poles.

After that, whenever we could catch a small party

of men, Turks excepted (for that would have been to give the Turks more information than we could expect to get from them), Ranjoor Singh would ask questions about Wassmuss. Most of them would glance toward the mountains at mention of his name, but few had much to tell about him. However, bit by bit, our knowledge of his doings and his whereabouts kept growing, and we rode forward, ever toward the mountains now, wasting no time and plundering no more than expedient.

We saw no more living Armenians on all that long journey. The Turks and Kurds had exterminated them! We rode by burned villages, and through villages that once had been half-Armenian. The non-Armenian houses would all be standing, like to burst apart with plunder, but every single one that had sheltered an Armenian family would lie in ruins. God knows why! On all our way we found no man who could tell us what those people had done to deserve such hatred. We asked, but none could tell us.

One town, through which we rode at full gallop, had Armenian bodies still lying in the streets, some of them half-burned, and there were Kurds and Turks busy plundering the houses. Some of them came out to fire at us, but failed to do us any harm, and, the wind being the right way, we set a light to a dozen houses at the eastward end. Two or three miles away we stopped to watch the whole town go up in flames, and laughed long at the Turks' efforts to save their loot.

As we drew near enough to the mountains to see snow and to make out the lie of the different ranges, we ceased to have any fear of pursuit. There was plenty of evidence of Turkish armies not very far away; in fact, at Mosul there was gathering a very great army indeed; but they were all so busy killing and torturing and hunting down Armenians that they seemed to have no time for duty on that part of the frontier. Perhaps that was why the Germans had sent Wassmuss, in order that the Turks might have more leisure to destroy their enemies at home! Who knows? There are many things about this great war to which none know the answer, and I think the fate of the Armenians is one of them.

But who thought any more of Armenians when the outer spurs of the foot-hills began to close around us? Not we, at any rate. We had problems enough of our own. What lay behind us was behind, and the future was likely to afford us plenty to think about! Too many of us had fought among the slopes of the Himalayas now to know how difficult it would be for Turks to follow us; but those mountaineers, who are nearly as fierce as our mountaineers of northern India, and who have ever been too many for the Turks, were likely to prove more dangerous than anything we had met yet.

We had enough food packed on our captured mules to last us for perhaps another eight days when we at last rode into a grim defile that seemed to lead between the very gate-posts of the East—two great mountains, one on either hand, barren, and ragged, and hard. We were being led at that time by a Kurdish prisoner, who had lain by the wayside with the belly-ache. Our Greek doctor had physicked him, and he was now compelled to lead us under Ranjoor Singh's directions, with his hands made fast behind him, he riding on a mule with one of our men on either hand. By that time Ranjoor Singh had picked up enough information at different times, and had added enough of it together to know whither we must march, and the Kurd had nothing to do but obey orders.

We had scarcely ridden three hundred yards into the defile of which I speak, remarking the signs of another small body of mounted men who had preceded us, when fifty shots rang out from overhead and we took open order as if a shell had burst among us. Nobody was hit, however, and I think nobody was intended to be hit. I saw that Ranjoor Singh looked unalarmed. He beckoned for Abraham, who looked terrified, and I took Abraham by the shoulder and brought him forward. There came a wild yell from overhead, and Ranjoor Singh made Abraham answer it with something about Wassmuss. In the shouting that followed I caught the word Wassmuss many times.

Presently a Kurdish chief came galloping down, for all the world as one of our Indian mountaineers would ride, leaping his horse from rock to rock as if he and the beast were one. I rode to Ranjoor Singh's side, to protect him if need be, so I heard what followed, Abraham translating.

"Whence are ye?" said the Kurd. "And whither? And what will ye?" They are inquisitive people, and they always seem to wish to know those three things first.

"I have told you already, I ride from Farangistan,*

---

*Europe.

and I seek Wassmuss. These are my men," said Ranjoor Singh.

"No more may reach Wassmuss unless they have the money with them!" said the Kurd, very truculently. "Two days ago we let by the last party of men who carried only talk. Now we want only money!"

"Who was ever helped by impatience?" asked Ranjoor Singh.

"Nay," said the Kurd, "we are a patient folk! We have waited eighteen days for sight of this gold for Wassmuss. It should have been here fifteen days ago, so Wassmuss said, but we are willing to wait eighteen more. Until it comes, none else shall pass!"

I was watching Ranjoor Singh very closely indeed, and I saw that he saw daylight, as it were, through darkness.

"Yet no gold shall come," he answered, "until you and I shall have talked together, and shall have reached an agreement."

"Agreement?" said the Kurd. "Ye have my word! Ride back and bid them bring their gold in safety and without fear!"

"Without fear?" said Ranjoor Singh. "Then who are ye?"

"We," said the Kurd, "are the escort, to bring the gold in safety through the mountain passes."

"So that he may divide it among others?" asked Ranjoor Singh, and I saw the Kurd wince. "Gold is gold!" he went on. "Who art thou to let by an opportunity?"

"Speak plain words," said the Kurd.

"Here?" said Ranjoor Singh. "Here in this defile,

where men might come on us from the rear at any minute?"

"That they can not do," the Kurd answered, "for my men watch from overhead."

"Nevertheless," said Ranjoor Singh, "I will speak no plain words here."

The Kurd looked long at him—at least a whole minute. Then he wiped his nose on the long sleeve of his tunic and turned about. "Come in peace!" he said, spurring his horse.

Ranjoor Singh followed him, and we followed Ranjoor Singh, without one word spoken or order given. The Kurd led straight up the defile for a little way, then sharp to the right and uphill along a path that wound among great boulders, until at last we halted, pack-mules and all, in a bare arena formed by a high cliff at the rear and on three sides by gigantic rocks that fringed it, making a natural fort.

The Kurd's men were mostly looking out from between the rocks, but some of them were sprawling in the shadow of a great boulder in the midst, and some were attending to the horses that stood tethered in a long line under the cliff at the rear. The chief drove away those who lay in the shadow of the boulder in the midst, and bade Ranjoor Singh and me and Abraham be seated. Ranjoor Singh called up the other daffadars, and we all sat facing the Kurd, with Abraham a little to one side between him and us, to act interpreter. That was the first time Ranjoor Singh had taken so many at once into his confidence and I took it for a good sign, although unable to ignore a twinge of jealousy.

"Now?" said the Kurd. "Speak plain words!"

"You have not yet offered us food," said Ranjoor Singh.

The Kurd stared hard at him, eye to eye. "I have good reason," he answered. "By our law, he who eats our bread can not be treated as an enemy. If I feed you, how can I let my men attack you afterward?"

"You could not," said Ranjoor Singh. "We, too, have a law, that he with whom we have eaten salt is not enemy but friend. Let us eat bread and salt together, then, for I have a plan."

"A plan?" said the Kurd. "What manner of a plan? I await gold. What are words?"

"A good plan," said Ranjoor Singh.

"And on the strength of an empty boast am I to eat bread and salt with you?" the Kurd asked.

"If you wish to hear the plan," said Ranjoor Singh. "To my enemy I tell nothing; however, let my friend but ask!"

The Kurd thought a long time, but we facing him added no word to encourage or confuse him. I saw that his curiosity increased the more the longer we were silent; yet I doubt whether his was greater than my own! Can the sahib guess what Ranjoor Singh's plan was? Nay, that Kurd was no great fool. He was in the dark. He saw swiftly enough when explanations came.

"I have three hundred mounted men!" the Kurd said at last.

"And I near as many!" answered Ranjoor Singh. "I crave no favors! I come with an offer, as one leader to another!"

The Kurd frowned and hesitated, but sent at last for bread and salt, for all our party, except that he ordered his men to give none to our prisoners and none to the Syrians, whom he mistook for Turkish soldiers. If Ranjoor Singh had told him they were Syrians he would have refused the more, for Kurds regard Syrians as wolves regard sheep.

"Let the prisoners be," said Ranjoor Singh, "but feed those others! They must help put through the plan!"

So the Kurd ordered our Syrians, whom he thought Turks, fed too, and we dipped the flat bread (something like our Indian chapatties) into salt and ate, facing one another.

"Now speak, and we listen," said the Kurd when we had finished. Some of his men had come back, clustering around him, and we were quite a party, filling all the shadow of the great rock.

"How much of that gold was to have been yours?" asked Ranjoor Singh, and the Kurd's eyes blazed.

"Wassmuss promised me so-and-so much," he answered, "if I with three hundred men wait here for the convoy and escort it to where he waits."

"But why do ye serve Wassmuss?" asked Ranjoor Singh.

"Because he buys friendship, as other men buy ghee, or a horse, or ammunition," said the Kurd. "He spends gold like water, saying it is German gold, and in return for it we must harry the British and Russians."

"Yet you and I are friends by bread and salt," said

Ranjoor Singh, "and I offer you all this gold, whereas he offers only part of it! Nay, I and my men need none of it—I offer it all!"

"At what price?" asked the Kurd, suspiciously. Doubtless men who need no gold were as rare among these mountains as in other places!

"I shall name a price," said Ranjoor Singh. "A low price. We shall both be content with our bargain, and possibly Wassmuss, too, may feel satisfied for a while."

"Nay, you must be a wizard!" said the Kurd. "Speak on!"

"Tell me first," said Ranjoor Singh, "about the party who went through this defile two days ahead of us."

"What do you know of them?" asked the Kurd.

"This," said Ranjoor Singh. "We have followed them from Mosul, learning here a little and there a little. What is it that they have with them? Who are they? Why were they let pass?"

"They were let pass because Wassmuss gave the order," the Kurd answered. "They are Germans—six German officers, six German servants—and Kurds—twenty-four Kurds of the plains acting porters and camp-servants—many mules—two mules bearing a box slung on poles between them."

"What was in the box?" asked Ranjoor Singh.

"Nay, I know not," said the Kurd.

"Nevertheless," said Ranjoor Singh, "my brother is a man with eyes and ears. What did my brother hear?"

"They said their machine can send and receive a

message from places as far apart as Khabul and Stamboul. Doubtless they lied," the Kurd answered.

"Doubtless!" said Ranjoor Singh. By his slow even breathing and apparent indifference, I knew he was on a hot scent, so I tried to appear indifferent myself, although my ears burned. The Kurds clustering around their leader listened with ears and eyes agape. They made no secret of their interest.

"They said they are on their way to Khabul," the Kurd continued, "there to receive messages from Europe and acquaint the amir and his ruling chiefs of the true condition of affairs."

"How shall they reach Afghanistan?" asked Ranjoor Singh. "Does a road through Persia lie open to them?"

"Nay," said the Kurd. "Persia is like a nest of hornets. But they are to receive an escort of us Kurds to take them through Persia. We mountain Kurds are not afraid of Persians."

"Which Kurds are to provide the escort?" Ranjoor Singh asked him, and the Kurd shook his head.

"Nay," he said, "that none can tell. It is not yet agreed. There is small competition for the task. There are better pickings here on the border, raiding now and then, and pocketing the gold of this Wassmuss between-whiles! Who wants the task of escorting a machine in a box to Khabul?"

"Nevertheless," said Ranjoor Singh, "I know of a leader and his men who will undertake the task."

"Who, then?" said the Kurd.

"I and my men!" said Ranjoor Singh; and I held my breath until I thought my lungs would burst.

"Persia!" thought I. "Afghanistan!" thought I. "And what beyond?"

"Ye are not Kurds," the chief answered, after he had considered a while. "Wassmuss said the escort must consist of three hundred Kurds or he will not pay."

"The payment shall be arranged between me and thee!" said Ranjoor Singh. "You shall have all the gold of this next convoy, if you will ride back to Wassmuss and agree that you and your men shall be the escort to Afghanistan."

"Who shall guard this pass if I ride back?" the Kurd asked.

"I!" said Ranjoor Singh. "I and my men will wait here for the gold. Leave me a few of your men to be guides and to keep peace between us and other Kurds among these mountains. Ride and tell Wassmuss that the gold will not come for another thirty days."

"He will not believe," said the Kurd.

"I will give you a letter," said Ranjoor Singh.

"He will not believe the letter," said the Kurd.

"What is that to thee, whether he believes it or not?" said Ranjoor Singh. "At least he will believe that Turks brought you the letter, and that you took it to him in good faith. Will he charge you with having written it?"

"Nay," said the Kurd, nodding, "I can not write, and he knows it."

"Do that, then," said Ranjoor Singh. "Ride and agree to be escort for these Germans and their machine to Afghanistan. Leave me here with ten or a dozen of your men, who will guide me after I have the gold to where you shall be camping with your Germans somewhere just beyond the Persian border. I will arrange to overtake you after dusk—perhaps at midnight. There I will give you the gold, and you shall ride away. I and my men will ride on as escort to the Germans."

"What if they object?" said the Kurd.

"Who? The men with the box, or Wassmuss?" asked Ranjoor Singh.

"Nay," said the Kurd, "Wassmuss will be very glad to get a willing escort. He is in difficulty over that. There will be no objection from him. But what if the men with the box object to the change of escorts?"

"We be over two hundred, and they thirty!" answered Ranjoor Singh, and the Kurd nodded.

"After all," he said, "that is thy affair. But how am I to know that you and your men will not ride off with the gold? Nay, I must have the gold first!"

Ranjoor Singh shook his head.

"Then I and my men will stay here and help seize the gold," the Kurd said meaningly.

"Nay!" said Ranjoor Singh. "For then you would fight me for it!"

"Thou and I have eaten bread and salt together!" said the Kurd.

"True," said Ranjoor Singh, "therefore trust me, for I am a Sikh from India."

"I know nothing of Sikhs, or of India," said the Kurd. "Gold I know in the dark, by its jingle and weight, but who knows the heart of a man?"

"Then listen," said Ranjoor Singh. "If you and your men seize the gold, you must bear the blame. When the Turks come later on for vengeance, you will hang. But if I stay and take the gold, who shall know who I am? You will be able to prove with the aid of Wassmuss that neither you nor your men were anywhere near when the attack took place."

"Then you will make an ambush?" said the Kurd.

"I will set a trap," said Ranjoor Singh. "Moreover, consider this: You think I may take the gold and keep it. How could I? Having taken it from the Turks, should I ride back toward Turkey? Whither else, then? Shall I escape through Persia, with you and your Kurds to prevent? Nay, we must make a fair bargain as friend with friend—and keep it!"

"If I do as you say," said the Kurd, "if I take this letter to Wassmuss, and agree with him to escort those Germans across Persia, what, then, if you fail to get the gold? What if the Turks get the better of you?"

"Dead men can not keep bargains!" answered Ranjoor Singh. "I shall succeed or die. But consider again: I have led these men of mine hither from Stamboul, deceiving and routing and outdistancing Turkish regiments all the way. Shall I fail now, having come so far?"

"Insha' Allah!" said the Kurd, meaning, "If God wills."

"Since when did God take sides against the brave?" Ranjoor Singh asked him, and the Kurd said nothing; but I feared greatly because they seemed on the verge of a religious argument, and those Kurds are fanatics. If anything but gold had been in the balance against him, I believe that Kurd would have defied us, for, although he did not know what Sikhs might be, he knew us for no Musselmen. I saw his eyes look inward, meditating treachery, not only to Wassmuss, but to us, too. But Ranjoor Singh detected that quicker than I did.

"Let us neglect no points," he said, and the Kurd brought his mind back with an effort from considering plans against us. "It would be possible for me to get that gold, and for other Kurds—not you or your men, of course, but other Kurds—to waylay me in the mountains. Therefore let part of the agreement be that you leave with me ten hostages, of whom two shall be your blood relations."

The Kurd winced. He was a little keen man, with a thin face and prominent nose; not ill-looking, but extremely acquisitive, I should say.

"Wassmuss holds my brother hostage!" he answered grimly, as if he had just then thought of it.

"I have a German prisoner here," said Ranjoor Singh, with the nearest approach to a smile that he had permitted himself yet, "and Wassmuss will be very glad to exchange him against your brother when the time comes."

"Ah!" said the Kurd, and—

"Ah!" said Ranjoor Singh. He saw now which way the wind blew, and, like all born cavalry leaders, he pressed his advantage.

"Do the Turks hold any of your men prisoner?" he asked.

"Aye!" said the Kurd. "They hold an uncle of mine, and my half-brother, and seven of my best men. They keep them in jail in fetters."

"I have five Turkish prisoners, all officers, one a bimbashi, whom I will give you when I hand over the gold. The Turks will gladly trade your men against their officers," Ranjoor Singh assured him. "You shall have them and the German to make your trade with."

It was plain the Kurd was more than half-convinced. His men who swarmed around him were urging him in whispers. Doubtless they knew he would keep most, if not all, of the gold for himself, but the safety of their friends made more direct appeal and I don't think he would have dared neglect that opportunity for fear of losing their allegiance. Nevertheless, he bargained to the end.

"Give me, then, ten hostages against my ten, and we are agreed!" he urged.

"Nay, nay!" said Ranjoor Singh. "It is my task to fight for that gold. Shall I weaken my force by ten men? Nay, we are already few enough! I will give you one—to be exchanged against your ten at the time of giving up the gold in Persia."

"Ten!" said the Kurd. "Ten against ten!"

"One!" said Ranjoor Singh, and I thought they would quarrel and the whole plan would come to nothing. But the Kurd gave in.

"Then one officer!" said the Kurd, and I trembled, for I saw that Ranjoor Singh intended to agree to that, and I feared he might pick me. But no. If I had thought a minute I would not have feared, yet who thinks at such times? The men who think first of their charge and last of their own skin are such as Ranjoor Singh; a year after war begins they are still leading. The rest of us must either be content to be led, or else are superseded. I burst into a sweat all over, for all that a cold wind swept among the rocks. Yet I might have known I was not to be spared.

After two seconds, that seemed two hours, he said to the Kurd, "Very well. We are agreed. I will give you one of my officers against ten of your men. I will give you Gooja Singh!" said he.

Sahib, I could have rolled among the rocks and laughed. The look of rage mingled with amazement on Gooja Singh's fat face was payment enough for all the insults I had received from him. I could not conceal all my merriment. Doubtless my eyes betrayed me. I doubt not they blazed. Gooja Singh was sitting on the other side of Ranjoor Singh, partly facing me, so that he missed nothing of what passed over my face—as I scarcely intended that he should. And in a moment my mirth was checked by sight of his awful wrath. His face had turned many shades darker.

"I am to be hostage?" he said in a voice like grinding stone.

"Aye," said Ranjoor Singh. "Be a proud one! They have had to give ten men to weigh against you in the scale!"

"And I am to go away with them all by myself into the mountains?"

"Aye," said Ranjoor Singh. "Why not? We hold ten of theirs against your safe return."

"Good! Then I will go!" he answered, and I

knew by the black look on his face and by the dull rage in his voice that he would harm us if he could. But there was no time just then to try to dissuade Ranjoor Singh from his purpose, even had I dared. There began to be great argument about the ten hostages the Kurd should give, Ranjoor Singh examining each one with the aid of Abraham, rejecting one man after another as not sufficiently important, and it was two hours before ten Kurds that satisfied him stood unarmed in our midst. Then he gave up Gooja Singh in exchange for them; and Gooja Singh walked away among the Kurds without so much as a backward look, or a word of good-by, or a salute.

"He should be punished for not saluting you," said I, going to Ranjoor Singh's side. "It is a bad example to the troopers."

"Kuch—kuch—," said he. "No trouble. Black hearts beget black deeds. White hearts, good deeds. Maybe we all misjudged him. Let him prove whether he is true at heart or not."

Observe, sahib, how he identified himself with us, although he knew well that all except I until recently had denied him title to any other name than traitor. "Maybe we all misjudged," said he, as much as to say, "What my men have done, I did." So you may tell the difference between a great man and a mean one.

"Better have hanged him long ago!" said I. "He will be the ruin of us yet!" But he laughed.

"Sahib," I said. "Suppose he should get to see this Wassmuss?"

"I have thought of that," he answered. "Why should the Kurds let him go near Wassmuss? Unless they return him safely to us we can execute their hostages; they will run no risk of Wassmuss playing tricks with Gooja Singh. Besides, from what I can learn and guess from what the Kurds say, this Wassmuss is to all intents and purposes a prisoner. Another tribe of Kurds, pretending to protect him, keep him very closely guarded. The best he can do is to play off one tribe against another. Our friend said Wassmuss holds his brother for hostage, but I think the fact is the other tribe holds him and Wassmuss gets the blame. I suspect they held our friend's brother as security for the gold he is to meet and escort back. There is much politics working in these mountains."

"Much politics and little hope for us!" said I, and at that he turned on me as he never had done yet. No, sahib, I never saw him turn on any man, nor speak as savagely as he did to me then. It was as if the floodgates of his weariness were down at last and I got a glimpse of what he suffered—he who dared trust no one all these months and miles.

"Did I not say months ago," he mocked, "that if I told you half my plan you would quail? And that if I told the whole, you would pick it to pieces like hens round a scrap of meat? Man without thought! Can I not see the dangers? Have I no eyes—no ears? Do I need a frog to croak to me of risks whichever way I turn? Do I need men to hang back, or men to lend me courage?"

"Who hangs back?" said I. "Nay, forward! I will die beside you, sahib!"

"I seek life for you all, not death," he answered, but he spoke so sadly that I think in that minute his hope and faith were at lowest ebb.

"Nevertheless," I answered, "if need be, I will die

beside you. I will not hang back. Order, and I obey!" But he looked at me as if he doubted.

"Boasting," he said, "is the noise fools make to conceal from themselves their failings!"

What could I answer to that? I sat down and considered the rebuff, while he went and made great preparation for an execution and a Turkish funeral. So that there was little extra argument required to induce one of our Turkish officer prisoners—the bimbashi himself, in fact—to write the letter to Wassmuss that Ranjoor Singh required. And that he gave to the Kurdish chief, and the Kurd rode away with his men, not looking once back at the hostages he had left with us, but making a great show of guarding Gooja Singh, who rode unarmed in the center of a group of horsemen. That instant I began to feel sorry for Gooja Singh, and later, when we advanced through those blood-curdling mountains I was sorrier yet to think of him borne away alone amid savages whose tongue he could not speak. The men all felt sorry for him too, but Ranjoor Singh gave them little time for talk about it, setting them at once to various tasks, not least of which was cleaning rifles for inspection.

I took Abraham to interpret for me and went to talk with our ten hostages, who were herded together apart from the other ten armed Kurds. They seemed to regard themselves as in worse plight than prisoners and awaited with resignation whatever might be their kismet. So I asked them were they afraid lest Gooja Singh might meet with violence, and they replied they were afraid of nothing. They added, however, that no man could say in those mountains what this day or the next might bring forth.

Then I asked them about Wassmuss, and they rather confirmed Ranjoor Singh's guess about his being practically a prisoner. They said he was ever on the move, surrounded and very closely watched by the particular tribe of Kurds that had possession of him for the moment.

"First it is one tribe, then another," they told me. "If you keep your bargain with our chief and he gets this gold, we shall have Wassmuss, too, within a week, for we shall buy the allegiance of one or two more tribes to join with us and oust those Kurds who hold him now. Hitherto the bulk of his gold has been going into Persia to bribe the Bakhtiari Khans and such like, but that day is gone by. Now we Kurds will grow rich. But as for us"—they shrugged their shoulders like this, sahib, meaning to say that perhaps their day had gone by also. I left them with the impression they are very fatalistic folk.

There was no means of knowing how long we might have to wait there, so Ranjoor Singh gave orders for the best shelter possible to be prepared, and what with the cave at the rear, and plundered blankets, and one thing and another we contrived a camp that was almost comfortable. What troubled us most was shortage of fire-wood, and we had to send out foraging parties in every direction at no small risk. The Kurds, like our mountain men of northern India, leave such matters to their womenfolk, and there was more than one voice raised in anger at Ranjoor Singh because he had not allowed us to capture women as well as food and horses. Our Turkish prisoners laughed at us for not having stolen women, and Tugendheim vowed he had never seen such fools.

But as it turned out, we had not long to wait. That very evening, as I watched from between two great boulders, I beheld a Turkish convoy of about six hundred infantry, led by a bimbashi on a gray horse, with a string of pack-mules trailing out behind them, and five loaded donkeys led by soldiers in the midst. They were heading toward the hills, and I sent a man running to bring Ranjoor Singh to watch them.

It soon became evident that they meant to camp on the plains for that night. They had tents with them, and they pitched a camp three-quarters of a mile, or perhaps a mile away from the mouth of our defile, at a place where a little stream ran between rocks. It was clear they suspected no treachery, or they would never have chosen that place, they being but six hundred and the hills full of Kurds so close at hand. Nevertheless, they were very careful to set sentries on all the rocks all about, and they gave us no ground for thinking we might take them by surprise. Seeing they outnumbered us, and we had to spare a guard for our prisoners and hostages, and that fifty of our force were Syrians and therefore not much use, I felt doubtful. I thought Ranjoor Singh felt doubtful, too, until I saw him glance repeatedly behind and study the sky. Then I began to hope as furiously as he.

The Turks down on the plain were studying the

sky, too. We could see them fix bayonets and make little trenches about the tents. Another party of them gathered stones with which to reenforce the tent pegs, and in every other way possible they made ready against one of those swift, sudden storms that so often burst down the sides of mountains. Most of us had experienced such storms a dozen times or more in the foot-hills of our Himalayas, and all of us knew the signs. As evening fell the sky to our rear grew blacker than night itself and a chill swept down the defile like the finger of death.

"Repack the camp," commanded Ranjoor Singh. "Stow everything in the cave."

There was grumbling, for we had all looked forward to a warm night's rest.

"To-night your hearts must warm you!" he said, striding to and fro to make sure his orders were obeyed. It was dark by the time we had finished. Then he made us fall in, in our ragged overcoats—aye, ragged, for those German overcoats had served as coats and tents and what-not, and were not made to stand the wear of British ones in any case—unmounted he made us fall in, at which there was grumbling again.

"Ye shall prove to-night," he said, "whether ye can endure what mules and horses never could! Warmth ye shall have, if your hearts are true, but the man who can keep dry shall be branded for a wizard! Imagine yourselves back in Flanders!"

Most of us shuddered. I know I did. The wind had begun whimpering, and every now and then would whistle and rise into a scream. A few drops of heavy rain fell. Then would come a lull, while we could feel the air grow colder. Our Flanders experience was likely to stand us in good stead.

Tugendheim and the Syrians were left in charge of our belongings. There was nothing else to do with them because the Syrians were in more deathly fear of the storm than they ever had been of Turks. Nevertheless, we did not find them despicable. Unmilitary people though they were, they had marched and endured and labored like good men, but certain things they seemed to accept as being more than men could overcome, and this sort of storm apparently was one of them. We tied the mules and horses very carefully, because we did not believe the Syrians would stand by when the storm began, and we were right. Tugendheim begged hard to be allowed to come with us, but Ranjoor Singh would not let him. I don't know why, but I think he suspected Tugendheim of knowing something about the German officers who were ahead of us, in which case Tugendheim was likely to risk anything rather than continue going forward; and, having promised him to the Kurdish chief, it would not have suited Ranjoor Singh to let him escape into Turkey again.

The ten Kurds who had been left with us as guides and to help us keep peace among the mountains all volunteered to lend a hand in the fight, and Ranjoor Singh accepted gladly. The hostages, on the other hand, were a difficult problem; for they detested being hostages. They would have made fine allies for Tugendheim, supposing he had meditated any action in our rear. They could have guided him among the mountains with all our horses and mules and supplies. And suppose he had made up his mind to start through the storm to find Wassmuss with their aid, what could have prevented him? He might betray us to Wassmuss as the price of his own forgiveness. So we took the hostages with us, and when we found a place between some rocks where they could have shelter we drove them in there, setting four troopers to guard them. Thus Tugendheim was kept in ignorance of their whereabouts, and with no guides to help him play us false. As for the Greek doctor, we took him with us, too, for we were likely to need his services that night, and in truth we did.

We started the instant the storm began—twenty minutes or more before it settled down to rage in earnest. That enabled us to march about two-thirds of the way toward the Turkish camp and to deploy into proper formation before the hail came and made it impossible to hear even a shout. Hitherto the rain had screened us splendidly, although it drenched us to the skin, and the noise of rain and wind prevented the noise we made from giving the alarm; but when the hail began I could not hear my own foot-fall. Ranjoor Singh roared out the order to double forward, but could make none hear, so he seized a rifle from the nearest man and fired it off. Perhaps a dozen men heard that and began to double. The remainder saw, and followed suit.

The hail was in our backs. No man ever lived who could have charged forward into it, and not one of the Turkish sentries made pretense at anything but running for his life. Long before we reached their posts they were gone, and a flash of lightning showed the tents blown tighter than drums in the gaining wind and white with the hailstones. When we reached the tents there was hail already half a foot deep underfoot where the wind had blown it into drifts, and the next flash of lightning showed one tent—the bimbashi's own—split open and blown fluttering into strips. The bimbashi rushed out with a blanket round his head and shoulders and tried to kick men out of another tent to make room for him, and failing to do that he scrambled in on top of them. Opening the tent let the wind in, and that tent, too, split and fluttered and blew away. And so at last they saw us coming.

They saw us when we were so close that there was no time to do much else than run away or surrender. Quite a lot of them ran away I imagine, for they disappeared. The bimbashi tried to pistol Ranjoor Singh, and died for his trouble on a trooper's bayonet. Some of the Turks tried to fight, and they were killed. Those who surrendered were disarmed and driven away into the storm, and the last we saw of them was when a flash of lightning showed them hurrying helter-skelter through the hail with hands behind their defenseless heads trying to ward off hailstones. They looked very ridiculous, and I remember I laughed.

I? My share of it? A Turkish soldier tried to drive a bayonet through me. I think he was the last one left in camp (the whole business can only have lasted three or four minutes, once we were among them). I shot him with the repeating pistol that had once been Tugendheim's—this one, see, sahib—and believing the camp was now ours and the fighting over, I lay down and dragged his body over me to save me from hailstones, that had made me ache already in every inch of my body. I rolled under and pulled the body over in one movement; and seeing the body and thinking a Turk was crawling up to attack him, one of our troopers thrust his bayonet clean through it. It was a goodly thrust, delivered by a man who prided himself on being workmanlike. If the Turk had not been a fat one I should not be here. Luckily, I had chosen one whose weight made me grunt, and because of his thickness the bayonet only pierced an inch or two of my thigh.

I yelled and kicked the body off me. The trooper made as if to use the steel again, thinking we were two Turks, and my pointing a pistol at him only served to confirm the belief. But next minute the lightning showed the true facts, and he came and sat beside me with his back to the hail, grinning like an ape.

"That was a good thrust of mine!" he bellowed in my ear. "But for me that Turk would have had your life!"

When I had cursed his mother's ancestors for a dozen generations in some detail the truth dawned on him at last. I took his weapon away from him while he bound a strip of cloth about my thigh, for I knew the thought had come into his thick skull to finish me off and so save explanation afterward. I would gladly have let him go with nothing further said, for I knew the man's first intention had been honest enough, but did not dare do that because he would certainly suppose me to be meditating vengeance. So I flew into a great rage with him, and drove him in front of me until we found a dead mule —whether killed by hail or bullet I don't know—and he and I lay between the mule's legs, snuggling under its belly, until the storm should cease and I could take him before Ranjoor Singh.

I did not know where the gold was, nor where anything or anybody was. I could see about three yards, except when the lightning flashed; and then I could see only stricken plain, with dead animals lying about, and fallen tents lumpy with the men who huddled underneath, and here and there a live animal with his rump to the hail and head between his fore-legs.

When the storm ceased, suddenly, as all such mountain hail-storms do, I ordered my trooper in front of me and went limping through the darkness shouting for Ranjoor Singh, and I found him at last, sitting on the rump of a dead donkey with the ten boxes of gold coin beside him—quite little boxes, yet only two to a donkey load.

"I have the gold," he said. "What have you?"

"A stab," said I, "and the fool who gave it me!" And I showed my leg, with the blood trickling down. "I had killed a Turk," said I, "and this muddlehead with no discernment had the impudence to try to finish the job. Behold the result!"

He was one great bruise from head to foot from hailstones, yet with all he had to think about and all his aches, he had understanding enough to spare for my little problem. He saw at once that he must punish the man in order to convince him his account with me was settled.

"Be driver of asses," he ordered, "until we reach Persia! There were five asses. One is dead. It is good we have another to replace the fifth!"

There goes the trooper, sahib—he yonder with the limp. He and I are as good friends to-day as daffadar and trooper can be, but he would have slain me to save himself from vengeance unless Ranjoor Singh had punished him that night. But my tale is not of that trooper, nor of myself. I tell of Ranjoor Singh. Consider him, sahib, seated on the dead ass beside ten chests of captured gold, with scarcely a man of us fit to help him or obey an order, and himself bleeding in fifty places where the hail had pierced his skin. We were drenched and numbed, with the spirit beaten out of us; yet I tell you he wiped the blood from his nose and beard and made us save ourselves!

CHAPTER VIII

Once in a lifetime. Once is enough!—HIRA SINGH.

Well, sahib, our journey was not nearly at an end, but my tale is; I can finish it by sundown. After that fight there was no more doubt of us; we were one again—one in our faith in our leader, and with men so minded such a man as Ranjoor Singh can make miracles seem like details of a day's work.

Turks who had been bayoneted and Turks slain by hailstones lay all about us, and we should have been dead, too, only that the hail was in our backs. As it was, ten of our men lay killed and more than thirty stunned, some of whom did not recover. Our little Greek doctor announced himself too badly injured to help any one, but when Ranjoor Singh began to choose a firing party for him, he changed his mind.

The four living donkeys were too bruised by the hail to bear a load, but the Turks had had some mules with them and we loaded our dead and wounded on those, gathered up the plunder, told off four troopers to each chest of gold, and dragged ourselves away. It was essential that we get back to the hills before dawn should disclose our predicament, for whatever Kurds should chance to spy us would never have been restrained by promises or by ritual of friendship from taking prompt advantage. A savage is a savage.

The moon came out from behind clouds, and we

cursed it, for we did not want to be seen. It shone on a world made white with hail—on a stricken camp—dead animals—dead men. We who had swept down from the hills like the very spirit of the storm itself returned like a funeral cortège, all groaning, chilled to the bone by the searching wind, and it was beginning to be dawn when the last man dragged himself between the boulders into our camping ground. We looked so little like victors that the Syrians sent up a wail and Tugendheim began tugging at his mustaches, but Ranjoor Singh set them at once to feeding and grooming animals and soon disillusioned them as to the outcome of the night.

Now we began to pray for time, to recover from the effects of hail and chill. Some of the men began to develop fevers, and if Ranjoor Singh had not fiercely threatened the doctor, things might have gone from bad to worse. As it was, three men died of something the matter with their lungs, and five men died of wounds. Yet, on the other hand, we did not desire too much time, because (surest of all certainties) the Turks were going to send regiments in a hurry to wreak vengeance. Before noon, somebody rallied the remnants of the convoy we had beaten and brought them back to bury dead and look for property, and they looked quite a formidable body as I watched them from between the boulders. They soon went away again, having found nothing but tents torn to rags; but I counted more than four hundred, which rather lessened my conceit. It had been the storm that night that did the work, not we.

We could not burn our dead, for lack of sufficient

wood, although we drove the Syrians out of camp to gather more; so we buried them in a trench, and covered them, and laid little fires at intervals along the new-stamped earth and set light to those. We did not bury them very deep, because a bayonet is a fool of a weapon with which to excavate a grave and a Syrian no expert digger in any case; so when the fires were burned out we piled rocks on the grave to defeat jackals.

The Kurdish chief returned on the fifth day and by that time, although most of us still ached, some of us looked like men again, and what with the plunder we had taken, and the chests of gold in full view, he was well impressed. He began by demanding the gold at once, and Ranjoor Singh surprised me by the calm courtesy with which he refused.

"Why should my brother seek to alter the terms of our bargain?" he asked.

For a long time the Kurd made no answer, but sat thinking for some excuse that might deceive us. Then suddenly he abandoned hope of argument and flew into a rage, spitting savagely and pouring out such a flood of words that Abraham could hardly translate fast enough.

"That pig you gave me for a hostage played a trick!" he shouted. "He and a man of mine knew Persian. They talked together. Then in the night they ran away, and your hostage went to Wassmuss, and has told him all the truth and more untruth into the bargain than ten other men could invent in a year! So Wassmuss threw in my teeth that letter you gave me, and I was laughed out of countenance by a heritage of spawn of Tophet! And what has Wasmuss done but persuade three hundred Kurds of a tribe who are my enemies to accept this duty of escort at a great price! And so your Germans are gone into Persia already! Now give me the gold and my hostages back, and I will leave you to your own devices!"

It was an hour before Ranjoor Singh could calm him, and another hour again before cross-examination induced him to tell all the truth; and the truth was not reassuring. Wassmuss, he said, probably did not know yet that we had taken the gold, but the news was on the way, for spies had talked in the night with the ten Kurds whom he left with us to be guides and to help us keep peace. We had given those ten a Turkish rifle each and various other plunder, because they helped us in the fight, and they had promised in return to hold their tongues. But a savage is a savage, and there is no controverting it.

"What is Wassmuss likely to do?" Ranjoor Singh asked.

"Do?" said the Kurd. "He has done! He has set two tribes by the ears and sent them down to surround you and hem you in and starve you to surrender! So give me the gold, that I may get away with it before a thousand men come to prevent, and give me back my hostages!"

If what was happening now had taken place but a week before, Ranjoor Singh would have found himself in a fine fix, for all except I would have there and then denounced him for a bungler, or a knave. But now the other daffadars who clustered around him and me said one to the other, "Let us see what our sahib makes of it!" The men sent word to know what was being revealed through two long hours of talk, and Chatar Singh went back to bid them have patience.

"Is there trouble?" they asked, and he answered "Aye!"

"Tell our sahib we stand behind him!" they answered, and Chatar Singh brought that message and I think it did Ranjoor Singh's heart good,—not that he would not have done his best in any case.

"You have lost my hostage, and I hold yours," he told the Kurd, "so now, if you want yours back you must pay whatever price I name for them!"

"Who am I to pay a price?" the Kurd demanded. "I have neither gold nor goods, nor anything but three hundred men!"

"Where are thy men?" asked Ranjoor Singh.

"Within an hour's ride," said the Kurd, "watching for the men who come from Wassmuss."

"You shall have back your hostages," said Ranjoor Singh, "when I and my men set foot in Persia!"

"How shall you reach Persia?" laughed the Kurd. "A thousand men ride now to shut you off! Nay, give me the gold and my men, and ride back whence you came!"

Then it was Ranjoor Singh's turn to laugh. "Sikhs who are facing homeward turn back for nothing less than duty!" he answered. "I shall fight the thousand men that Wassmuss sends. If they conquer me they will take the gold and your hostages as well."

The Kurd looked amazed. Then he looked

thoughtful. Then acquisitive—very acquisitive indeed. It seemed to me that he contemplated fighting us first, before the Wassmuss men could come. But Ranjoor Singh understood him better. That Kurd was no fool—only a savage, with a great hunger in him to become powerful.

"My men are seasoned warriors," said Ranjoor Singh, "and being men of our word first and last, we are good allies. Has my brother a suggestion?"

"What if I help you into Persia?" said the Kurd.

But Ranjoor Singh was wary. "Help me in what way?" he asked, and the Kurd saw it was no use to try trickery.

"What if I and my men fight beside you and yours, and so you win through to Persia?" asked the Kurd.

"As I said," said Ranjoor Singh, "you shall have back your hostages on the day we set foot in Persia."

"But the gold!" said the Kurd. "But the gold!"

"Half of the gold you shall have on the third day after we reach Persia," said Ranjoor Singh.

Well, sahib, as to that they higgled and bargained for another hour, Ranjoor Singh yielding little by little until at last the bargain stood that the Kurd should have all the gold except one chest on the seventh day after we reached Persia. Thus, the Kurds would be obliged to give us escort well on our way. But the bargaining was not over yet. It was finally agreed that after we reached Persia, provided the Kurds helped us bravely and with good faith, on the first day we would give them back their hostages; on the third day we would give them Tugendheim, to trade with Wassmuss against the Kurd's brother (thus keeping Ranjoor Singh's promise to Tugendheim to provide for him in the end); on the fifth day we would give them our Turkish officer prisoners, to trade with the Turks against Kurdish prisoners; and on the seventh day we would give them the gold and leave to go. We ate more bread and salt on that, and then I went to tell the men.

But I scarcely had time to tell them. Ranjoor Singh had out his map when I left him, and he and the Kurd were poring over it, he tracing with a finger and asking swift questions, and the Kurd with the aid of Abraham trying to understand. Yet I had hardly told the half of what I meant to say when Ranjoor Singh strode past me, and the Kurd went galloping away between the boulders to warn his own men, leaving us not only the hostages but the ten guides also.

"Make ready to march at once—immediately—*ek dum!*" Ranjoor Singh growled to me as he passed, and from that minute until we were away and well among the hills I was kept too busy with details to do much conjecturing. A body of soldiers with transport and prisoners, wounded and sick, need nearly as much herding as a flock of sheep, even after months of campaigning when each man's place and duty should be second nature. Yet oh, it was different now. There was no need now to listen for whisperings of treason! Now we knew who the traitor had been all along—not Ranjoor Singh, who had done his best from first to last, but Gooja Singh, who had let no opportunity go by for defaming him and making trouble!

"This for Gooja Singh when I set eyes on him!" said not one trooper but every living man, licking a cartridge and slipping it into the breech chamber as we started.

We did not take the track up which the Kurdish chief had galloped, but the ten guides led us by a dreadful route round almost the half of a circle, ever mounting upward. When night fell we camped without fires in a hollow among crags, and about midnight when the moon rose there was a challenge, and a short parley, and a Kurd rode in with a message from his chief for Ranjoor Singh. The message was verbal, and had to be translated by Abraham, but I did not get to hear the wording of it. I was on guard.

"It is well," said Ranjoor Singh to me, when he went the rounds and found me perched on a crag like a temple minaret, "they are keeping faith. The Wassmuss men are in the pass below us, and our friends deny them passage. At dawn there will be a fight and our friends will probably give ground. Two hours before dawn we will march, and come down behind the Wassmuss men. Be ready!"

The sahib will understand now better what I meant by saying Anim Singh has ears too big for his head. Because of his big ears, that could detect a foot-fall in the darkness farther away than any of us, he had been sent to share the guard with me, and now he came looming up out of the night to share our counsels; for since the news of Gooja Singh's defection there was no longer even a pretense at awkwardness in approaching Ranjoor Singh. Anim Singh had been among the first to fling distrust to the winds and to make the fact evident.

But into those great ears, during all our days and weeks and months of marching, Gooja Singh had whispered—whispered. The things men whisper to each other are like deeds done in the dark—like rats that run in holes—put to shame by daylight. So Anim Singh came now, and Ranjoor Singh repeated to him what he had just told me. Anim Singh laughed.

"Leave the Kurds to fight it out below, then!" said he. "While they fight, let us eat up distance into Persia, gold and all!"

Ranjoor Singh, with the night mist sparkling like jewels on his beard, eyed him in silence for a minute. Then:

"I give thee leave," he said, "to take as many men as share that opinion, and to bolt for your skins into Persia or anywhither! The rest of us will stay and keep the regiment's promise!"

That was enough for Anim Singh. I have said he is a Sikh with a soldier's heart. He wept, there on the ledge, where we three leaned, and begged forgiveness until Ranjoor Singh told him curtly that forgiveness came of deeds, not words. And his deeds paid the price that dawn. He is a very good man with the saber, and the saber he took from a Turkish officer was, weight and heft and length, the very image of the weapon he was used to. Nay, who was I to count the Kurds he slew. I was busy with my own work, sahib.

The fight below us began before the earliest color of dawn flickered along the heights. And though we started when the first rifle-shot gave warning, hiding our plunder and mules among the crags in charge of the Syrians, but taking Tugendheim with us, the way was so steep and devious that morning came and found us worrying lest we come too late to help our friends—even as once we had worried in the Red Sea!

But as we had come in the nick of time before, even so now. We swooped all unexpected on the rear of the Wassmuss men, taking ourselves by surprise as much as them, for we had thought the fight yet miles away. Echoes make great confusion in the mountains. It was echoes that had kept the Wassmuss men from hearing us, although we made more noise than an avalanche of fighting animals. Straightway we all looked for Wassmuss, and none found him, for the simple reason that he was not there; a prisoner we took told us afterward that Wassmuss was too valuable to be trusted near the border, where he might escape to his own folk. There is no doubt Wassmuss was prisoner among the Kurds,—nor any doubt either that he directs all the uprising and raiding and disaffection in Kurdistan and Persia. As Ranjoor Singh said of him—a remarkable man, and not to be despised.

Seeing no Wassmuss, it occurred to me at last to listen to orders! Ranjoor Singh was shouting to me as if to burst his lungs. The Kurds were fighting on foot, taking cover behind boulders, and he was bidding me take my command and find their horses.

I found them, sahib, within an ace of being too

late. They had left them in a valley bottom with a guard of but twenty or thirty men, who mistook us at first for Kurds, I suppose, for they took no notice of us. I have spent much time wondering whence they expected mounted Kurds to come; but it is clear they were so sure of victory for their own side that it did not enter their heads to suspect us until our first volley dropped about half of them.

Then the remainder began to try to loose the horses and gallop away, and some of them succeeded; but we captured more than half the horses and began at once to try to get them away into the hills. But it is no easy matter to manage several hundred frightened horses that were never more than half tamed in any case, and many of them broke away from us and raced after their friends. Then I sent a messenger in a hurry to Ranjoor Singh, to say the utmost had been attempted and enough accomplished to serve his present purpose, but the messenger was cut down by the first of a crowd of fugitive Kurds, who seized his reins and fought among themselves to get his horse.

Seeing themselves taken in the rear, the Kurds had begun to fall back in disorder, and had actually burst through our mounted ranks in a wild effort to get to their own horses; for like ourselves, the Kurds prefer to fight mounted and have far less confidence in themselves on foot. Ranjoor Singh, with our men, all mounted, and our Kurdish friends, were after them—although our friends were too busy burdening themselves with the rifles and other belongings of the fallen to render as much aid as they ought.

I left my horse, and climbed a rock, and looked for half a minute. Then I knew what to do; and I wonder whether ever in the world was such a running fight before. I had only lost one man; and it was quite another matter driving the Kurds' horses up the valley in the direction they wished to take, to attempting to drive them elsewhere. Being mounted ourselves, we could keep ahead of the retreating Kurds very easily, so we adopted the same tactics again and again and again.

First we drove the horses helter-skelter up the valley a mile or two. Then we halted, and hid our own horses, and took cover behind the rocks to wait for the Kurds; and as they came, making a good running fight of it, dodging hither and thither behind the boulders to try to pick off Ranjoor Singh's men, we would open fire on their rear unexpectedly, thus throwing them into confusion again,—and again,—and again.

We opened fire always at too great distance to do much material damage, I thinking it more important to preserve my own men's lives and so to continue able to demoralize the Kurds, and afterward Ranjoor Singh commended me for that. But I was also acutely aware of the risk that our bullets might go past the Kurds and kill our own Sikhs. I am not at all sure some accidents of that nature did not happen.

So when we had fired at the Kurds enough to make them face about and so expose their rear to Ranjoor Singh, we would get to horse again and send the Kurdish horses galloping up the pass in front of us. Finally, we lost sight of most of the Kurdish horses, although we captured one apiece—which is all a man can manage besides his own and a rifle.

By that time it was three in the afternoon already and the pass forked about a dozen different ways, so that we lost the Kurds at last, they scattering to right and left and shooting at us at long range from the crags higher up. We were all dead beat, and the horses, too, so we rested, the Kurds continuing to fire at us, but doing no damage. They fired until dusk.

Our own three hundred Kurdish friends were not very far behind Ranjoor Singh, and I observed when they came up with us presently that he took up position down the pass behind them. They were too fond of loot to be trusted between us and that gold! They were so burdened with plunder that some of them could scarcely ride their horses. Several had as many as three rifles each, and they had found great bundles of food and blankets where the enemy's horses had been tethered. Their plundering had cost them dear, for they had exposed themselves recklessly to get what their eyes lusted for. They had lost more than fifty men. But we had lost more than twenty killed, and there was a very long tale of wounded, so that Ranjoor Singh looked serious as he called the roll. The Greek doctor had to work that night as if his own life depended on it—as in fact it did! We made Tugendheim help him, for, like all German soldiers, he knew something of first aid.

Then, because the Kurds could not be trusted on such an errand, Ranjoor Singh sent me back with fifty men to bring on the Syrians and our mules and belongings, and the gold. He gave me Chatar Singh to help, and glad I was to have him. A brave good daffadar is Chatar Singh, and now that all suspicion of our leader was weaned out of him, I could ask for no better comrade on a dark night. Night did I say? That was a night like death itself, when a man could scarcely see his own hand held thus before his face—cold and rainy to make matters worse.

We had two Kurds to show us the way, and, I suppose because our enemies had had enough of it, we were not fired on once, going or coming. Our train of mules clattered and stumbled and our Syrians kept losing themselves and yelling to be found again. Weary men and animals ever make more noise than fresh ones; frightened men more than either, and we were so dead weary by the time we got back that my horse fell under me by Ranjoor Singh's side.

Of all the nights I ever lived through, except those last we spent in the trench in Flanders before our surrender, that was the worst. Hunger and cold and fear and weariness all wrought their worst with me; yet I had to set an example to the men. My horse, as I have told, fell beside Ranjoor Singh; he dragged me to my feet, and I fell again, dizzy with misery and aching bones. Yet it was beginning to be dawn then, and we had to be up and off again. Our dead were buried; our wounded were bound up; the Kurds would be likely to begin on us again at any minute; there was nothing to wait there for. We left little fires burning above the long grave (for our men had brought all our dead along with them, although our Kurdish friends left theirs behind them) and I took one of the captured horses, and Ranjoor Singh led on. I slept on the march. Nay, I had no eyes for scenery just then!

After that the unexpected, amazing, happened as it so often does in war. We were at the mercy of any handful who cared to waylay us, for the hillsides shut us in, and there was cover enough among the boulders to have hidden a great army. It was true we had worsted the Wassmuss men utterly; I think we slew at least half of them, and doubtless that, and the loss of their horses, must have taken much heart out of the rest. But we expected at least to be attacked by friends of the men we had worsted—by mountain cutthroats, thieves, and plunderers, any fifty of whom could have made our march impossible by sniping us from the flanks.

But nothing happened, and nobody attacked us. As we marched our spirit grew. We began to laugh and make jokes about the enemy hunting for lost horses and letting us go free. For two days we rode, and camped, and slept a little, and rode on unmolested, climbing ever forward to where we could see the peaks that our friendly chief assured us were in Persia. For miles and miles and everlasting miles it seemed the passes all led upward; but there came a noon at last when we were able to feel, and even see—when at least we knew in our hearts that the uphill work was over. We could see other ranges, running in other directions, and mountains with tree-draped sides. But chiefly it was our hearts that told us we were really in sight of Persia at last.

Then wounded and all gathered together, with Ranjoor Singh in the midst of us, and sang the

Anand, our Sikh hymn of joy, our Kurdish friends standing by and wondering (not forgetting nevertheless to watch for opportunity to snatch that gold and run!)

And there, on the very ridge dividing Persia from Asiatic Turkey, it was given to us to understand at last a little of the why and wherefore of our marching unmolested. We came to a crack in a rock by the wayside. And in the crack had been thrust, so that it stood upright, a gnarled tree-trunk, carried from who knows how far. And there, crucified to the dry wood was our daffadar Gooja Singh, with his flesh all tortured and torture written in his open eyes—not very long dead, for his flesh was scarcely cold—although the birds had already begun on him. Who could explain that? We sat our horses in a crowd, and gaped like fools!

At last I said, "Leave him to the birds!" but Ranjoor Singh said "Nay!" Ramnarain Singh, who had ever hated Gooja Singh for reasons of his own, joined his voice to mine; and because they had no wish to offend me the other daffadars agreed. But Ranjoor Singh rose into a towering passion over what we said, naming me and Ramnarain Singh in one breath as men too self-righteous to be trusted!

"What proof have we against him?" he demanded.

"Try him by court martial!" Ramnarain Singh screwed up courage to answer. "Call for witnesses against him and hear them!"

"Who can try a dead man by court martial?" Ranjoor Singh thundered back. "He left us to go and be our hostage, for our safety—for the safety of your ungrateful skins! He died a hostage, given by us to savages. They killed him. Are ye worse savages than they? Which of our dead lie dishonored anywhere? Have they not all had burning or else burial? Are ye judges of the dead? Or are ye content to live like men? Take him down, and lay him out for burial! His brother daffadars shall dig his grave!"

Aye, sahib. So he gave the order, and so we obeyed, saying no more, but digging a trench for Gooja Singh with bayonets, working two together turn and turn about, I, who had been all along his enemy, doing the lion's share of the work and thinking of the talks he and I had had, and the disputes. And here was the outcome! Aye.

It was not a very deep trench but it served, and we laid him in it with his feet toward India, and covered him, and packed the earth down tight. Then we burned on the grave the tree to which he had been crucified, and piled a great cairn of stone above him. There we left him, on the roof of a great mountain that looks down on Persia.

It was perhaps two hours, or it may have been three, after burying Gooja Singh (we rode on in silence, thinking of him, our wounded groaning now and then, but even the words of command being given by sign instead of speech because none cared to speak) that we learned the explanation, and more with it.

We found a good place to camp, and proceeded to make it defensible and to gather fuel. Then some of the women belonging to our Kurdish friends overtook us, and with them a few of our Kurdish wounded and some unwounded ones who had returned to glean again on the battle-field. These brought with them two prisoners whom we set in the midst, and then Abraham was set to work translating until his tongue must have almost fallen out with weariness. Bit by bit, we pieced a tale together that had reason in it and so brought us understanding.

Our first guess had been right; the Turks had already sent (some said a full division) to wreak vengeance for our plundering of the gold. The Kurds of those parts, who fight among themselves like wild beasts, nevertheless will always stand together to fight Turks; therefore those who had been attacking us were now behind us with thousands of other Kurds from the tribes all about, waiting to dispute the passes with the common enemy. They considered us an insignificant handful, to be dealt with later on. The women said the battle had not begun; and the prisoners bade our Kurds swallow tribal enmity and hurry to do their share! The chief listened to them, saying nothing. Has the sahib ever watched a savage thinking while lust drew him one way and pride another? Truly an interesting sight!

But the rest of the men were too interested to learn the reason of Gooja Singh's torture and death to care for the workings of a Kurdish chief's conscience. They crowded closer and closer, interrupting with shouted questions and bidding each other be still. So Ranjoor Singh said a word to Abraham and he changed the line of questioning. The truth was soon out.

Gooja Singh, it seemed, probably not believing we

had one chance in a million, decided to contrive safety for himself. So with one Kurd to help him, he escaped in the night, and went and found Wassmuss in a Kurdish village in the mountains. He told Wassmuss who we were, and whence we were, and what we intended. So Wassmuss (who must be a very remarkable man indeed), although a prisoner, exerted so much persuasion forthwith that three hundred Kurds consented to escort the party of Germans there and then to Afghanistan. He promised them I know not what reward, but the point is they consented, and within eight hours of Gooja Singh's arrival the German party was on its way.

Then Wassmuss sent the thousand Kurds to deal with us; but, as I have told, we beat them. And that made the Kurds who held Wassmuss prisoner extremely angry with Gooja Singh; so they made him prisoner, too. And then, by signal and galloper and shouts from crag to crag came word that the Turks were marching in force to invade the mountains, and instantly they turned on Gooja Singh and would have torn him in pieces for being a spy of the Turks, sent on ahead to prepare the way. But some cooler head than the rest urged to put him to the torture, and they agreed.

Whether or not Gooja Singh declared under torture that we were Turks we could not get to know, but it is certain that the Kurds decided we were Turks, whatever Wassmuss swore to the contrary; and doubtless he swore furiously! And because they believed us to be Turks, they let us be for the present, sure that we would try to make our way back if they could keep the main Turkish forces from regaining touch with us. And Gooja Singh they presently crucified in a place where we would almost surely see him, thinking thus to surprise us with the information that all was known, and to frighten us into a state of comparative harmlessness—a favorite Kurdish trick.

That did not account for everything. It did not account for our victory over Turks in the hail-storm and our plunder of the Turks' camp and capture of the gold. But none had seen that raid because of the storm, and the spies who had said they talked with our men in the night were now disbelieved. Our presence in the hills and Gooja Singh's escape was all set down to Turkish trickery; and doubtless they did not believe we truly had gold with us, or they would have detached at least a party to follow us up and keep in touch.

The clearest thing of all that the disjointed scraps of tale betrayed was that we were in luck! If the Kurds believed us to be Turks, they were likely to let us wander at will, if only for the very humor and sport of hunting us down when we should try to break back. "No need to waste more labor setting this camp to rights!" said I. "We shall rest a little and be up and away again!" And the wounded groaned, and some objected, but I proved right. Ranjoor Singh was no man to study comfort when opportunity showed itself. We rested two hours, and during those two hours our friend the Kurdish chief made up his mind, and he and Ranjoor Singh struck a new bargain.

"Give me the gold!" said he. "Keep the hostages

and ten of my men to guide you, and send them back when you are two days into Persia. I go to fight against the Turks!"

Well, they bargained, and bargained. Ranjoor Singh offered him his choice of a chest of gold then and there, or four-fifths of the whole in Persia; and in the end he agreed to take three chests of gold then and there, and to leave us the hostages and thirty men to see us on our way. "For," said Ranjoor Singh, "how should the hostages and my prisoners return to you safely otherwise?"

So we kept two chests of gold, and found them right useful presently. And we said good-by to him and his men, and put out our own fires and rode eastward. And of the next few days there is nothing to tell except furious marching and very little sleep—nor much to eat either.

Once we were well into Persia we bought food right and left, paying fabulous prices for it with gold from our looted chests. Here and there we traded a plundered rifle for a new horse, sometimes two new horses. Here and there a wounded man would die and we would burn his body (for now there was fuel in plenty). Day after day, night after night, Ranjoor Singh kept in the saddle, hunting tirelessly for news of the party of Germans on ahead of us. Their track was clear as daylight, and on the fifth day (or was it the sixth) after we entered Persia he learned at last that we were only a day or two behind them. Like us, they were in a hurry; but unlike us, they had no Ranjoor Singh to force the pace and do the scouting, so that for all their long lead we were overtaking them.

Like us, they seemed wary of the public eye, for they followed lonely routes among the wooded foothills; but their Kurdish horsemen left a track no blind man could have missed, and although they plundered a little as they went, they spent gold, too, like water, so that the villagers were in a strange mood. Most of the plundering was done by their Kurdish escort who, it seemed, kept returning to steal the money paid by the Germans for provisions. Sometimes when we offered gold we would be mocked. But on the whole, we began to have an easy time of it —all but the wounded, who suffered tortures from the pace we held. We secured some carts at one village and put our wounded in them, but the carts were springless, and there were no roads at all, so that it was better in those days to be a dead man than a sick or wounded one! There was no malingering!

After a few days (I forget how many, for who can remember all the days and distances of that long march?) Abraham got word of a great Christian mission station where thousands of Christians had sought safety under the American flag. He and his Syrians elected to try their fortune there, and we let them go, all of us saluting Abraham, for he was a good brave man, fearful, but able to overcome his fear, and intelligent far beyond the ordinary. We let the Syrians take their rifles and some ammunition with them, because Abraham said they might be called on perhaps to help defend the mission.

Not long after that, we let our Kurds go, giving up our Turkish officer prisoners and Tugendheim as well. We all knew by that time what our final goal was, and Tugendheim begged to be allowed to go with us all the way. But Ranjoor Singh refused him.

"I promised you to the Kurd, and the Kurd will trade you to Wassmuss against his brother," he said. "Tell Wassmuss whatever lies you like, and make your peace with your own folk however you can. Here is your paper back."

Tugendheim took the paper. (You remember, sahib, he had signed a receipt in conjunction with the Turkish mate and captain of that ship in which we escaped from Stamboul.) Well, he took the paper back, and burned it in the little fire by which I was sitting facing Ranjoor Singh.

"Let me go with you!" he urged. "It will be rope or bullet for me if ever I get back to Germany!"

"Nevertheless," said Ranjoor Singh, "I promised to deliver you to Wassmuss when we made you prisoner in the first place. I must keep my word to you!"

"I release you from your word to me!" said Tugendheim.

"And I promised you to the Kurdish chief."

"The Kurdish chief?" said Tugendheim. "What of him? What of it? Why, why, why—he is a savage—scarcely human—not to be weighed in the scales against a civilized man! What does such a promise as that amount to?" And he stood tugging at his mustaches as if he would tear them out.

"I have some gold left," said Ranjoor Singh, when

he was sure Tugendheim had no more to say, "and I had seriously thought of buying you for gold from these Kurds. There may be one of them who would take on himself the responsibility of speaking for his chief. But since you hold my given word so light as that I must look more nearly to my honor. Nay, go with the Kurds, Sergeant Tugendheim!"

Tugendheim made a great wail. He begged for this, and he begged for that. He begged us to give him a letter to Wassmuss explaining that we had compelled him by threats of torture. He begged for gold. And Ranjoor Singh gave him a little gold. Some of us put in a word for him, for on that long journey he had told many a tale to make us laugh. He had suffered with us. He had helped us more than a little by drilling the Syrians, and often his presence with us had saved our skins by convincing Turkish scouts of our bona fides. We thought of Gooja Singh, and had no wish that Tugendheim should meet a like fate. So, perhaps because we all begged for him, or perhaps because he so intended in the first place, Ranjoor Singh relented.

"The Persians hereabouts," he said, "all tell me that a great Russian army will come down presently from the north. Have I heard correctly that you meditated escape into Russia?"

Tugendheim answered, "How should I reach Russia?"

"That is thy affair!" said Ranjoor Singh. "But here is more gold," and he counted out to him ten more golden German coins. "You must ride back with these Kurds, but I have no authority over them.

They are not my men. They seem to like gold more than most things."

So Tugendheim ceased begging for himself and rode away rather despondently in the midst of the Kurds; and we followed about a day and a half behind the German party with their strange box-full of machinery. There were many of us who could talk Persian, and as we stopped in the villages to beg or buy curdled milk, and as we rounded up the cattle-herdsmen and the women by the wells, we heard many strange and wonderful stories about what the engine in that box could do. I observed that Ranjoor Singh looked merry-eyed when the wildest stories reached him; but we all began to reflect on the disastrous consequences of letting such crafty people reach Afghanistan. For, as doubtless the sahib knows, the amir of Afghanistan has a very great army; and if he were to decide that the German side is after all the winning one he might make very much trouble for the government of India.

And now there was no longer any doubt that the machine slung in the box between two mules was a wireless telegraph, and that most of the other mules were loaded with accessories. The tales we heard could not be made to tally with any other explanation. And what, said we, was to prevent the Germans in Stamboul from signaling whatever lies they could invent to this party in Afghanistan, supposing they should ever reach the country? Yet when we argued thus with Ranjoor Singh, he laughed.

And then, after about a week of marching, came Tugendheim back to us, ragged and thirsty and nearly dead, on a horse more dead than he. He had bought himself free from the Kurds with the gold Ranjoor Singh gave him; but because he had no more gold the Persians had refused to feed him. "How should he find his way alone to meet the Russians," he said, "whose scouts would probably shoot him on sight in any case?" So we laughed, and let him rest among our wounded and be one of us,—aye, one of us; for who were we to turn him away to starve? He had served us well, and he served us well again.

Has the sahib heard of Bakhtiari Khans? They are people as fierce as Kurds, who live like the Kurds by plundering. The Germans ahead of us, doubtless because Persia is neutral in this war and therefore they had no conceivable right to be crossing the country, chose a route that avoided all towns and cities of considerable size. And Persia seems to have no army any more, so that there was no official opposition. But the Bakhtiari Khans received word of what was doing, and after that there were new problems. But for the fact that Tugendheim was with us in his ragged German uniform we should have had more trouble than we did.

At first the Khans were content with blackmail, holding up the Germans at intervals and demanding money. But I suppose that finally their money all gave out, and then the Kahns put threats into practise. But before actual skirmishing began the Khans would come to us, after getting money from the Germans, and it was only the fact that we had Tugendheim to show that convinced them we belonged to the party ahead. Ranjoor Singh claimed that our transit fee had been paid for us already, and the Khans did not deny it.

But they caught up the Germans again and demanded money from them because of us who were following, and I have laughed many a time to think of the predicament that put them in. For could they deny all knowledge of us? In that case they might be denying useful allies in their hour of need. If the Bakhtiari Khans should annihilate us their own fate would not be likely to tremble in the balance very long. Yet if they admitted knowledge of us, what might that not lead to? And how was it possible for them to know really who we were in any case?

Finally, they sent one of their Kurdish servants back to find us and ask questions. And to him we showed Tugendheim, and spoke to him at great length in Persian, of which he understood very little; so that when he overtook his own party again (if he ever did, for the Kahns were on the prowl and very cruel and savage), they may have been more in the dark about us than ever.

At last the Bakhtiari Khans began guerrilla warfare, and the Kurds who were escorting the Germans retaliated by burning and plundering the villages by which they passed—which incensed the Khans yet more, because they did not belong to that part of Persia and had counted on the plunder for themselves. From time to time we caught a Bakhtiari Khan, and though they spoke poor Persian, some of us could understand them. They explained that the Persian government, being very weak, made use of them to terrorize whatever section of the country seemed rebellious—surely a sad way to govern a land!

There were not very many of the Khans. They are used to raiding in parties of thirty to fifty, or perhaps a hundred. I think there were not many more of them than of the German party and us combined; and at that the Bakhtiari Khans were all divided into independent troops. So that the danger was not so serious as it seemed. But guerrilla warfare is very trying to the nerves, and if we had not had Ranjoor Singh to lead us we should have failed in the end; for we were fighting in a strange land, with no base to fall back on and nothing to do but press forward.

The Kurds, too, who escorted the Germans, began to grow sick of it. Little parties of them began to pass us on their way home, giving us a wide berth, but passing close enough, nevertheless, to get some sort of protection from our proximity, and the numbers of those parties grew and grew until we laughed at the thought of what anxiety the Germans must be suffering. Yet Ranjoor Singh grew anxious, too, for the Khans grew bolder. It began to look as if neither Germans nor we would ever reach half-way to the Afghan border. Ranjoor Singh was the finest leader men could have, but we were being sniped eternally, men falling wounded here and there until scarcely one of us but had a hurt of some kind—to say nothing of our sick. Men grew sick from bad food, and unaccustomed food, and hard riding and exposure. Our little Greek doctor took sick and died, and we had nothing but ignorance left with which to treat our ailments. We began to be a sorry-looking regiment indeed. Nevertheless, the ignorance helped, for at least we did not know how serious our wounds were. I myself received one bullet that passed through both ankles, and it is not likely I shall ever walk again without a limp. Yet if I can ride what does that matter so long as the government has horses? And if a man limps in both feet wherein is he the loser? Mine was a slight wound compared to some of them. We had come to a poor pass, but Ranjoor Singh's good sense saved the day again.

There came a day when the Bakhtiari Khans gave us a terrible last attention and then left us—as it turned out for good (although we did not know then it was for good). We watched their dust as their different troops gathered together and rode away southward. I suppose they had received word of better opportunity for plunder somewhere else; they took little but hard knocks from us, and doubtless any change was welcome. When we had seen the last of them, and had watched the vultures swoop down on a horse they had left behind, we took new heart and rode on; and it so happened that the Germans chose that occasion for a rest. Their dwindling Kurdish escort was growing mutinous and they took advantage of a village with high mud walls to get behind cover and try to reestablish confidence. Perhaps they, too, saw the Bakhtiari Khans retiring in the distance, for we were close behind them at that time—so close that even with tired horses we came on them before they could man the village wall. We knocked a hole in the wall and had a good wide breach established in no time, to save ourselves trouble in case the gates should prove too strongly held; and leaving Anim Singh posted in the breach with his troop, Ranjoor Singh sent a trooper with a white flag to the main gate.

After ten or fifteen minutes the German commanding officer rode out, also with a white flag, and not knowing that Ranjoor Singh knew German, he spoke English. (Tugendheim had taken his tunic off and—all sweaty and trembling had hidden behind the ranks disguised with a cloth tied about his head.) I sat my horse beside Ranjoor Singh, so I heard all.

"Persia is neutral territory!" said the German.

"Are you, then, neutral?" asked Ranjoor Singh.

"Are you?" asked the German. He was a handsome bullet-headed man with a bold eye, and I knew that to browbeat or trick him would be no easy matter. Nevertheless he still had so many Kurds at his back that I doubted our ability to get the better of him in a fight, considering our condition.

"I could be neutral if I saw fit," answered Ranjoor Singh, and the German's eyes glittered.

"If you are neutral, ride on then!" he laughed. I saw his eye teeth. It was a mean laugh.

"What are you doing here?" asked Ranjoor Singh.

"Minding my business," said the German pointedly.

"Then I will mind mine and investigate," said Ranjoor Singh, and he turned to me as if to give an order, at which the German changed his tactics in a hurry.

"My business is simple," said the German. "Perfectly simple and perfectly neutral. We have a wireless installation with us. It is all ready to set up in this village. In a few moments we shall be receiving messages from Europe, and then we shall inform the inhabitants of these parts how matters stand. As neutrals they are entitled to that information." Their eyes met, each seeking to read the other's mind, and the German misunderstood, as most Germans I have met do misunderstand.

"Before we can receive a message we shall send one," said the German. "Before I came out to meet you, I gave the order to get in touch with Constantinople and signal this: That we are being interfered with and our lives are endangered on neutral territory by troops belonging to British India, and therefore that all British Indian prisoners-of-war in Germany should be made hostages for our safety. That means," he went on, "that unless we signal every day that all is well, a number of your countrymen in Germany corresponding to the number of my party will be lined up against a wall and shot."

"So that message has been sent?" asked Ranjoor Singh.

"Yes," said the German.

"Then send this message also," said Ranjoor Singh: "That the end has certainly come. Then close up your machine because unless you wish to fight for your existence there will be no more messages sent or received by you between here and Afghanistan."

I thought that a strange message for Ranjoor

Singh to bid him send. I did not believe that one of us, however weary, was willing to accept relief at the price of our friends' lives. Nevertheless, I said nothing, having learned it is not wise to draw too swift conclusions when Ranjoor Singh directs the strategy.

But the German evidently thought so, too, for his eyes looked startled, and I took comfort from that.

"I understand you wish to reach Afghanistan?" asked Ranjoor Singh.

"That is our eventual destination," said the German.

"Very well," said Ranjoor Singh. "Pack up your machine. Then I will permit your journey to the Afghan border, unhampered by me, on two conditions."

"What two conditions?" asked the German.

"That your machine shall remain packed up until you reach Afghanistan, and that your doctor shall divide his services until then equally between your men and mine."

"And after that, what?" asked the German.

"I have nothing to do with Afghanistan," said Ranjoor Singh. "Keep the bargain and you are free as far as I am concerned to do what you like when you get there."

So we had a doctor again at last, for the German agreed to the terms. Not one of us but needed medical aid, and the men were too glad to have their hurts attended, to ask very many questions; but they were certainly surprised, and suspicious of the new arrangement, and I did not dare tell them what I had overheard for fear lest suspicion of Ranjoor Singh be reawakened. I refused even to tell the other daffadars, which caused some slight estrangement between them and me. However, Ranjoor Singh was as conscious of that risk as I, and during all the rest of the long march he kept their camp and ours, their column and ours half an hour's ride apart—sometimes even farther—sometimes half a day apart, to the disgust of the doctor, who had that much more trouble, but with the result of preventing greater friction.

To tell of all that journey across Persia would be but to remember weariness—weariness of horse and men. Sometimes we were attacked; more often we were run away from. We grew sick, our wounds festered and our hearts ached. Horses died and the vultures ate them. Men died, and we buried or burned their bodies according or not as we had fuel. We dried, as it were, like the bone-dry trail we followed, and only Ranjoor Singh's heart was stout; only he was brave; only he had a song on his lips. He coaxed us, and cheered us, and rallied us. The strength of the regiment was but his strength, and as for the other party, who hung on our flank, or lagged behind us or preceded us by half a day, their Kurds deserted by fives and tens until there was scarcely a corporal's guard remaining.

They must have been as weary as we, and as glad as we when at last at the end of a long drawn afternoon, we saw an Afghan sentry.

Has the sahib ever seen an Afghan sentry?

This one was gray and old and sat on his gray

pony like a huddled ape with a tattered umbrella over his shoulder and his rifle across his knees. He looked less like a sentry than like a dead man dug up and set there to scare the birds away. But he was efficient, no doubt of that. He had seen us and passed on word of us the minute we showed on the sky-line, and the hills all about him were full of armed men waiting to give us a hot reception if necessary and to bar farther progress in any case.

So there we had to camp, just over the Afghan border, but farther apart from the Germans than ever—two, three miles apart, for now it became Ranjoor Singh's policy to know nothing whatever about them. The Afghans provided us with rations and sent us one of their own doctors dressed in the uniform of a tram-car conductor, and their highest official in those parts, whose rank I could not guess because he was arrayed in the costume of a city of London policeman, asked innumerable questions, first of Ranjoor Singh and then of each of us individually. But we conferred together, and stuck to one point, that we knew nothing. Ranjoor Singh did not know better than we. The more he asked the more dumb we became until, perhaps with a view to loosing our tongues, the Afghans who mingled among us in the camp began telling what the Germans were saying and doing on the rise two miles away.

They had their machine set up, said they. They were receiving messages, said they, with this wonderful wireless telegraph of theirs. They kept receiving hourly news of disasters to the Allied arms by land and sea. And we were fearfully disturbed about all this, because we knew how important it must be for India's safety that Afghanistan continue neutral. And why should such savages continue neutral if they were once persuaded that the winning side was that of the Central Powers? Nevertheless, Ranjoor Singh continued to grow more and more contented, and I wondered. Some of the men began to murmur.

In that camp we remained, if I rightly remember, six days. And then came word from Habibullah Kahn, the Afghan amir, that we might draw nearer Khabul. So, keeping our distance from the Germans, we helped one another into the saddle (so weak most of us were by that time) and went forward three days' march. Then we camped again, much closer to the Germans this time, in fact, almost within shouting distance; and they again set up their machine, causing sparks to crackle from the wires of a telescopic tower they raised, to the very great concern of the Afghans who were in and out of both camps all day long. One message that an Afghan told me the Germans had received, was that the British fleet was all sunk and Paris taken. But that sort of message seemed to me familiar, so that I was not so depressed by it as my Afghan informant had hoped. He went off to procure yet more appalling news to bring me, and no doubt was accommodated. I should have had burning ears, but that about that time, their amir came, Habibullah Kahn, looking like a European in his neatly fitting clothes, but surrounded by a staff of officers dressed in greater variety of uniforms than one would have believed to exist. He had brought with him his engineers to view this wonderful machine, but before approaching either camp—perhaps to show impartiality—he sent for the German chief and one, and for Ranjoor Singh and one. So, since the German took his doctor, Ranjoor Singh took me, he and I both riding, and the amir graciously excusing me from dismounting when I had made him my salaam and he had learned the nature of the wound.

After some talk, the amir asked us bluntly whence we came and what our business might be, and Ranjoor Singh answered him we were escaped prisoners of war. Then he turned on the German, and the German told him that because the British had seen fit to cut off Afghanistan from all true news of what was happening in the world outside, therefore the German government, knowing well the open mind and bravery and wisdom of the amir and his subjects, had sent himself at very great trouble and expense to receive true messages from Europe and so acquaint with the true state of affairs a ruler and people with whom Germany desired before all things to be on friendly terms.

After that we all went down in a body, perhaps a hundred men, with the amir at our head, to the German camp; and there the German and his officers displayed the machine to the amir, who, with a dozen of his staff around him, appeared more amused than astonished.

So the Germans set their machine in motion. The sparks made much crackling from the wires, at which the amir laughed aloud. Presently the German chief read off a message from Berlin, conveying the kaiser's compliments to his highness, the amir.

"Is that message from Berlin?" the amir asked, and I thought I heard one of his officers chuckle.

"Yes, Your Highness," said the German officer.

"Is it not relayed from anywhere?" the amir asked, and the German stared at him swiftly—thus, as if for the first time his own suspicion were aroused.

"From Stamboul, Your Highness—relayed from Stamboul," he said, as one who makes concessions.

The amir chuckled softly to himself and smiled.

"These are my engineers," said he, "all college trained. They tell me our wireless installation at Khabul, which connects us through Simla with Calcutta and the world beyond, is a very good one, yet it will only reach to Simla, although I should say it is a hundred times as large as yours, and although we have an enormous dynamo to give the energy as against your box of batteries."

The Germans, who were clustered all about their chief, kept straight faces, but their eyes popped round and their mouths grew stiff with the effort to suppress emotion.

"This, Your Highness, is the last new invention," said the German chief.

"Then my engineers shall look at it," said the amir, "for we wish to keep abreast of the inventions. As you remarked just now, we are a little shut off from the world. We must not let slip such opportunities for education." And then and there he made his engineers go forward to inspect everything, he scarce concealing his merriment; and the Germans stood aside, 'looking like thieves caught in the act while the workings were disclosed of such a wireless apparatus as might serve to teach beginners.

"It might serve perhaps between one village and the next, while the batteries persisted," they said, reporting to the amir presently. The amir laughed, but I thought he looked puzzled—perplexed, rather than displeased. He turned to Ranjoor Singh:

"And you are a liar, too?" he asked.

"Nay, Your Royal Highness, I speak truth," said Ranjoor Singh, saluting him in military manner.

"Then what do you wish?" asked the amir. "Do you wish to be interned, seeing this is neutral soil on which you trespass?"

"Nay, Your Royal Highness," answered Ranjoor Singh, with a curt laugh, "we have had enough of prison camps."

"Then what shall be done with you?" the amir asked. "Here are men from both sides, and how shall I be neutral?"

The German chief stepped forward and saluted. "Your Royal Highness, we desire to be interned," he said. But the amir glowered savagely.

"Peace!" said he. "I asked you nothing, one string of lies was enough! I asked thee a question," he said, turning again to Ranjoor Singh.

"Since Your Royal Highness asks," said Ranjoor Singh, "it would be a neutral act to let us each leave your dominions by whichever road we will!"

The amir laughed and turned to his attendants, who laughed with him.

"That is good," said he. "So let it be. It is an order!"

So it came about, sahib, that the Germans and ourselves were ordered hotfoot out of the amir's country. But whereas there was only one way the Germans could go, viz, back into Persia, there to help themselves as best they could, the road Ranjoor Singh chose was forward to the Khyber Pass, and so down into India.

Aye, sahib, down into India! It was a long road, but the Afghans were very kind to us, providing us with food and blankets and giving some of us new horses for our weary ones, and so we came at last to Landi Kotal at the head of the Khyber, where a long-legged English sahib heard our story and said "Sha-bash!" to Ranjoor Singh—that means "Well done!" And so we marched down the Khyber, they signaling ahead that we were coming. We slept at Ali Masjib because neither horses nor men could move another yard, but at dawn next day we were off again. And because they had notice of our coming, they turned out the troops, a division strong, to greet us, and we took the salute of a whole division as we had once taken the salute of two in Flanders, Ranjoor Singh sitting his charger like a graven image, and we—one hundred three-and-thirty men and the prisoner Tugendheim, who had left India eight hundred strong—reeling in the saddle from sickness and fatigue while a roar went up in Khyber throat such as I scarcely hope to hear again before I die. Once in a lifetime, sahib, once is enough. They had their bands with them. The same tune burst on our ears that had greeted us that first night of our charge in Flanders, and we—great bearded men—we wept like little ones. They played *It Is a Long, Long Way to Tipperary.*

Then because we were cavalry and entitled to the same, they gave us *Bonnie Dundee* and the horses cantered to it; but some of us rolled from the saddle in sheer weakness. Then we halted in something like a line, and a general rode up to shake hands with Ranjoor Singh and to say things in our tongue that may not be repeated, for they were words from heart to heart. And I remember little more, for I, too, swooned and fell from the saddle.

* * * * * * *

The shadows darkened and grew one into another. Hira Singh sat drawing silently in the dust, with his injured feet stretched out in front of him. A monkey in the giant tree above us shook down a little shower of twigs and dirt. A trumpet blared. There began much business of closing tents and reducing the camp to superhuman tidiness.

"So, sahib," he said at last, "they come to carry me in. It is time my tale is ended. Ranjoor Singh they have made bahadur. God grant him his desire! May my son be such a man as he, when his day comes.

"Me! They say I shall be made commissioned officer—the law is changed since this great war began. Yet what did I do compared to what Ranjoor Singh did? Each is his own witness and God alone is judge. Does the sahib know what this war is all about?

"I believe no two men fight for the same thing. It is a war in each man's heart, each man fighting as the spirit moves him. So, they come for me. Salaam, sahib. Bohut salaam. May God grant the sahib peace. Peace to the sahib's grandsons and great-grandsons. With each arm thus around a trooper's neck will the sahib graciously excuse me from saluting?"

THE END